Circling
Back *to* You

Also by Julie Tieu

The Donut Trap

Circling Back to You

A NOVEL

JULIE TIEU

AVON

An Imprint of HarperCollinsPublishers

CIRCLING BACK TO YOU. Copyright © 2022 by Julie Tieu. All rights reserved. Printed in the United States of America. No part of this book may be used or reproduced in any manner whatsoever without written permission except in the case of brief quotations embodied in critical articles and reviews. For information, address HarperCollins Publishers, 195 Broadway, New York, NY 10007.

HarperCollins books may be purchased for educational, business, or sales promotional use. For information, please email the Special Markets Department at SPsales@harpercollins.com.

FIRST EDITION

Designed by Diahann Sturge

Title page and chapter opener illustration © lukpedclub / Shutterstock, Inc.

Library of Congress Cataloging-in-Publication Data has been applied for.

ISBN 978-0-06-306984-8

22 23 24 25 26 LSC 10 9 8 7 6 5 4 3 2 1

To David

Circling Back to You

CHAPTER 1

CADENCE

December

C adence could not be late to community service. It didn't matter as much whenever she showed up ten (or fifteen) minutes late to work. After five years of late nights in the Prism Realty office, she felt entitled to give herself a few more minutes to get ready in the morning. But today, Cadence woke up, slapped on some eye cream, and ran out the door because she had enough decency to show up—she checked her phone—*almost* on time for community service.

For months, HR "gently reminded" Cadence that she still had a paid day off to volunteer, and if she didn't use it before the end of the year, she would lose it. Okay, getting paid while performing free labor sounded like an oxymoron to her, and it was perhaps morally compromising to be pressured to do good, not out of the kindness of their hearts but for the sake of thinly veiled corporate PR. Still, spending her Friday packing food boxes for the needy was more appealing than tackling her hemorrhaging inbox and warding off brokers trying to close deals before the New Year.

Cadence's Prism polo shirt chafed her skin as she jogged. It had a minimal design, with the company's logo of nesting triangles stitched on the front pocket, which aimed to provide an approachable yet professional appearance. She'd never worn it before and found it buried behind much prettier blouses. It was given out one year in a misguided attempt to build morale, the thought being that having hundreds of employees wear the same black shirt at company picnics and team-building activities would create a sense of unity. Honestly, the higher-ups put too much faith in an unbreathable, yet moisture-wicking shirt.

When Cadence walked through the doors of the food bank, she found herself feeling lost. Holiday music boomed over the enormous warehouse brimful of volunteers decked out in garish sweaters, weaving through pallets of produce. There didn't seem to be any rhyme or reason to the madness. It was like Santa's Workshop, but instead of toys, there were yams. Crates and crates of yams. Cadence checked her phone as she caught her breath. She swiped away the calendar notification reminding her that she was supposed to arrive nine minutes ago, and tapped on her work email. There were probably instructions in her email confirmation. She might have known if she had actually read it.

"Hello." A woman wearing a San Francisco–Marin Food Bank jacket approached Cadence with a clipboard. "I'm Gaby, the volunteer coordinator. I can check you in. Who are you here with?"

Cadence relaxed her shoulders, relieved that she didn't have to scour her unread emails. "Prism Realty," she answered.

"Last name?"

"Lim."

Gaby flipped to the third page, turned the clipboard around, and tapped on Cadence's printed name. "Can I have you sign on this line? And then I can walk you over to your group."

Cadence scribbled on the line next to her name. She scanned the list before returning it, checking to see who had arrived before her. Just as she saw his name, Matt bellowed from across the warehouse.

"LIM!" He waved both arms to get Cadence's attention, as if she could miss him. In the years they had worked together, she'd grown accustomed to seeing Matt in suits, tailored to fit his lean body. But today Matt Escanilla, Prism Realty's top-selling broker, had literal bells on, jingle-jangling on his garland-green sweater and topped off with a red Santa hat.

When she acknowledged him with a single wave, Matt gestured at the empty spot next to him at the end of a row of foldable tables that were set up for an assembly line.

Cadence ignored the fluttery feeling in her stomach, blaming it on the light breakfast she ate that morning. She thanked Gaby as she handed back the clipboard and excused herself, crossing the warehouse floor, greeting her colleagues along the way. There was Sonya Bhatt from Accounting, bagging carrots. Kevin Lewis, fellow analyst, who silently nodded when she said hi. Apparently, he was still annoyed after their heated conversation over the merits of VLOOKUP versus INDEX MATCH. Frank Mendez from Finance, who traded in his business formal wear for dad jeans. It was a look.

"Hey," Cadence said. She dropped her purse underneath the table and unbuttoned her coat as she assumed her station.

"Good morning." Matt beamed as he greeted her. It had to be unnatural to possess so much energy in the morning. As she thought this, he presented her with a cup of coffee. "For last night."

Cadence quickly accepted it before Matt said another word, but it was too late. She caught Sonya averting her eyes, pretending like she wasn't eavesdropping. Cadence suppressed her instinct to explain that the coffee was a thank-you gift for the last-minute data she supplied for Matt's upcoming meeting with a VIP client. It would only open a can of worms with the other brokers whose requests were still sitting in her inbox.

"I didn't expect to see you here," Cadence said before taking a sip.

"Why not?" Matt loaded the cardboard box in front of him with packaged stuffing mix and cans of green beans, then pushed it over to Frank. "'Tis the season of giving, or have you forgotten?"

Had she offended him? She was about to apologize when she caught Matt assessing her all-black outfit, down to her boots. Cadence pulled her coat over her polo, muttering, "I didn't know I was supposed to wear an ugly Christmas sweater."

If Matt wasn't offended before, he was now. "What are you calling ugly?"

Cadence took another sip, avoiding the question because nothing about Matt was ugly. Sure, he had confidence in spades, affording him to wear this foolish getup with ease. But unlike the other brokers in the office, Matt never felt entitled to Cadence's time and politely asked whenever he needed a favor. Unlike her, Matt always took his family's calls, especially if it was his lola, patiently listening while she spoke in long stretches. Cadence didn't mean to listen in on their conversations, but it wasn't hard to catch the staccato of his lola's Tagalog accent when their cubicles were right next to each other. With his gregarious nature, Matt was popular among clients, which was why he was in the running for a promotion to lead Prism's new office in L.A.

Though she was an analyst, it didn't take genius to determine that the best-case scenario was for her to not invest her heart in a man who was about to leave for sunnier climes. And when Matt would inevitably leave, Cadence wouldn't have to worry about harboring a silly infatuation. In the meantime, she needed to pull herself together and keep her feelings in lockdown.

Matt prompted her again by sweeping a hand across his ridiculous sweater, creating an audible shimmer. The man was basically a walking, talking wind chime.

The corners of Cadence's lips twitched, but she refused to smile. It would only encourage him. She set aside her cup, gathered a box, and faced the warehouse, diverting her attention to packing canned goods. It was easier to talk to him when she wasn't looking at him.

"I swear I didn't know," she asserted.

"It was in the email."

"So? This is a work-related event and I'm wearing a work-appropriate outfit," she replied, prim and proper. "It's not like I have a"—her nose wrinkled—"tinsel-covered sweater laying around." Cadence passed along her box, trying to keep the pace of the assembly line.

"How do you not have one already? Do you not get invited to parties?"

"Not ones requiring me to buy something that I'll only wear once a year. I don't have enough closet space for that." Her tiny studio apartment didn't have much space for anything. She flicked a bell on his sleeve. "This can't possibly be machine washable."

"Where is your holiday spirit, Scrooge?" Matt chuckled, slightly bewildered at her attitude.

"Bah humbug." Cadence leaned into her grumpiness. It was the last defense against her inconvenient attraction. She slid another box, but before she let go, Matt slapped his hands on the sides, catching her fingers underneath. It couldn't have lasted for more than a second, but it was long enough for a blush to creep up her neck. By the time she glanced at him, Matt had maneuvered his Santa hat onto her head.

"There," he said, running a hand through his mussed-up hair. "So you don't look like a Christmas ghost."

Cadence touched the white fur that ran along the edge of the red cap. It was still warm from Matt, enough to melt her resolve. Before she could stop it, her lips curled into a small smile.

In turn, Matt's smirk stretched into a satisfied grin. At least one of them was happy about it. Cadence hated that no matter how much she fortified her brain with formal education, it easily turned into mush over his not-ugly mouth.

"All right, lovebirds. Stop lollygagging," Frank complained, knocking on their table. "You're slowing things down."

Cadence's laugh sounded forced even to her own ears. "Oh, Frank. You're so funny. We're not—"

Matt's eyebrows sank toward the center of his face. He must have known something was up because no bigger lies had ever been spoken. Frank had the personality of tap water. Call her a coward, but Cadence couldn't bear to have Matt watch her lie her way out of this conversation.

Her eyes darted across the room, checking for anyone who could have heard Frank's unwarranted statement. Kevin appeared vaguely interested and Sonya had begun texting someone. It could have been anyone—her husband or her teenage kids. She could have been putting in her lunch order or responding to one of her accountant friends—Cadence didn't know all of their names, but they looked like a tight clique—or worse, any of the administrative assistants, who could smell juicy gossip a mile away. Cadence had to contain the situation somehow. Minimize it. Close the loop.

"We're just friends," Cadence announced, even though she had never referred to Matt as one to his face. They weren't *really* friends, since she never saw him outside of the office, but they were friend-*ly*. Matt was merely a friendly office friend that Cadence sometimes wanted to f—

"Friends," Matt casually repeated, nodding in lukewarm agreement, like it was a novel idea to him too.

This was for the best. Soon Matt would leave for L.A. without having to worry that his professional legacy would be overshadowed by rumors. Cadence feared that she wouldn't be so lucky. Through this oddly public admission, with Kevin, Sonya, Frank, and onlooking high school students trying to rack up volunteer hours for college applications as their witnesses, Matt and Cadence set the record straight that they were officially, for better or for worse, friends.

For insurance purposes, Cadence added, "Besides, I'm dating someone."

"Oh . . . congrats?" Matt narrowed his eyes, confused rather than questioning.

"Mm-hmm." Her lie needed to be strengthened with another lie. Cadence blurted out the first name she could think of. "Karl."

Matt bit his tongue, trying not to laugh at her reference to the pervasive Bay Area fog. "Oh, Karl. *Riiiiight*." Bells tinkled as he crossed his arms and shifted on his feet. "I remember you telling me about him. Didn't you say he was giving you the *cold* shoulder?"

"He's not great with texting, no."

"Hmm. Do you think it's because he's getting a little . . . you know. *Gray?*"

"Matt. Don't be ageist."

"I don't see any boxes being made," Frank chimed in with a not-so-subtle nudge. "Let's go. I have to catch my kid's holiday pageant."

"You heard the guy," Cadence said, ready to end this conversation. Their colleagues were too, having resumed their tasks after losing interest in Matt and Cadence's dumb jokes.

But before she could jump back into the assembly line and fulfill her good deed of the day, Matt caught Cadence's eyes, and with a hint of a smile, he mouthed, *You okay?*

It was times like these that reminded Cadence why she found Matt so likable. It was a quick, earnest check-in before they moved on.

Cadence nodded. She *was* okay. More than okay. She had gained a new friend, a good one, and those were hard to come by.

CHAPTER 2

MATT

You got this.

"Hey, Matt. Need help there?"

Sonya rocked back and forth on her heels, no doubt waiting for Matt to stop hogging the printer.

"Nah, I got it. That's a nice scarf, Sonya!"

She preened at the compliment. "I'll come back later."

Matt resumed his print job and his pre-meeting pep talk.

You. Got. This.

The printer halted to the sound of a crunch. What he'd got was a paper jam. Shit.

Matt reminded himself that there was no reason to be nervous. He did his homework this weekend, scouring the internet, mining out all possible minutiae about his famously private client, Percy Ma.

From what he'd gathered, Percy had the deceptive appearance of a typical quiet, geeky start-up co-founder who operated behind the scenes. Like the other guy who co-founded Facebook with Mark Zuckerberg. iStan, the app Percy co-founded, was objectively genius. It offered a platform that cultivated fandoms, making it easier to share photos, videos, and fanfic. It was like a virtual 24/7 Comic Con, attracting fervent users from every fandom, from the mainstream stuff to the obscure. After iStan took Asia by storm, Percy became iStan's COO and oversaw its global expansion. He made it look easy, since he was fluent in five languages and rubbed elbows with the rich and famous, traveling on his private jet and teeing off in exclusive resorts. Percy was arrogance personified, wrapped in a zip-up hoodie, straight-legged jeans, and New Balances.

Last night Matt was sure that he discovered everything there was to know about Percy. He could write the unauthorized biography of Percy Ma—or at the very least, his Wikipedia page.

So why was Matt blanking one hour before their first meeting?

"What are you doing?"

Matt glanced up from where he was crouched on the floor, his arm halfway inside the fucking printer, grasping on to a tiny corner of his document. His first thought when he saw Cadence standing outside the breakroom, in her usual pencil skirt and a knit sweater she once described as saffron (whatever that meant), was *What kind of coupon is she printing now?* She'd already done several foodie tours. A ferry to Angel Island? One of those bus tours that took her to all the mostly free landmarks around the city? He was about to tell her that it would be more eco-friendly if she saved coupons to her phone until he saw that in her hands was a Trader Joe's entrée.

Was it time for lunch already? How much time did he waste trying to get his files to print?

Matt checked the watch on his free hand and smoothed down

his tie as he breathed a sigh in relief. It was nine-fifteen and the pasta entrée in Cadence's hands was still frozen.

"Hold on. I almost," Matt grunted, "got it." He yanked out a crinkled sheet of paper with demographic data for a building on Sansome Street, which, if the day goes as planned, will be the future U.S. headquarters for iStan.

"Why are you printing this?" Cadence asked, identifying the smeared rendition of her spreadsheet. "Percy Ma doesn't strike me as the type to want hard copies."

Says the person who printed every single report because it was easier on her eyes.

"You'd be surprised how many clients appreciate holding a glossy folder brochure while they tour a property." Matt stood up and shut the printer door. It whirred as his flyers reprinted. "It also saves me in case I forget something." A real concern at the moment.

"Ah."

"But it was outdated and I couldn't get them reprinted in time for today's meeting. I was going to throw this in." Matt wiped a spot of ink off his forearm. After he unrolled his sleeve, he twisted his wrist to button his cuff, which was easier said than done since his fingers were trembling. He was losing it. "Can you help me with this?"

Cadence's head snapped up like she got caught online shopping at her desk. Her hands tightened around her lunch. "I-I better put this away."

Matt paused and rewound the last few seconds. Had he done something to cause Cadence to retreat into the breakroom? Matt prided himself in his ability to read people—it was helpful in his line of work—but Cadence was hard to figure out sometimes. He started at Prism a few months after Cadence, and for as long as he'd known her, Matt found Cadence to be self-contained. It was like she was allergic to small talk. It took multiple attempts until Matt figured out that somewhere underneath her unsmiling exterior, Cadence had a wry sense of humor. He would never go as far as to tell her to smile more, but he wished that she would, because when she did, it was nice.

Matt finally managed to get the stubborn button on his own. Cadence returned and gathered the finished copies from the printer tray. "Is that an eight?"

He stepped closer and glanced over her shoulder as he shuffled into his suit blazer, squinting at the bullet point Cadence had her finger on. "I think it's a percent sign . . . or a six?"

Her back straightened. "No. It's an eight," she confirmed with a strained voice. "I should know. I verified this for you."

Was she pissed? Matt backed up to give her some space. Cadence continued to scrutinize his printouts, with a smattering of pink appearing on her cheeks. Maybe she could forgive him, given the circumstances. "I'm sorry. You know how I am before big meetings. And this one is the biggest one."

Matt paid his dues. Years of cold calls, building a wide network of brokers, investors, and clients, closing deals, and topping his personal best sales records all led to this next rung on his career ladder. The fact that it would take him closer to his family was icing on the cake.

"Half of these numbers aren't clear." Cadence flipped the sheet to scan the other side.

"I used Quick Print." Et tu, Xerox machine? Matt compulsively checked his watch again. "I'm in a rush."

Cadence's face softened with a touch of pity. "I can resend you the file, so that it's at the top of your inbox." She patted her peacoat pockets for her phone.

"You don't have to do that," Matt said, dabbing the sheen of sweat off his forehead. Either that paper jam gave him the workout of his life or the pressure was settling in. Matt closed his eyes and took a deep breath, flapping the sides of his blazer to cool himself down while pumping himself up.

Prism's top-selling broker, two years in a row.

SF Monthly's Fifth Most Eligible Bachelor. In the real estate category, but hey, it counts—

A comforting hand landed on the nape of his neck. Matt's eyes flew open to find Cadence, frozen within inches of him. Maybe because he'd never seen her up close before or because she wasn't shooing him away claiming that she was in the middle of a spreadsheet, but when her doe eyes widened, he realized for the first time that they were a striking dark brown, etched with amber.

"S-Sorry." Cadence delicately removed herself, backing away with her hands up. "It was"—she nervously gesticulated at her own lapels in reference to Matt's suit—"flipped up."

It was cute.

"It's fine," he said, reassuring an adorably embarrassed Cadence. Her face was the color of Mars. "Really, I should thank you. I wouldn't have made a good impression."

"Here." Cadence thrust the printouts in Matt's general direction, her eyes looking over his shoulder. "I wrote my extension on the letterhead. Just in case. Good luck today."

"Thanks, but you didn't need to." Cadence was already walking away before he could finish his sentence. If he had more time, he would have liked to tell her that it wasn't an empty platitude. He didn't want her to think that he took her help for granted, but also, he already knew her extension. It was only one digit apart from his.

MATT ENVIED WOMEN who power walked to work in running shoes, lugging an office-appropriate pair in their large purses. His Italian leather shoes pinched his toes after he had walked through fourteen floors of office space. It was hard to gauge Percy Ma's reaction when he was surrounded with an entourage of staff members. Initially, Matt found it promising that Percy brought along a team of designers to sketch ideas during the tour, but they kept disrupting Matt's sales pitch with questions about the history of the French Beaux-Arts building.

"There are more tenants occupying the building than I expected," said Ms. Huang, the project manager for iStan's U.S. expansion. That was how she introduced herself. Matt wasn't even on a first-name basis with his client's gatekeeper.

Matt cleared his throat, which did nothing to get Ms. Huang's attention. He pushed past the minor setback, following behind her as she perused their surroundings. "As I mentioned before, the building was retrofitted seven years ago, so it is in sound condition. The landlord would be amenable to any construction that was necessary to configure the space according to the company's needs, so long as it doesn't affect the facade, given that it's a historical building. The location is optimal. It's next to a BART station, which would be convenient for employees."

Ms. Huang stopped at a window, peering out toward the bay. Matt was beginning to feel like he was losing to the sea lions.

Matt could not be deterred. He had to secure this deal. The economy dipped during the first quarter of the year, affecting his sales. Though he had a good rapport with Prism's CEO, Sadie Chan, Matt ultimately had to impress the board of directors to get promoted, and he was not without competition.

"The tenants occupying the retail space on the first floor will be vacating by the end of the month. As for the rest, their leases will expire within the next six months. Picture this." He pointed his outstretched arm toward the empty top floor. "This space would be for C-suite offices."

Percy Ma, who had been using Matt's brochure as a fan, shrugged. "I like to have a cubicle among the engineers."

To each their own.

The designers scattered about, minding their own business as they took pictures and jotted notes. The sound of their stylus pens tapping and gliding across their iPads echoed through the empty floor. It had been a long time since Matt felt this uncertain during a showing, and he didn't like it one bit. He had to kick things up a notch if he wanted to tip things in his favor.

"Do you like basketball, Percy?" Matt's cousins would call him a sellout if they heard him right now. "I could arrange for a club suite for tonight's Warriors game."

"That won't be necessary," Ms. Huang interjected, signaling to the team to gather around. "We have a busy schedule, touring other buildings in the area."

Matt tried not to take offense, but it wasn't often that he was brushed off in a professional or personal context. Under normal circumstances, he had no problem brokering deals to clients who had a marked interest in something he was offering. But it was clear that this showing ran past its desired time for both parties, so he conceded.

"Understood."

"Thank you for showing us around. We'll be in touch." Ms. Huang herded the team toward the elevator. The showing was wrapping up too quickly. Before it escaped him, Mat made it his purpose to shake Ms. Huang's hand before she stepped into the elevator, though she treated it like an afterthought. He reached for Percy's, but a moat of bodies stood in the way. "Please let me know if you have any further questions," Matt practically shouted as the doors began to close. "You have my contact information. You can reach me anytime," he added, trying not to sound too desperate.

Once the doors closed, Matt's shoulders sagged from the botched meeting. What was he going to tell Sadie? She was the one who referred Percy to him, like a test he just failed. He needed a minute to think. He loosened his tie as he sat at a nearby bench and checked his messages to buy himself some time before he returned to the office. Automatically, he tapped on his cousins' group chat.

CELINE: Matt. Mom and Dad want to know when you're coming down for Christmas.
AJ: Secret Santa, the noise-canceling headphones are my top choice

Crap. Matt was AJ's Secret Santa. He made a note to buy AJ's gift.

MATT: This Saturday.

GERALD: Okay, AJ. Socks it is

CELINE: They're excited you'll be down through New Year's

Matt was excited too, especially since he had missed Thanksgiving. He had long accepted his fate to hustle around the clock, since he worked on commission. Missing birthdays and a holiday here and there were all part of the sacrifice toward his successful career. It was easier to do during his twenties, when his cousins were spread out in colleges or first jobs in different cities across California. But now that they'd all settled back in the L.A. area and started families, Matt was beginning to feel like a spectator in the nosebleed section, watching his extended family grow from afar.

JASON: Maleena wants to know if we're doing White
Elephant again

AJ: oh hell no

MISSY: FML

CELINE: What's wrong?

MISSY: finals

GERALD: you got this. don't be so dramatic

MISSY: ☹

That was Matt's cue to exit. He loved his cousins, but he hated when the conversation veered off track and people were having separate conversations simultaneously, throwing off the sequence of texts. The group was getting too big. He closed the chat as a new text came in.

CADENCE: It's actually a 9.

Matt must not have recovered from his post-showing fog because it took him a while to remember what Cadence was talking about. It was out of his hands, since he gave away all his brochures.

MATT: Don't worry about it. Meeting's over.
CADENCE: How did it go?

Most days, Matt could roll with the punches, but to have Cadence in his corner, asking about his meeting, was like a breath of fresh air in this competitive environment.

MATT: Could have gone better.
MATT: I'll tell you when I get back to the office.
CADENCE: You know where to find me.

CHAPTER 3

CADENCE

C adence, can I pick your brain for a second?" Kevin announced uninvited, breaching the entrance to Cadence's cramped cubicle. "I want to go over the valuation on 6062 Post Street."

Cadence didn't have time for Kevin and the impatient whistling sounds coming from his nostrils. There were two more weeks left in the year, and based on the emails that flooded her inbox, nobody cared that the holidays were around the corner. Investors were getting nervous. Interest rates were projected to increase in the next year. Every client wanted to be prioritized. Therefore, Kevin's wanting to "go over" his valuation analysis, which was likely his way to settle their ongoing argument, was not an urgent matter.

"I'm busy," Cadence answered as she continued typing the rest of her email.

Kevin stomped out, mumbling under his breath, irked by Cadence's clipped reply. Matt once suggested that Kevin's requests to pick her brain were his way of asking for help without admitting it. Cadence couldn't give Kevin the benefit of the doubt. If she was willing to lend her expertise in the spirit of collegiality, the least Kevin could do was not be a dick about it. She didn't care if Kevin was promoted to senior analyst. It didn't mean she was at his beck and call.

This was not what Cadence envisioned when she made the jump into real estate. She blamed real estate TV shows for editing out the boring behind-the-scenes parts—like her job—and making it seem like a deal closed so quickly. In reality, a number of things could drag a deal for months. That's where her role as an analyst came in.

She reviewed every document, analyzing to make sure there weren't any hidden problems with the property, that the financing checked out, that it was valued properly. Decisions were made based on her analyses, so the information had to be accurate, founded on sound data, and presented appropriately for her audience, whether it be a memo, a detailed report, or an attractive presentation with colorful graphs. Cadence consistently fulfilled these responsibilities and finished her work faster than the other analysts, which was a gift and a curse. She was highly sought after by all the brokers because time was money in this business. However, it also meant she did more work than the rest of her colleagues.

"Hey." Josie Hill handed Cadence a stack of envelopes over Cadence's monitor. "I stopped by the mailbox and picked these up for you." As Sadie's executive assistant, Josie never delivered anyone's mail, but she must have gotten fed up seeing Cadence's mail pile up. "Most of them are holiday cards."

Cadence pulled out a photo card of Stacy from marketing with her wife, son, and terrier mix posing in front of their trimmed Christmas tree. "I never know what to do with these. Am I supposed to pin them on my cubicle? I see all these people every day. Isn't that weird?"

"Don't you display cards around your house?"

Cadence's eyebrows furrowed as she considered where she could put these cards in her Mission District studio other than her recycle bin.

"Okay. I'll take that as a no. Remind me not to give you a Christmas card in the future." Josie rapped her fingers on the transparent cubicle divider that barricaded Cadence in. "I heard something interesting recently."

The drop in Josie's voice meant that either the whispers about layoffs had some footing or Josie was going to spill her thoughts on the latest spin-off of *The Bachelor*. *Bachelor on Holiday*? *Bachelor the Musical*? Cadence had no clue, but she braced herself for the worst.

"Prism *cares*."

Cadence wasn't following. Was that a secret code word for something? "What are you talking about?"

"The food bank?"

Oh. "What about it?"

"Are you and Matt a thing?"

Cadence gulped. Watching insanely tanned people date each other while indulging in song and dance was starting to sound like the preferred choice. "Excuse me?"

Josie perched over Cadence's cubicle with a gleam in her eyes. "Haven't you seen your email? It was in the newsletter."

Cadence tried to remain calm as her soul departed from her body, double-clicking on the company-wide(!) newsletter. After she skimmed the perfunctory welcome message from Sadie, her heart thrummed as she read the headline shouting in big, bold letters that PRISM CARES! Below it, there was the group photo Prism employees took with the hired Santa. Matt and Cadence were standing a close but respectable distance from each other. If Josie hadn't been watching, Cadence would have cropped the photo and sent it to her best friend, Maddie.

"Are you referring to this?" Cadence could play this cool. There was nothing to see here.

"I heard from Frank that there was something going on in this cozy corner over here."

Frank was going to get his reports with ugly paper clips from now on. "We're just friends," Cadence stated.

"So I've heard."

"Frank doesn't know what he's talking about." Cadence was coming up short on excuses when she was saved by her desk phone. "Excuse me. I have to take that."

Josie sniffed as she unlatched herself from the cubicle wall. If Cadence had any hope that she was off the hook, they were dashed when Josie's eyes ping-ponged between Cadence's and Matt's cubicle. Someone should put her in charge of surveillance.

Cadence picked up her phone once Josie disappeared around the corner. "Hello? Cadence speaking."

"It's Tristan."

Cadence's ears perked up. It wasn't like her older brother to call so soon. They touched base once a month primarily at their dad's request. It was his only way to keep tabs on her from three hundred miles away. "Why are you calling me at work?"

"I'm setting up Dad's new phone. Just checking if this is the right number."

"Oh. Okay." Cadence softened her tone out of empathy. She tried to teach her dad how to use a computer once. They didn't get past left-clicking and right-clicking. Tristan had the patience of a monk to live with their father and deal with him on a daily basis.

"Dad wants to know if you're coming home for Christmas."

"No. I have to work on the twenty-sixth. Saving my vacation days for January and February." In years past, Cadence combined her visit home for her mom's death anniversary and Lunar New Year, but no such luck for her upcoming trip.

"Okay."

Patience of a monk but talked like a robot.

"Is everything okay?"

"Yeah."

"Uh, okay."

Tristan hung up before she could say goodbye. Cadence wondered why they went through the motions when they were mature enough to admit that their phone calls had regressed into a brief verbal checklist. She considered creating an online form that Tristan could complete each month instead.

1. How are you? ☐ Fine ☐ Not Fine. Explain:_____
2. How is Dad? ☐ Fine ☐ Not Fine. Explain:_____
3. Did you get this month's money transfer? ☐ Yes ☐ No
4. Do you need more money? ☐ Yes ☐ No
5. Other:_____

The form would be simpler and could efficiently populate a spreadsheet.

Cadence flipped through her stack of holiday cards, glancing at every happy family photo with a tinge of envy. Her mother would roll in her grave if she knew how distant their family had become. With that hum of guilt, Cadence wondered if she could spare a few vacation days for Christmas or arrange to work remotely.

Cadence began to compose a new email to her supervisor, Bill, but was prompted with a message that he was out of the office until January 2. This was so like him, coming and going as he pleased. Cadence never knew when Bill was ever in the office. He didn't even tell anyone that he was taking time off.

Cadence sifted through her mail again. If Bill was out of the office, then that meant that she should have received her bonus by now. In the haystack of photo cards, she found a small envelope addressed to her in Bill's scraggly handwriting. To her dismay, it was not the standard letter-size envelope that would have encased a piece of Prism's official letterhead indicating an end-of-year bonus. Inside, there was a small notecard from Bill's personal stationery.

Keep up the good work. Happy New Year!

—Bill

Behind the note was a fifty-dollar gift card to the tourist-trap chocolate shop at Fisherman's Wharf. What kind of bullshit was this? Yes, Prism had a tough year, and Cadence was grateful to have avoided the last round of layoffs. But after all the transactions she worked on, this was how Bill was going to show his appreciation? Cadence would have rather taken the fifty dollars in cash. She didn't understand why people thought cash gifts were impersonal. It couldn't be less personal than a card that didn't even include her name.

Cadence leaned back in her ergonomic chair and shut her eyes, wondering why she was pushing herself to work hard when the only thing waiting for her at the end was overpriced chocolates. That wasn't the carrot that brought Cadence to Prism Realty five years ago. It was a chance encounter, running into Sadie after Cadence burned herself out at her last job doing market research in New York. Cadence sat through Sadie's keynote address at a women's leadership conference in awe. Cadence wanted to be like Sadie—independent, decisive—a person who gave zero fucks about how others perceived her. Cadence took a chance and emailed Sadie, telling her how inspired she was by her remarks. To her surprise, Sadie replied and encouraged her to apply for a position at Prism.

It was supposed to be the beginning of a new chapter. Cadence took it as a sign to finally come back to California after her mother had bugged her for years to move closer to home. Cadence didn't have prior real estate experience, but she was confident in her ability to adapt her skills to her new environment. But things took off to a rocky start.

When Cadence started at Prism, she saw Sadie only in passing. Sadie was at the very top of the organizational chart, whereas Cadence was somewhere on a branch above intern but below everyone else, including the rest of the research team. Then a few months later, her mom died suddenly from a heart attack. When Cadence flew home to San Gabriel for the funeral, she thought the loss would bring her closer to her family, but instead, everyone moved on in separate ways. Tristan spent more time with his high school sweetheart girlfriend, Linda. Dad retired from running his shop, where he sold Buddhist ceremonial items. Cadence went back to work.

Work kept her busy. Work allowed her to send money home. Work passed her over for a promotion and gave her fifty-fucking-dollar gift cards.

"Work can fuck itself," Cadence muttered under her breath.

"And here I thought I had a bad day."

Cadence winced at the sound of Matt's voice. He had to be close if he heard her. She cracked an eye open to find Matt, amused, hovering above her.

"What happened?" Cadence pushed herself up, dusted off her latest existential crisis, and tried to forget that Matt's upside-down face was the stuff of *Spider-Man*-kiss dreams. "They didn't like the property?"

"They weren't overly enthusiastic, let's put it that way." Matt exhaled as he plopped down on his chair and ran his hand through his inky hair.

Cadence felt that she should say something encouraging as Matt sulked, losing himself to his phone. Isn't that what a friend should do? "I bet you did great." Matt shrugged as he thumbed on. She gave her next attempt some more oomph. "You'll get them next time! You . . . tried your best?"

"You don't sound so sure of yourself." Matt chuckled, though it sounded disheartened. "We'll see. What about you? What's got you down in the dumps?"

Cadence took a precautious glance and made sure no one was around before she wheeled herself toward Matt's desk. She passed the gift card to Matt over the low, sliding plastic partition that divided their desks and whispered, "Check out my bonus."

Matt flipped it between his fingers. "What the fuck is this?"

"Right?!" Validation washed over Cadence. "You can keep it. Gift it. Take some chocolates home for your lola."

"What about you? You can use it. Aren't you going home for the holidays?"

"No. I'm scheduled to work on Christmas Eve and the twenty-sixth."

"Call in sick."

Cadence shrugged. "My family isn't big on Christmas." Tristan was probably going to spend the day with his girlfriend, and her dad didn't celebrate Christmas. She would rather save herself the trouble and the cost of airfare than spend the day having uncomfortable conversations with her dad. She could do that just as well from San Francisco. "Even if I wanted to, I have so much to close out before New Year's."

Luckily, Matt dropped it. He thanked her for the gift card and slipped it into his pocket. "Are you going to the holiday party?"

"Yup." Cadence was going to milk Prism for all the free food and booze it was worth. "You?"

Matt nodded. "You bringing Karl?"

Cadence ran her tongue over her teeth to stifle her smile. She hadn't planned for Karl to be a thing. "Nah. He's not great at parties. Too gloomy."

"He sounds *nebulous.*"

Cadence tried not to laugh over how proud Matt was of his corny reply, like he'd been saving it in his back pocket. She failed.

"What about you?" Matt seemed dumbstruck by her question, so she elaborated. "Are you bringing someone?"

"*Oh.*" A frown. "No."

"You're not dating anyone?" Cadence had to ask because when else would such an opportunity present itself? Their newly minted friendship hadn't translated yet into commiserating over dating app woes at the watercooler.

"*Well . . .*"

The sky-high pitch in his voice was all Cadence needed to know. "The Prism holiday party wouldn't be my choice to bring a date anyway." She dug her heels into the carpet and pushed herself back to the safety of her desk. "How good of a time can you really have when your boss is around?"

"I don't know." Matt tilted his head in thought while he held her gaze. "We seem to do all right."

Cadence's brain was overheating. She had a litany of defense mechanisms for his saunters into the office, the clean citrus-woodsy scent of his cologne, and his baseline sales speak that generally sounded flirtatious. Those were easy to bat away because those were part of Matt's MO. Unintentional. This she couldn't register.

Her phone rang again and Cadence welcomed the distraction. This time she remembered to check the caller ID before she picked up. She didn't recognize the number. "Hi. Cad—"

A man's voice plowed past Cadence's greeting and jumped straight into questions that she had no context for. She tried to find a moment to interject politely, but the guy did not let up.

"Excuse me!" she pressed, bringing the man to a stop. "I think you have the wrong number."

"Is this not extension 1147?"

"It is," Cadence gritted out as professionally as she could. His tone left much to be desired.

"And who are you?" Before she could answer, the rude man continued, "It doesn't matter. Can you transfer me to Matt? Or anyone who could explain Prism's absurd market analysis for the Financial District?"

"I compiled the analysis, and I can tell you exactly how it was calculated if you'd like." Nothing made Cadence's blood boil faster than a condescending man who didn't know what he was talking about. This fucker chose the wrong day to question Cadence's expertise. She let him have it, explaining the rationale and data collection process for her analysis. She dumbed down every excruciating detail of each number, formula, and cell, connecting the dots for him to lead his pea brain to the same conclusion. *Absurd, my ass.*

There was a long pause before the man spoke again. His brain probably needed time to catch up. "That was very informative, *Miss . . . ?*"

Cadence's eye twitched at the patronizing emphasis on her prefix. "Lim. Cadence Lim." Let's see if the man liked a taste of his own medicine. "Do you have any questions, *Mister . . . ?*"

The man snorted, incredulous. "Ma. Percy Ma."

CHAPTER 4
MATT

Matt braved a glance over to Cadence's desk. She'd had squabbles with Kevin before, but this phone call was different. It was like watching a master class in assertive verbal takedowns. Cadence deliberately walked through her analysis firmly, laced with enough acid in her voice for it to burn. She showed such restraint, Matt wondered if the poor person on the other line knew that they just got owned. Personally, he wasn't sure if he should be scared of Cadence or if he should give her a high five.

"Oh." Cadence's hand strangled the phone cord as her face fell. She cleared her throat. "Please hold," she said with a hollow voice, void of the fighting spirit she exhibited seconds ago. She pressed a button on her phone as her body folded. "Um . . . Matt?"

Uh-oh.

Cadence's hand shook as she held out her phone, wincing like she just swallowed a bitter pill. "M-mister . . . Percy Ma is on the line for you."

Matt jumped out of his seat, his fight-or-flight response tuning out her apologies for not knowing how to transfer the call. He loosened his tie and inhaled deeply before he picked up the phone. "Percy. This is Matt."

"I had a very interesting phone call with your colleague."

"Oh, did you?" Matt matched Percy's cool tone while he mentally prepared himself for groveling.

"Yes, she made some compelling points. Clarified things, though I'm curious how you wrote the wrong phone number on your own materials, Matt."

"Oh, my mistake," Matt lied, clamping his hand around Cadence's armrest to keep her from shrinking away. She got them into this mess, so she had to woman up here.

"I'll cut to the chase," Percy said. "We both know that there's more inventory out there, but the Sansome building has a unique charm. If we can hash out some better terms and move this along, we can have a deal." Matt silently fist-pumped the air. "I'm traveling back to Shenzhen, so my assistant will set up a meeting. Over email," Percy added, "assuming it's the correct email."

"Ha-ha, good one." Lovely. Getting dunked on by a soon-to-be billionaire was on his bingo card. "Thanks so much." Matt hung up the phone and crossed his arms, waiting for Cadence to look at him in the eye and face the consequences of her actions. "Well? What do you have to say for yourself?"

Cadence didn't seem to know what to do with her hands. They eventually clasped around her neck like she was about to stop, drop, and roll. "Listen . . ."

"I'm all ears."

"I don't know what came over me. I know how important this deal was and I'm so, *so* sorry. What do I need to do to fix this?

Should I apologize to him over email or do I"—she swallowed—
"need to get Sadie involved?"

"I don't know how to break it to you, Lim." Matt rubbed his
chin, indulgently feigning his consideration. "Percy said you
made some *interesting* comments. Comments that turned the tables around and threw a wrench in my strategy. You're gonna have
to help me out here . . ." Matt tried not to laugh when Cadence
cringed and nodded as if to accept her verdict. "There's so much
to prep before we meet with Percy's team."

Cadence's head shot up, her face a kaleidoscope of emotions—
confusion, relief, then disbelief as something dawned on her. "You
got the . . . !" Her hands sprung out as Matt nodded, her fingers
curling, air-wringing Matt's neck. "I felt so bad!"

"You should because it could have gone south real fast, but"—
Matt grabbed Cadence's wrists and lifted her fists up like she just
won the heavyweight championship—"we did it!"

Cadence's arms were limp as he shook them in celebration. "I
hate you."

"No, you don't." Matt let go of her hands before he wore down
her patience. "So, conference room tonight? What do you want for
dinner? I'm buying."

"Shh! Keep it down." Cadence scanned their surroundings.
"People can hear you."

"What? What's the big deal?"

"There's rumors about . . ." Cadence flicked her finger, pointing
at him and then herself. *Oh.* What was so bad about that? "Forget
it." She rubbed her wrists. "I can't."

"Why? You got a hot date with Karl? Where is he taking you
now? Alcatraz?"

Cadence glared at Matt for the dig at her local tourist hobby. "Just because I'm single doesn't mean my evenings are free for the taking."

"Come on. That's not what I meant. You can't bail on me now after you went all She-Hulk on Percy Ma. We're lucky that he liked it, and I could use some of that magic at the meeting. So what do you say?"

Cadence swiveled her chair to face her computer. Over her shoulder, she said, "You owe me."

What else was new? "I'll add it to my tab."

LATER THAT EVENING, Matt walked through Prism's front doors with his fingers hooked under a tight double-knotted plastic bag containing multiple steaming-hot takeout containers. He hoped Thai food would quell Cadence's hangry feelings or else he'd lose more than the blood supply to his index fingers.

"I come bearing gifts," he announced to nobody in the dark, empty office. With its white walls and modern Scandinavian furniture, it resembled an upgraded IKEA showroom. Matt crossed the main office floor, the motion-sensing lights flickering on behind him.

"Finally! What took you so long?" Cadence's voice was muffled by the closed conference room doors.

"I'm starving," she exclaimed without looking up from her laptop. She was in her usual seat at the far end of the conference table. According to her, it was the best seat because she was farsighted and could see the screen better from a distance. Never mind the fact that it was the closest to the conference room door and it allowed her to sneak in when she ran a few minutes late, which was always. Everyone in the office knew it too, which was why the seat was always reserved for her.

"Take a break." Matt shrugged off his coat and blazer and slid the pad thai toward her. It was nearing ten o'clock (two P.M. in Shenzhen, where iStan was based), and they needed carbs if they wanted to get through this call.

Cadence cracked open the compostable lid of her to-go box, inhaling dreamily. "Before I forget." She tossed this month's issue of *SF Monthly* on the table. "Congratulations, San Francisco's Fifth Most Eligible Bachelor."

"Fifth? Who were one through four?" he demanded, half serious.

Cadence flipped through the pages until she found Matt's profile. "'Matt Escanilla: Breaking Ground and Hearts Across the Peninsula,'" she read out loud. "Seriously? Who did you have to pay for this?" She jammed her finger at Matt's glossy image, in his slim-fit navy suit, a foot propped up on a shovel. His teeth were on full display. The sunlight filtered across his tawny skin as he stood on the corner of Sutter Street, where he brokered a deal for a start-up whose name ended with *-ly*.

"The writer is a friend of my client's. Can't blame her if she thinks I'm a catch."

Cadence skimmed the rest of the article, then glanced at him. "She needs to book an appointment with her optometrist or make more Filipino friends, because you look nothing like Manny Jacinto."

It couldn't have been more than a few seconds, but something about being the target of her gaze made him feel anxious. Normally, when a woman's eyes traveled up and down in his direction, he took that as a sign of interest. From Cadence, it felt like . . . What did this feel like?

Cadence shook her head after her assessment. "Same lean body type, but I doubt your cheekbones could cut glass. Where is the journalistic integrity here?"

Disappointment. It felt like disappointment. The day had not been good for his ego.

"Whatever. It's not like there's a lot of Filipino representation in media. It was either him or the Jabbawockeez, and nobody knows what they look like behind the masks. Besides, don't you think it's good publicity for the company?"

"The front desk did receive a few calls inquiring about your services this morning. Not sure if they're all real estate related," Cadence answered dryly. She unsheathed her wooden chopsticks and split them neatly in half, dusting off the splinters that landed on her skirt. "So, am I done for the night?"

Matt hesitated a second before taking his usual seat to her left. Why was she in such a hurry? "Can we review what you discussed with Percy? In case it comes up."

"It's all in the report. I'm sure that even *you* could figure it out."

"Hey!" Matt pointed his fork at her with the intention of rebutting her insult, but since he needed her, he let it go. "Numbers are only numbers until we give them meaning. It's the story that connects the dots, that excites us about the possibilities and warns us about the consequences. That's where you excel, pun intended, and why I asked you to be here."

Matt's admission seemed to embarrass Cadence because she averted her eyes, flicking them back to her laptop screen. He didn't mean to make her feel uncomfortable, so he picked up an angel wing in awe. "Have you ever seen anything so perfect? A stuffed, deep-fried, *boneless* chicken wing."

"You and your fear of bones. You're such a child sometimes," she teased. She dumped the entire plastic sauce cup of sambal on her noodles and mixed everything together into one big gloppy mess. "For the record, I agreed to this because you said you'd pick up dinner and my fridge is empty."

"You're saying you're doing this for the free food?"

Of course she would. Cadence brought her own lunch on most days, usually consisting of a frozen Trader Joe's entrée, eaten at her desk, except when the office catered lunch. For someone who wore designer clothes, she was awfully frugal.

"What can I say?" She peeked up from her laptop with a sidelong glance. "I'm a cheap date."

Date? Matt knew it was a figure of speech, but the word rang in his head. It wasn't like the concept of dating Cadence was new. When Matt first met Cadence, he found her attractive, but she never seemed interested in anything besides work. Then when Frank called them lovebirds, Cadence made it clear that they were just friends. So be it. Matt didn't mind if it meant spending more time with her.

Even as Matt watched her burn her insides, slurping chili-laden noodles into her mouth, he still found her cute, with that long hair that she casually tousled to the right. Matt spent many meetings distracted by Cadence's hair tsunami and the way it somehow reverted back to its normal state once she stood up, like it followed its own laws of physics.

"I can feel your eyes judging me," Cadence said in between bites. "I haven't eaten since lunch."

Matt held his breath. How long had he been staring at her?

"No, I wasn't. I was—" Matt needed to change the subject fast. His eyes landed on her laptop screen. "Is that what you were 'working' on? Dress shopping?"

"Jeez, so judgy tonight. It's for the holiday party next week. Last minute, I know. I need to decide on one quick." She clicked open the cart, revealing the dresses in contention.

Matt was sure any dress she chose would be fine. Cadence had good taste. Her colorful outfits looked effortlessly put together. He could always spot her among their dark-suited colleagues.

"Whoa." Matt nearly choked on his food when he saw the steep price tag of a shimmery gold-sequined cocktail dress fit for a red carpet. "That dress costs as much as my suit."

Cadence raised an eyebrow. "And?"

"And . . ." Matt saw the look on her face and he was not going to dig himself into his own grave. "You know what? You"—he pointed at her with his fork—"you deserve it."

"Mm-hmm. That's what I thought." Cadence clicked on the next dress in her cart. "Is the color too Christmassy?" she mused. "I don't want to look like Mrs. Claus."

Mrs. Claus was not where Matt's thoughts were going as he envisioned Cadence in the formfitting crimson dress, his hand moving down the curve of her exposed back.

"Whatever you pick will look nice." Matt kept his voice level until it caught in his throat at the end, cracking ever so slightly. Jesus, that hadn't happened since he was a teenager. Matt stuck his fork into his pad see ew and tried to stop thinking about how nice she looked in anything.

Or nothing.

Matt shook the stray thought out of his head. He regretted bringing up her online shopping. His phone buzzed on the table from an incoming text, saving him from this minefield of cocktail dresses.

"I didn't know your grandma texted you this late," Cadence joked.

Matt wondered how many conversations with Lola Cadence had overheard through their flimsy cubicle partition. Lola called a lot, but thankfully she wasn't into texting.

With a sideways glance, Cadence caught the text preview. "Oh, my bad. Definitely not grandma."

Matt hurriedly picked up his phone.

MIKI: last night was fun. drinks later?

"Miki as in fifth-floor receptionist Miki? From that beauty start-up?" Cadence asked with wide, knowing eyes.

"Who's being judgy now? What's wrong with Miki?" He couldn't explain why he was feeling defensive. Cadence never showed interest in his dating life before, and last he checked, there wasn't anything wrong with dating someone who happened to work in the same building.

"Nothing is wrong with Miki. She's nice, but—"

"But what?"

"She's, like, the third person you've dated from there, isn't she? All I'm saying is, any more and they're going to think you're easy," she said with a straight face until her smiling eyes gave her away. "Please don't ruin things with her. This morning, in the elevator, she offered to hook me up with some skin-care samples."

Matt gasped, clutching his imaginary pearls. "You're using me for free moisturizer? I feel so cheap!"

"Don't. Their stuff is expensive." She angled her face, elongating her elegant neck. "Look," she said, pointing at her eye. "I'm starting to get dark circles and fine lines. 'Asian don't raisin' is a lie." Her finger glided down the curve of her cheek. "And then here, I'm starting to get laugh lines."

Matt had no idea what she was talking about. To him, her face looked flawless. "How can you have laugh lines? You hardly smile, let alone laugh."

"Maybe it's because you're not funny. Have you ever thought about that?" Cadence dabbed her napkin at the corners of her mouth. "Whew. The spice kicked in." She began to fan her face and ran her tongue across her burning, glistening full lips.

What wouldn't he do to get branded by that mouth? Matt took a long sip of his chilled water, which proved to be a poor substitute for a cold shower.

Cadence checked the time on her phone. "We still have a few minutes before the call. Do you want to go over the numbers one more time? That way, you might make it for drinks."

"Drinks?"

"Yeah," she said while closing out her browsers. "With Miki? Don't tell me you forgot about her already. I swear, Matt. Can you wait until I get some samples before you—"

"Wait." An open file on Cadence's laptop caught his eye. "Is that your résumé?" Cadence swiftly minimized the file. "Are you looking for another job?" Matt couldn't hide his surprise. Cadence had complained about work before, but nothing that made him think that she would leave.

"I'm thinking about it." She proceeded to pull up the documents for the conference call, moving on.

When she didn't elaborate, Matt asked, "Where are you applying to?" The question came out more pointed than he expected, so to soften it, he added, "Maybe I can refer you."

"I don't know yet. It was one thing to watch Kevin get promoted before me, but not getting a bonus was a wake-up call. I've been here for five years. If there's no growth for me here, then I should keep my options open, right? There's nothing keeping me here anyway."

"Sure." Matt looked down at his food, though he didn't feel hungry anymore. He couldn't blame her for wanting something more. She was too smart for her job, and her supervisor, Bill, delegated his work to her constantly. It made sense for her to go somewhere that valued her talents, but for some reason, when he thought of Cadence, he associated her with Prism and San Francisco. The thought of her leaving left him with a sense of dread he didn't fully understand.

THE NEXT MORNING, Matt waited at the corner coffee shop for his drink and the coffee he owed Cadence. It was one of the countless coffees he owed her for helping him out over the years, and at this rate, he'd have to supply her caffeine fix in perpetuity.

His phone rang as the barista presented his drinks. Matt quickly inserted his earbuds and accepted the call before it went to voice mail.

"Hi. It's Matt," he said, expecting it to be a client.

"I know it's you, Matt. I'm the one who called you," Lola said matter-of-factly. "Have you eaten yet?"

"Yes." Matt closed his eyes and took a deep breath. He loved his grandma dearly. She helmed their family even when Lolo was alive. But her calls were becoming more frequent. The fact that she lived three hundred and seventy-eight miles away in Eagle Rock didn't save him from her reminders that he was still single.

"I'm sorry, Lola. I'm about to head to the office. I'll make it up to you when I come home for Christmas."

"You know what would make me happy? It is not a present or anything that would fit under a tree."

"Oh, gosh," Matt muttered to himself. He could not use the Lord's name in vain in his grandma's presence.

"Matt. Please, my dear Matt. I know you're a handsome boy and you need to sow some wild oats, but it's time to settle down, yeah? You're no spring chicken anymore. When are you going to get married? Everyone else is married and has kids."

"That's not true," Matt countered. "Not Missy."

"Of course not Missy," Lola hissed. "She's still in college."

"AJ doesn't have kids." Matt grabbed his drinks and walked down the block toward the office.

"Not now, but maybe soon."

"What do you mean, 'maybe soon'?"

Lola huffed. "AJ and George are looking into adoption. You would know that if you came home for Thanksgiving, Matthew John Escanilla."

Ah, she busted out the full name. Matt had to tread carefully.

"So, are you seeing anyone special right now?"

Matt tried to think of a new variation of the same old excuse. It wasn't his fault that his job kept him working through the evenings, when normal people liked to meet up. He never felt like he was missing out, not when it was easy to find someone to grab late-night drinks with and have casual sex with when he was in the mood for it. Lola didn't need to know this, though.

Matt stopped outside his office building. He could imagine Lola clasping her hands in prayer as she asked that question. He didn't want to disappoint her, but he was sure his recent fling with Miki didn't qualify her as "someone special."

"Matt!"

He looked up and found Cadence jogging toward him. The forest-green scarf tucked into her black wool coat covered half of her face. From the top half, her eyes lit up. Unfortunately, they were looking at the drinks in his hands.

"Thanks for picking up coffee," she said, twisting each cup until she found the one labeled *IOU*. She held it preciously in her bare hands, absorbing its warmth. "I don't know about you, but I'm so tired after last night. Don't tell anyone I stayed here with you. If word gets around, I'll *never* hear the end of it."

"Who is that?"

The sound of Lola's voice in his ear startled Matt. For a split second, he forgot that he was on the phone with her.

Cadence smiled with a delight he'd never seen before. *Is that your grandma?* she mouthed. After Matt nodded, Cadence leaned close to his ear. She was so close, he worried that she might have noticed his hard swallow.

"Hi, Lola," she said cheerily. "Matt's told me so much about you!" Stepping back, she beamed at him like she found it so sweet that he was talking to his grandma first thing in the morning. If only she knew how much her seemingly innocuous introduction complicated things for him.

"I'll head up first. See you there." She held up her coffee to say thanks and then walked briskly into the building.

"Matt. Who was that?" Lola repeated, with a weighted curiosity.

"That was . . ." Images of Cadence flashed before his eyes. The way her voice grew louder while she was arguing about Excel formulas with the other analysts. How she was composed and pragmatic during meetings, but relaxed when it was just the two of them.

"Someone special," he admitted.

Lola clapped her hands. "Thank the Lord! Tell me more about her."

"Um . . . she's smart and nice," he said wistfully. "And—"

And she was just a friend. Matt couldn't get himself to say it out loud, because being a friend didn't feel like enough anymore.

"And beautiful, yes?"

"Uh-huh," he agreed. Cadence was indeed beautiful, with her classically elegant face that could have served as a muse for paintings, with a default reserved expression that kept her shrouded in mystery. In front of him, Sadie's car turned into the underground garage. "Lola, I have to go to work."

"Try to bring your girlfriend down for Christmas." She said it sweetly enough, but she didn't leave him much of a choice.

"No promises. Love you, Lola." He hung up before she could threaten him anymore. What was he going to do? He didn't want to disappoint his grandma, but how could he bring Cadence? There weren't enough coffees in the world to convince Cadence to do it except for the off chance that she might want to be more than friends.

His suit suddenly felt too tight at the thought of broaching this topic with her. Finding women to date was one thing, but admitting feelings for someone as important to him as Cadence made him nervous. He worked too hard to become her friend to let it get weird over unrequited feelings. But as he entered the building, he was reminded of what pushed him through the long days. That rush when he converted his millionth cold call into a client and the thrill of closing a deal.

No risk, no reward, he told himself.

CHAPTER 5

MATT

The Prism Realty holiday party was a swanky ordeal at the Bently Reserve. Matt picked a champagne flute off a waiter's tray and surveyed the venue, soaking in its magnificent tall ceilings and grand neoclassic design. The place smelled like money, a remnant of its past life as a bank. The room had blue mood lighting along the walls, and the cascading crystal chandeliers glowed overhead, though the room still managed to look dim. If there hadn't been a decked-out twelve-foot Christmas tree centering the room, the venue could have easily passed for a nightclub. A nightclub full of real estate brokers.

Matt spotted Cadence standing by the dessert bar, chatting with Josie. Cadence didn't get the red dress, but Matt wasn't complaining. He tried to inconspicuously sip his champagne while he absorbed the image of Cadence wearing a black long-sleeved velvet wrap dress that clung to her curves in all the right ways. When she bent her right knee slightly to shift her weight, she exposed a thigh-high slit that left Matt parched. He polished off his champagne, disposed of his empty glass, straightened his tie, and made his way toward her.

"Hello, ladies." Josie lit up when Matt joined their conversation, extending an arm for a hug, accidentally sloshing her martini in the process. Matt leaned down and accepted. Cadence, on the other hand, was making eyes at the tower of macarons. "Sadie went all out this year."

"You'd never know that we had layoffs this year, would you?" Cadence said into her glass.

"That was the point," Josie quipped. "We should move to a better spot for Sadie's announcements."

She led them closer toward the stage as the lights dimmed over the ballroom and jazzy covers of Christmas songs waned. The crowd clapped when Sadie stepped up to the microphone.

"Good evening, everyone!" Sadie shouted over lingering applause. "I'll keep my remarks short so that you all can resume the party. Credit to Josie, who put this soiree together." Josie waved, eliciting another round of applause. "We've had a roller coaster of a year and I believe I can speak on behalf of the board of directors when I say that we could not have pulled through without all of you standing here. That's why we've gathered tonight. To celebrate your work and accomplishments. I will say that we had some bright spots this year. Without further ado—because I know this is the real reason why you all came tonight, besides the open bar"—she paused for laughs—"the top five brokers with the most sales this year were . . ."

Cadence's arm brushed against his as she inched closer to whisper in his ear. "Are you getting your diplomatic Oscars clap ready for when you win?"

Matt smirked. "Hell no. I'm ready to assume my bragging rights for another year."

Cadence rolled her eyes at his hubris, but the truth was that it was anyone's game this year. There were no guarantees when you were working on commission, especially in a volatile economy. The only thing standing between Matt and this promotion was hard work. Pounding the pavement. Making deals happen. He just hoped he did enough to gain his ticket back to Southern California and closer to his family.

"In third place, Dana Fisher!" Sadie continued to rousing cheers. "And second place, Matt Escanilla!"

Matt's heart sank as he acknowledged the applause with a wave. What was worse than being the runner-up was that he knew whose name would be announced next. Everyone in the office liked to pit Matt and Hunter as rivals, but Matt always found it insulting. Rivals implied that they were similarly skilled competitors, but they weren't. Matt consistently had a high sales record, and he didn't need to have family connections to achieve it.

"That means, drumroll, please"—Sadie's voice rose with anticipation—"Prism Realty's top broker this year is Hunter Waterson! Congratulations, everyone! Please enjoy the rest of your night."

"Oh no." Cadence placed her hand on his arm. "Damn. I'm sorry, M—"

"Matt!"

Ah, fuck. Matt squared his shoulders as Hunter sidled next to him to rub his win in Matt's face. Since it was the holidays, Matt decided to play nice and reached for a handshake. "Hunter. Congrats, man."

Hunter gripped Matt's hand from the top like a claw machine in a fucking weirdo power move. "Better luck next year. When I get the director position in L.A., you'll get to move into my spot at the top of the sales list."

Matt clenched his jaw. "We'll see about that."

As Hunter let go of Matt's hand, his eyes dropped to Cadence. "Well, look who it is. Matt's *liiittle* helper," he drawled. "I almost didn't see you hiding down there."

Matt bristled at Hunter's condescending tone. He opened his mouth, ready to defend Cadence, when she beat him to the punch.

"Excuse me?" Cadence stood taller with the aid of her stilettos. "You might want to think twice before you come around with your next client."

"Loosen up, Cadence. It's a party." Hunter excused himself from the conversation to make his rounds, which was probably the smartest thing he had done this evening.

"That motherf—"

"Don't waste your time on that asshole." Matt removed the Cadence's glass of liquid courage and passed it on to a server. As much as he liked seeing Cadence riled up, it wouldn't have been good office politics, since Hunter was Bill's nephew. "He's not worth it."

"Matt, I've been looking for you." Sadie skated toward them from the stage, greeting passersby with a flashing wave that simultaneously shooed them away until she landed in between him and Cadence. "I wanted to commend you on your work on the iStan deal."

"I couldn't have done it without Cadence. She helped me work on the pitch."

"Yes, Cadence too," Sadie said, nodding in acknowledgment.

"I've only heard good things from Percy's team. It's a shame it's still pending because I know it would have been just the thing to put you in first place for sales. Now, that's neither here nor there. I'll let you in on a secret. The L.A. office is slated to open in April. The board of directors will decide who will take the lead on the Southern California region by February. So if I were you, Matt, I'd try to wrap up this deal as soon as possible."

"Understood. I'll get as much done as I can before I leave for Christmas." Matt had planned to take the week between Christmas and New Year's off to visit his family. He supposed he'd have to take work home, even if it earned him disapproving glares from his mom.

"That means you too, Cadence. I was surprised and not surprised to hear that Percy spoke highly of you."

"Oh, it was nothing," Cadence demurred. "He's exaggerating."

"Don't diminish your work," Sadie said, supportive and firm. "I'm glad to see you taking more initiative. Let's all touch base in the New Year." Sadie nodded at Josie, who jumped on her phone to set a reminder. "Now if you'll excuse me," Sadie said, linking arms with Josie, "we have things to discuss."

Josie tossed a pleading look over her shoulder as Sadie whisked her away.

"Poor Josie. She's always on call," Cadence said with a sympathetic frown. "Hey, you okay?"

"Yeah." Matt swallowed the crack in his voice. "Nothing like shirking all your responsibilities to get work done."

Cadence let out a resigned sigh. "Well, you won't be going about it alone."

"Sorry. I hope I didn't ruin any plans for you."

"Nah. I was going to be at work anyway. Now I'm just stuck with you."

"Wow." Matt placed a hand on his chest, smoothing his tie. "Kick me while I'm down, why don't you?"

"It's a compliment! If I had to be stuck anywhere, there are worse people than you."

Matt laughed. That was probably the nicest thing she'd ever said to him.

The DJ started bumping upbeat nineties hip-hop, causing their colleagues to holler. Cadence was feeling the music too, swaying along and mouthing the lyrics to no one but herself. Matt marveled at the rare sight.

When Cadence caught him staring at her, Matt thought she'd become embarrassed. Instead, they locked eyes. Her undivided attention was a gift bestowed to few, and Matt said nothing, fearing words would end the spell. When the song changed to Montell Jordan's "This Is How We Do It," Cadence shocked him again by stepping backward toward the dance floor with a sly smile, challenging him to follow her. He would be a fool not to.

So he danced toward her, dusting off his old boy-band dance moves, gaining some excited *woo*s from their colleagues. He couldn't care less about the crowd's reaction, not while Cadence bounced along to the music. She wasn't the best dancer in the technical sense, but she danced with an exhilarating, tipsy confidence, throwing up her hands as if she didn't have a care in the world. Matt committed the image to his memory.

As an audience started to form around them, Cadence leaned in over his shoulder. "I knew this would cheer you up." She gestured to the crowd, egging them to cheer louder. Matt felt a pinch of sadness at Cadence's well-intentioned but misguided pursuit to lift his spirits. This was one of the few instances where he didn't want to be in the spotlight. He would much rather have been alone with her. But the chants of *Go, Matt!* grew louder from the crowd, drowning out his thoughts. Not wanting to disappoint, he hammed it up and busted out his best moves.

Cadence began to back up to join the crowd as a spectator. Matt wasn't going to let her off the hook that easy. Before she made her escape, he pointed at her, challenging her to a dance battle. Matt went around pumping up the crowd. Cadence kept a nervous smile while she waved off the cheers of *Go, Cadence!*

"Show me what you got, Lim! Or are you afraid to lose to this?" he shouted, taunting her while he dragged his hands down his chest.

Cadence crossed her arms and narrowed her eyes, fuming at him. He knew having this much attention annoyed her. However, as he'd hoped, she dropped her arms and strode toward him. Challenge accepted.

Matt couldn't take his eyes off her. That slightly mischievous face. The way her hips swayed while she took determined steps. He didn't know what song was playing anymore. Matt gulped as Cadence closed the distance between them. He stuffed his hands into his pockets to stand his ground. The square-off culminated with a hand served to his face before she swirled back around, flicking her hair in Matt's face in the process. Cadence riled up the crowd, whose noise reached deafening levels when the DJ transitioned into the intro to Salt-N-Pepa's "Push It."

Cadence threw all her energy into rolling her body while cranking her finger guns with cheesy precision. When you added in the surprise factor, there was no contest. Cadence had already won. Matt clutched his chest when she shot him with an "Oh baby baby." To the crowd it looked like he was accepting defeat, but he could have sworn his heart stopped when she bit her lip to stop her playful smile. The whole act put him in agony. The crowd cheered louder for Cadence, officially declaring her the winner. She clasped her hands, bowed before the dance floor cleared, and made her way to the bar as the music transitioned back into a Christmas song.

Now or never, Matt.

He had to seize the moment, while the mood worked in his favor. He reached for her arm. Maybe he could lead her to the lobby or outside where they could talk alone, away from curious eyes.

Unfortunately, Josie got to Cadence first. "Um, hello? Who are you and what have you done to Cadence?" she asked while she clutched Cadence's shoulder with one hand, the other holding a nuclear-green martini. "That was ah-mazing! Wasn't it, Matt?"

He smiled, even though he was internally cursing Josie for ruining the magic. "What about me?" he asked, feigning offense.

"Oh, please," Josie said. "It's not always about you, Matt. Let Cadence have her moment."

Matt dismissed Josie's presence and leaned toward Cadence. "Hey. Can I talk to you for a second?" To throw Josie off, he added, "The iStan team countered on some terms that I'd like to go over with you."

"I'm off the clock," Cadence chided. She swung her head toward the buffet. "I think I'll get another plate and head out early."

Josie gripped Cadence's arm. "Aww! Don't go yet! I want to see more of Fun Cadence!"

Cadence tried to shake Josie off. "Are you saying I'm not normally fun?"

"Um . . . I don't know how to answer that without insulting you," Josie answered too honestly.

"Let the lady eat," Matt said. He tugged Cadence's elbow to extricate her from Josie's hold, but no dice.

"Aww!" Josie palmed her face. "Are you rescuing your work wife?"

"Oh my god. I'm done." Cadence yanked her arm to free herself.

"No, come back!" Josie stumbled forward to stop Cadence and in the process sloshed her drink down the front of Cadence's dress.

Cadence gasped and froze. Green apple martini dripped down her legs and pooled on the floor.

"I'm so sorry!" Josie hugged Cadence's neck. "I'll pay for your dry cleaning."

"It's fine," Cadence said, even though it wasn't. To Matt, she mouthed, *Get her off me!*

"How much did you drink?" he muttered to himself as he struggled to pull Josie off.

Cadence dried herself with napkins from the bar, disgusted when they stuck to her sticky hands. "I'm going to head out."

Matt shifted Josie onto a nearby stool. "Let me take you home."

"No, I got a ride," Cadence said, holding up her phone. "Make sure she's okay."

The night couldn't end like this. Matt caught her arm before she left.

"Hey," he said, hot from his belly. He searched her heart-shaped face, trying to find a glimmer of the woman who danced with abandon. Who, for a small window of time, let him see a new side of her. But she stood there, confused, gazing at him with those sad, disarming doe eyes as if she couldn't wait to get out of there. "Merry Christmas. Get home safe."

"Merry Christmas," she replied. Matt barely heard her over the Christmas song Michael Bublé was crooning over the speakers. The smooth velvet from her dress crossed his palm and slipped through his fingers as she backed away and left the party.

"Maaaatt," Josie said, leaning against his shoulder. He never thought his name could be stretched into multiple syllables. "When are you and Cadence going to hook up? We have bets riding on this."

Matt glared at her in disbelief. If only Josie knew that she had cock-blocked her chances of winning. "We're just friends."

"Yeah, right. More like Asian Jim and Asian Pam."

Matt scoffed. "Wouldn't that make you Dwight?"

"Affirmative." Josie giggled into a hiccup.

Matt changed his mind. Josie was being more of a Meredith. He motioned to the bartender to cut her off from drinks. While Josie sobered up, Matt checked his phone. There were multiple updates in the cousins' group chat.

CELINE: Matt. Did you tell Lola you're bringing a girlfriend for Christmas? Mom and Dad keep asking me about it.

Damn it.

GERALD: Word?
GERALD: Is she hot?

CELINE: Shut up, Gerry

CELINE: Who is she?

JUSTINE: Supposedly, Matt's girlfriend talked to Lola on the phone. Is that true?

GERALD: I didn't know blow-up dolls could talk

MISSY: ew!

JASON: Shut up, Gerry

AJ: Shut up, Gerry!

AJ: Imaginary girlfriends don't count either, Matt

GERALD: lol

Matt scrolled and scrolled, finding more of the same shit-talking from his cousins. Damn Gerald. This was his fault. Matt counted on Gerald to stay single so there was someone else Lola could bother. What was his family's fascination with his love life? He had plenty of friends who were still single in their mid-thirties. Hadn't they factored in that with this business, sales didn't fall into his lap? He had to make his own opportunities, by building relationships and outsmarting his competition. That shit took time!

Above all, he was doing it for them. He hated that he was missing out on family gatherings and watching his nieces and nephews grow. Matt couldn't wait to return to L.A. with a promotion in hand. Then he'd have it all.

A successful career.

His family close by.

And love?

Maybe he'd have to settle for two out of three.

CHAPTER 6
CADENCE

The Prism office during the week leading up to Christmas dwindled until two groups of people remained—those who didn't have vacation days left and those who worked because they had to. They had no other choice. It was easy to tell which employee belonged to which group. Those in the former group killed time watching holiday movies in an inconspicuous window on their monitor, while the latter group had devolved into hunched, sedentary creatures who subsisted on popcorn from the holiday tins and food gifts from corporate vendors.

By Christmas Eve, the office was a ghost town after everyone called in sick. Those who went to work that day were either a trouper or a sucker. Cadence knew where she belonged. She'd spent the week performing her due diligence, glued to her monitor to the point where it stung to blink. Meanwhile, Matt was running around town, trying to chase someone at the Department of Building Inspection to get an answer about the LED screen iStan wanted to hang on the facade, among other unconventional build-out concerns.

Cadence lurched to her desk at nine-thirty (what was time,

anyway?) in search of the freebie coffee Matt had begun to leave on her desk in the mornings. Instead, she found none and groaned when her desk phone rang. It was Tristan. Against her better judgment, she picked it up despite not having her morning caffeine.

"What's up?" Cadence asked as she lowered herself into her chair.

"Is that how you pick up the phone?"

Cadence groaned again and massaged the throbbing spot on her forehead. It was too early in the morning for Dad's gruff Hakka to stab her ears with accusations. In Hakka, she replied, "Why are you calling me at work?"

"Humph. You don't pick up my calls when I call from my cell phone." Cadence couldn't argue with that because it was true. "You said you couldn't come home because of work, so I'm making sure you're at work."

Cadence's eye twitched. "Is there something wrong?"

"Why does there have to be something wrong?" Dad snorted. Cadence could imagine him picking his nose with his pinkie. "I can't call you anymore to say hi?"

Cadence knew that her proud father would not call her at work if there wasn't anything important to say. If she wanted him to tell her in the least circuitous way, she'd have to comply with playing the part of the obedient, good daughter so that he could feel self-important. Forget it, he had enough friends for that. Cadence didn't have time for this shit. "Dad, I have work to do. If you're not going to tell me—"

"What kind of company makes you work on Christmas Eve?" he complained.

"Most companies! Why do you care? You don't celebrate Christmas!"

"So what? You don't like days off?"

Cadence pivoted before they went even more off tangent. "I'm coming home for Mom's death anniversary. I will see you then."

Dad replied with a heavy *mmm*. "When you come home, remember to go in the front house."

The front house? Cadence's two-story childhood home sat on the back of a concrete lot that was longer than it was wide. It towered behind a smaller one-story front house, which had been a rental property to provide a safety net for Dad. "Why would I go to the front house?"

"Because your brother and I moved in here."

Cadence sighed. He was really making her work for information. "Why?"

"Because I slipped on the stairs," he stated like he was telling her the weather.

"What?!" Cadence's heart raced. "Are you okay?"

"Yeah, fine. Go to work then. Bye."

Cadence hung up, wanting to pull her hair out. Her mom used to say that Cadence and her dad butted heads because they were so alike, but Cadence despised the comparison. Cadence would never leave their family in financial straits.

Cadence agitated her mouse to wake up her computer, banging it out of frustration when she became impatient.

"Can you keep it down over there?"

Cadence startled at Matt's muffled voice. She slid the partition and discovered Matt folded over his desk, wearing the same suit as the day before. She shook his arm. "Did you sleep here last night?"

"Stop yelling," Matt complained as he lifted his head, a pointy sticky tab stuck to his face, requesting a signature on his nose. He opened his mouth like he was about to say more, but only a gargle came out as he fell back asleep.

"You're exhausted. Go home and rest." Cadence peeled the tab off his face, which upon closer inspection had a muted pallor. She palmed his forehead. "Matt, you're *hot*."

"I know," he grumbled as he leaned forward into her hand.

Cadence pushed him back into his chair. "No, you're burning up."

Matt threw his arm over his eyes. "That's a Jonas Brothers song."

Cadence winced as he proceeded to sing—if that was the correct word for his incoherent mumbling—a song presumably by the aforementioned siblings. He must be delirious. "You need to go home."

"I wanna be Nick!" He pouted with a weak smile.

"Everybody wants to be Nick!" Cadence let out an exasperated sigh. It couldn't be that bad if Matt had his sense of humor intact. "Is there someone who can take you home?"

Matt removed his car keys from his pocket, foisting them on her. "Please? I'll owe you forever. All the coffees you want."

Cadence glanced around the empty office. She wasn't going to get much work done anyway. "All right." She took the keys. "Tell me where to go."

MATT'S APARTMENT WAS luxurious by Cadence's standard. Anything that had space for a couch and a sink bigger than her face was a palace in her book, but his building also had an elevator. A must-have when dragging a sick grown-ass man home.

"How long have you lived here?" Cadence said as she nudged Matt toward his bedroom. She didn't let her eyes wander, wanting to respect Matt's space and privacy, though she couldn't help but notice how all his furniture matched. Like he might have pointed at a furniture catalog and told a salesperson that he'd take the whole set. It was a stark contrast to Cadence's mishmash of bare essentials that had survived multiple cross-country moves.

"Four years." Matt shed his coat and fell face-first into his bed. "Moved here when I started at Prism."

"Um." Cadence scratched behind her ear. "You should change or take a shower or something." Her voice trailed off as she caught a glimpse of his sprawled body. She had to get out of there before she offered to help him take off his clothes. "D-Do you have medicine or should I go run out and get some?"

Matt mumbled something that sounded like *kitchen*.

Cadence backed out of the room and opened his cabinets one by one until she found flu medicine behind a collection of stainless steel tumblers. She tore a packet of tablets and poured a glass of water and brought them to his room.

She knocked on the open door. "I'm going to leave the medicine right next to you and head out."

"You're leaving?"

Cadence placed the glass and medicine on his nightstand. "You need to rest." Matt whined into his duvet. She tried to reason with him. "Matt. You're a thirty-four-year-old man and I trust that you can handle taking medication on your own."

Matt turned his head toward her, but his eyes were still closed. "How do you know my age?"

"Oh, puh-lease. You tell everybody when the office gets the birthday cake to celebrate the June birthdays."

"I don't know how old you are."

"You should never ask a lady her age." Matt cracked an eye

open and shot her an expectant look. "Fine. I'm thirty-one. Now that we settled that—"

"I'm *sick*," he appealed. This was exactly why Cadence compartmentalized her work life and her personal life. If she had enforced this boundary better, she would never have known that the Matt she knew from work was such a baby. "And it's Christmas Eve. You're going to ditch your sick friend on Christmas Eve?"

"Fine." It did sound bad when he put it that way. Cadence relented since he'd resorted to guilting her, but if she was going to stay, then she was going to focus on the task at hand. "Take your medicine, change your clothes *after I step out*, and go to sleep. I'll check on you later."

Cadence closed his bedroom door behind her, unclear about what she was going to do with herself. It didn't feel right to make herself at home and lounge on his couch watching TV.

She needed advice, so she texted her best friend, Maddie. They had been friends all their lives, and she knew Cadence better than anyone. Plus, Maddie was a mom now, so she would know what to do.

CADENCE: How do you treat the flu?

Maddie wouldn't mind the out-of-the-blue text. Between their busy jobs and Maddie's mom status, they'd come to terms with their ad hoc texts.

CADENCE: Merry xmas btw
MADDIE: Are you sick? Drink plenty of fluids! And chicken noodle soup!

It was sweet of Maddie to think that Cadence knew how to make chicken noodle soup.

> **CADENCE:** Do you have an easy recipe?
> **CADENCE:** No, I'm not sick. Taking care of a friend.
> **MADDIE:** 👀 Are we talking about your hot work friend?

Cadence should have known that Maddie would be on Team Matt after she had sent her that cropped photo of them at the food bank.

> **CADENCE:** Yeah.
> **MADDIE:** Here, try this.

Cadence tapped on the link Maddie sent, which led her to a sexy nurse costume on a discount Halloween website. How silly of her to forget the healing powers of thigh-high fishnet stockings.

> **MADDIE:** Bet that'll perk him right up.
> **CADENCE:** You're terrible. Love you.
> **MADDIE:** Happy to help!

Cadence opened Matt's fridge and found nothing useful. Water bottles. Condiments. Leftover takeout boxes. She checked his cabinets again in case there was a can of soup somewhere.

When she opened his small pantry, she felt like she hit the jackpot. There was a bag of rice. Screw chicken noodle soup. Cadence was going to make rice porridge, just as her mom made it. After rinsing a cup of rice in a pot, she filled it with water and put it on high heat until it boiled. Then she turned down the heat, stirring it as it simmered, cooking it low and slow to reach the right consistency. When it was done, Cadence turned off the burner and went to check on Matt.

"Hey, Matt?" Cadence knocked lightly on his door. "If you're up, I made food."

Matt opened the door, looking drowsy as he cinched a robe over his plaid pajama pants. He looked comfy, but very much sick. "You didn't have to cook."

"It's nothing." She returned to the kitchen to prepare a bowl.

He took a seat at his small dining table and Cadence placed a steaming serving in front of him.

"Literally nothing," Matt said as he examined the plain porridge.

Cadence handed him a spoon. "You didn't give me much to work with here, unless you want to eat it with leftover broccoli beef."

"I don't remember how old it is, so I'm gonna pass."

"Do you want soy sauce? Or fish sauce?"

Matt crinkled his nose as he rubbed his stomach. "On second thought, plain sounds good. Thanks."

"What are friends for?" Cadence took the seat across from him and watched him take a tentative slurp.

Matt's lips quirked into a wistful smile. "Who would have thought?"

"Why do you say that?"

He chuckled. "When I first met you, I didn't think you liked me at all. You always looked annoyed when I tried to talk to you."

"I can see why you thought that," she said, thinking back to that time. "I'm sorry if I wasn't very nice. I, uh . . . My mom passed away that year."

Cadence didn't know why she disclosed her mom's passing, because she never wanted to see that look of pity that was now on Matt's face. She was slipping, tired from the day, the week. But it was the most concise answer she could give rather than go into detail about her grieving the sudden loss of her mother. It had been easier to wall off her emotions because she was afraid of bursting into tears in the weeks following the funeral.

Matt put his spoon down. "I'm sorry. I didn't know."

"How could you? I never told you." Cadence preferred to keep her personal life private at work. One of the things she liked about starting a new job was that she could reinvent herself and build a reputation founded on her abilities. On the flip side, the thing she knew about quitting a job was that it was easier to do when she wasn't too attached. "You know what I thought when I first met you?" she said to take the focus off her. "Here comes another schmoozy broker. Every morning, you came in shooting your finger guns." Cadence pointed her fingers, imitating Matt. *Looking good, Frank! Send me your keto recipes. Sharon! Are those new earrings? They bring out your eyes!*

Matt scoffed. "That's called being friendly. You should try it sometime."

"Oh, please. Compliments from you are a dime a dozen."

"I thought you liked a good deal," Matt joked. Cadence leveled a look at him as she crossed her arms and leaned back in her seat. "So what? I never say anything I don't mean, and look where that's gotten us. We're friends, and dare I say, *best* friends?"

"Oh no." Cadence wagged her finger at the suggestion. This was where she drew the line. "I already have a best friend."

"Cadence. Why do you hurt me? Can't you see that I'm sick? I'm cold and hot at the same time, and to be honest, I can't tell the difference right now." Matt loosened his robe to cool off, shivering as he fanned himself.

Cadence's eyes inadvertently dipped to the point where his robe intersected until she willed them up.

"That doesn't sound good." Cadence gathered her coat before he noticed her drooling over the sliver of his exposed chest. "I better let you rest. I'll text you later."

"You're leaving?"

"I don't want to get sick," she said weakly. It was true. She didn't want to get sick, but the vulnerable expression on Matt's face made her want to take it back.

"I've never been alone on Christmas. I've always been with my family. Opening presents. Eating too much food. My sister, Celine, makes this cheesecake with Jell-O on top. I know it sounds weird, but she only makes it at Christmas and I'm not going to have any this year. And my cousins are a bunch of assholes, but I'm gonna miss them too. We always sing 'My Heart Will Go On' during karaoke."

His family sounded so sweet, and it was unfortunate that Matt couldn't go home, but he could hardly hold himself up. Cadence was afraid he was going to fall face-first into his bowl.

"They'll understand, and you're not fit to travel. It would be irresponsible to spread your germs."

Matt pouted as his eyes closed, heavy with sleep. "If you were trying to comfort me, it didn't work."

"What do you want me to say?"

"I don't know." He coughed into his elbow and it sounded like every horror movie sound effect rolled into one. His voice was hoarse when he was able to speak again. "That you believe in Christmas miracles?"

"Yeah . . . no." Cadence helped him to his feet and walked him to his room. Matt tucked himself under his duvet, turned on his side, and curled into a fetal position. She pressed the back of her hand on his face to check his temperature one last time. Before she removed it, Matt clasped his hand over it, holding it there, making her heart jump.

"Are you sure you can't stay?"

It wasn't a matter of *can't*. It was that she shouldn't. The longer she stayed there, allowing herself to get closer to Matt, the harder it was going to be when she watched him leave, and she suffered enough heartbreak to know not to do that to herself.

Matt seemed to sense her reluctance, because he let go and said, "I guess I'll have to eat that fifty-dollar box of chocolates all by myself."

Cadence chuckled as she removed her hand and checked her phone for the nearest BART station. "Please quarantine yourself until you're feeling better."

Matt grunted at her suggestion as he drifted back to sleep. "Merry Christmas, Cadence."

"Merry Christmas, Matt."

CHAPTER 7

CADENCE

January

New year, new me.

Not quite.

Cadence was not the type of person who made New Year's resolutions. She didn't believe that there was anything special about waiting until January to make positive changes for herself, but coincidentally, one week had passed and she was taking stock of all the things that could be better in her life. Nothing made her question her life choices more than being stuck in meetings that could have been reduced to an email, and there was no shortage of things that needed improvement. Her relationships. Her job. She really should floss more.

Cadence wrote a note in the margins of her legal pad to buy floss. It was the lowest-hanging fruit.

Under the conference table, Matt subtly knocked his knee to hers, bringing her mind back to the meeting. Cadence ignored the tingling feeling at the point of contact, since everyone around the table faced her, waiting expectantly for her. *Damn it. What did I miss?*

"Cadence," Bill repeated, "where are you on the Folsom deal?"

Cadence held back her own annoyed tone. "I sent the reports to Frank and Sonya." Bill should know. He was cc'd on the email. Cadence had spent the week underwriting that deal. There was no way she was taking work home during her vacation. "I'll have the memos updated by the end of the day."

"Good girl," he replied.

Good girl? Really? At thirty-one, Cadence was way past *girl*. Not to mention how belittling it was to hear it from an old white dude in an ugly pin-striped suit in front of her colleagues.

"Aw, Bill," Cadence said, feigning modesty, "when you compliment me like that, people might think you're playing favorites. Please make sure to throw Ari or Kevin a *good boy* once in a while."

Bill's face reddened, which made Cadence rethink her comment. That was the aggravating thing about microaggressions. They had to be dealt with in the moment before they festered into more egregious behavior. If she waited to confront Bill privately, it would have been easy for him to dismiss it altogether. But this attempt at bringing down the patriarchy earned her tense side-eye from every man around the table. Every man except one.

"Yeah, Bill," Matt chimed in. "I don't recall the last time you ever complimented me. Although I don't like *good boy*. Makes me feel like a puppy."

Cadence stifled a whimpering laugh. She was grateful that Matt backed her up, but was that the best he could come up with?

Bill opened his mouth, ready to give her a piece of his mind, when Josie knocked on the door and popped her head in. "Sorry to interrupt, Bill, but Sadie needs to see you."

"Very well." Bill shot Cadence a warning glare from across the room. "We were done here anyway." He left the conference room, the rest of the team filing out behind him. Fucking cowards.

Matt stood from his seat and closed his padfolio. "What's going on?"

Cadence tucked her reports under her arm and scrolled through emails on her phone for clues. "I'm sure you'll find out. Don't you have a meeting with Sadie this afternoon? To talk about your goals?"

"Not that." Matt walked alongside her, following her to the door. "What's going on with you? We haven't had much of a chance to catch up these days."

Cadence stopped short of the door, bumping shoulders with Matt as she turned to face him. She clutched her reports to her chest like they were her protective armor. No one was left in the room, so she couldn't fake a conversation out of there. She wanted to avert her gaze, but his whiskey-brown eyes pinned her in place, warming her from the inside out.

"Yeah, I know," she offered. Why didn't he grow a hairy mole on his face over the holidays? It would have made this stupid infatuation a lot easier to forget. "I'm trying to get everything done before I leave for vacation." Matt didn't seem to buy her cop-out answer, so she changed the topic. "Thanks for helping me back there with Bill."

She thought Matt would call her out on it, but he replied, "It's fine." Matt opened the door to an orchestra warm-up of phones ringing and keyboards clacking. "After you."

"Thanks." Cadence began to traverse the cubicle maze that centered Prism's open office floor.

"Isn't that what *best friends* are for?" he shouted from the doorway.

Cadence stumbled to a stop, knowing the entire office was waiting for her reaction. She was hoping he would forget this best friend campaign. She knew better than to feed into it, so she stalked toward her desk with blinders on. She did not want to see the amusement on her coworkers' faces.

Before she sat in her chair, Cadence pulled out the plastic screen that divided her cubicle from Matt's. It was laughable how flimsy and low it was. It wasn't going to keep him out of her hair, but it was her way to maintain some semblance of boundaries. Cadence logged back on to her computer and reviewed her to-do list, ignoring Matt when his loud typing announced his arrival. A few seconds later, a message from the Prism internal chat platform appeared on the bottom corner of her monitor.

MATT: How annoyed are you? Scale of 1 to 10.
CADENCE: Level 7. I'm telling you, aim for 5.
MATT: Why can't you embrace me for all that I am?

Cadence could count the ways she wanted to embrace him. She started to type out, "How could I wrap myself around that big head of yours?" and quickly deleted it. She shouldn't type anything that could be answered with "That's what she said." She drafted a new reply. "You're a handful." Nope, that didn't work, either.

CADENCE: Best friendship must be earned.

MATT: And what does that entail? A battery of tests?

MATT: Surviving a quest with increasingly dangerous encounters with unknown magical entities while discovering our powers within?

MATT: Or should we do a trust fall?

CADENCE: You're ridiculous.

MATT: Just say the word and I'll prove it to you

CADENCE: Let's circle back to this. Some of us have work to do.

She signed off before she spent the afternoon chatting. Harboring feelings for Matt was not conducive to her productivity. Not that her productivity mattered when she was still going nowhere while working under Bill's thumb. She'd probably pay for her earlier comment in some way, but she rage-submitted her résumé to ten jobs instead of worrying about it.

At the end of the day, Cadence had shut down every browser on her computer when Josie loomed over her monitor. "Sadie wants to see you before you leave."

"She does?" Normally, Cadence welcomed the chance to meet with Sadie, but not when she was about to head out. "How much time do I have?"

Josie knew Sadie's schedule by heart. It didn't stop Josie from making a show of it, dramatically turning her wrist to look at her imaginary watch. "You have a minute to get yourself together, but I wouldn't take too long." Josie waited to escort Cadence to Sadie's office. It must be urgent if Cadence had to be personally delivered.

Cadence watered the limp plant on her desk, hoping it would still be alive when she returned in two weeks. Before she turned toward Sadie's office, she peeked over the plastic divider and found an empty chair. Cadence couldn't make Sadie wait just so she could say goodbye to Matt before she left. She'd catch him on text. Cadence threw her purse over her shoulder and followed Josie down the hallway.

Josie opened Sadie's office door shortly after knocking. Sadie was in mid-conversation with someone, so Cadence quietly stepped inside, unsure of what she was walking herself into.

"Cadence. Come have a seat." Sadie stood in front of her desk and gestured to the empty chair next to . . . Matt?

"You wanted to see me, Sadie?" Cadence said, straightening out her skirt before settling into the mid-century modern chairs in front of Sadie's walnut desk. Matt grumbled a greeting of sorts behind his clasped hands while his knees bounced so fast, it shook the space around them. Cadence was starting to get motion sick. "What's going on?"

"Percy wants to back out of the deal." Matt groaned. "Fuck!"

"Why?" It wasn't the first time that a deal failed to close, but it gutted Cadence to pore over every last detail only to have it bite the dust.

"Percy cited the increasing requests for remote work from his employees," Sadie said. "From what I heard, he's already shopping for a new property."

"Good luck with that," Matt scoffed. He pushed himself up to his feet and started pacing around Sadie's office. "If he wants stay on the peninsula, then this is his best option."

Cadence had never seen Matt this stressed. When he'd lost

deals before, he'd huff and puff about it for a day or two, but nothing like this. "What can we do?"

"Matt and I had a lengthy phone call with Percy and he agreed to a meeting when he flies in for the TechXpo next week. It's being held at the L.A. Convention Center this year."

"Okay," Cadence said, unsure where she fit into this.

"I was thinking since you were traveling to L.A. for your vacation, you could assist Matt with some research."

"Excuse me?" Cadence lost the feeling of the ground underneath her feet.

Sadie failed to read the room and continued talking through her ideas. "And Matt can check up on our L.A. office and start networking and building our presence. You might want to reconnect with some clients that are based down there, but the marketing team started to put the word out. We already received calls from prospective clients across L.A. County that I can forward to you. There's one that I think Cadence could assist you wi—what's wrong?" That question was directed to Cadence and her dazed face. "You're going to L.A., right? For your mom's death anniversary," Sadie said as if the stars had aligned.

Matt returned to his seat. "Your mom's death anniversary?" The concerned tone of Matt's question gnawed at her. She never thought that the exact date of her mom's passing was need-to-know information.

Sadie's eyes darted between Matt and Cadence. "I thought you knew, Matt. What kind of work husband are you?"

Cadence winced. She hated the term *work husband*. Why was a romantic term used to refer to a positive professional relationship with a male colleague? That's all Matt was. A good colleague.

Cadence would happily refer to Matt as her "best colleague" instead of "work husband who stirs NSFW thoughts."

Sadie must have realized her faux pas, because she muttered to herself, "This is the last time I listen to Josie."

"How did you know?" Cadence asked, looking at her hands resting on her lap. "About my mom, I mean."

"I sent you flowers when your mom died," Sadie said, softening her tone. "I remember swinging by your desk to check how you were doing when you first started and I found out you had taken bereavement leave. I assumed that was why you were usually out of the office around this time."

"I don't know what to say." Cadence was touched at this unexpected moment of care from Sadie. "Thank you."

"You can thank me by getting Percy back on board. For any days you work, I'll credit your vacation day back to you," Sadie replied, getting back on task. "And, Cadence? If all goes well, I'd like to schedule a meeting with you and Bill to discuss your performance review." She turned to Matt. "Josie will set up your travel arrangements."

"Wait. Hold on." Matt dragged both of his hands through his hair. "What about—"

"What about what? Meetings and such?" Sadie leaned over and slipped her hand behind Matt's pocket square and pulled out his cell phone. "That's what this is for," she said, dropping the phone back into his blazer pocket. "I have to say, this was not the reaction I was expecting from you."

Matt grumbled as he rubbed his face. "This is very sudden."

"We've talked about this, Matt. You have stiff competition for the director position and some members of the board have their favorites. When it comes down to it, they will compare sales and clients to make their decisions, and that is where you need to focus. Think of the bigger picture, Matt. If you can get Percy to close this deal, we'll be in a better position if he ever decides to expand into L.A. So, are we good here?"

Matt nodded, though his mind seemed elsewhere.

"Good. Then it's settled. I'll see you both in two weeks. Don't let me down."

Cadence walked out of Sadie's office in a haze. What was she going to do? She wasn't looking forward to this vacation the same way she would have if it had been to an all-inclusive resort, but she took strange comfort in paying respects to her mom over uncomfortable meals with Tristan and Dad. She was never going to hear the end of it once Dad found out that she'd have to work.

"So," Matt began to say as he flapped his lapels and buttoned his blazer, "that went fucking well."

"Tell me about it. This blows." Even though four years had passed, the week of her mom's death anniversary was always a weird time for her. Cadence didn't really want to add work to the mix.

"Shit. What are you going to do? I didn't think—I didn't know about your mom."

"I know."

"What do you *want* to do? I don't want this to get in the way of your plans."

Cadence sighed. "My mom's anniversary is on Sunday, so if you don't mind, can we hold off on work until Monday?"

"Of course. You can let me know if you need more time."

"Thanks."

Cadence began to head out when Matt said, "So I guess we're going to be neighbors."

She stopped in the middle of the hallway. "Excuse me?"

"Josie will probably set us up in a hotel or something."

Cadence's eyes widened at his ludicrous suggestion and waved her hands, telling Matt to keep his voice down. "That's not gonna happen."

"But where are you going to stay? With your family?"

"Uh, yeah."

"Wouldn't it be easier to work together if we stayed in the same place?"

Cadence vehemently shook her head. It was hard enough seeing him in his robe a couple weeks ago, and she didn't have the fortitude to withstand being with him practically 24/7 for two weeks.

She grabbed his phone from his jacket pocket and dropped it back, mimicking Sadie. "You have this for meetings and such. Or email, Zoom, fax, or whatever."

Cadence impulsively reached behind his neck and swiped down his popped collar and flattened his lapel. She was just keeping a friend from looking unkempt. Matt smiled in gratitude. His eyes lingered on her face, inspecting it, to the point where Cadence feared that he might discover that she liked how nice his suit felt under her hands or that it let her get close enough to catch the faint scent of his cologne. Clean and refreshing, like drinking tropical fruit cocktails by the beach.

This was why Cadence couldn't have nice things. She had to keep her distance if she wanted to survive this trip. "I better go. I'll see you in L.A."

CHAPTER 8

MATT

"M att!" Hunter placed a condescending palm on Matt's shoulder, blocking his way into his cubicle. "Sorry about iStan. Listen, I'm speaking to a class at Berkeley tonight, if you want to drop by and pick up some pointers on closing deals."

Matt took shallow breaths. To remain calm, yes, but also because Hunter insisted on wearing an aggressively musky cologne that was marketed as "the essence of masculinity." Talk about overcompensating. If you asked Matt, there was no storied rivalry between Hunter and him. Celtics/Lakers, they were not. Hunter disliked Matt from the day Matt joined Prism Realty. It was like Hunter never learned that there was enough room in the sandbox for everyone.

"Thanks but no thanks." Matt brushed Hunter's hand away and tried to maneuver around him, but Hunter sidestepped into Matt's path.

"So, what's this about you going to L.A.?"

Hunter was so fucking transparent, like the thin white buttondown shirt he layered over his white tank top. Good. He should be scared that Matt was going after the director position.

"Percy invited me to TechXpo," Matt said coolly. "I don't know what you've heard, but we're still in talks."

"And that requires you to be out of the office for two weeks?"

Matt crossed his arms and widened his stance. "I'm planning to visit my family while I'm down there. Speaking of . . ." Matt's cell phone rang, just as he expected. He had texted his cousins about his work trip as he exited Sadie's office, and it would be only a matter of minutes before Lola found out. "I better take this," he said, excusing himself from this dreadful conversation.

"Hi, Lola," he said after accepting Lola's FaceTime call. Matt popped into the conference room for privacy. He couldn't hear Lola and was about to bring the phone up to his ear when his screen displayed an upward shot of his grandma's chin and nose. "Lola, hold up your phone so I can see your—"

"Jason told me you're visiting this weekend," she interrupted him. Matt wasn't sure if she didn't hear him earlier or if she was ignoring him or both. "That you'll be in town for two weeks. When were you going to tell me? Why did I have to hear it from Jason?"

"I just found out. I'm coming down for work."

"And? You're coming to Missy's birthday party next week, yes?"

It sounded like a question, but Matt knew that it was not a request. "Yes, I'll be there."

"And are you bringing your girlfriend?

"Girlfriend?"

"Your *special someone*?"

Cadence. "No," Matt said firmly. Matt once made the mistake of bringing a woman he was kind of dating to a family gathering and it blew up in his face. Questions about their relationship and his intentions. His aunties giving his date the third degree. He never wanted to experience that again, though a part of him wondered how Cadence would fit in with his family.

"Matthew," Lola scolded. "Help me understand."

"Understand what?"

"What is wrong with you? Why can't you find a girlfriend? Gerald said it's because you have a . . ." She hesitated for a second before whispering, "An f-boy haircut."

He couldn't help but smile at Lola's incapacity to curse, but he was going to punch Gerald in the nuts when he saw him. It wasn't Matt's fault that his barber buzzed the sides of his hair too short.

Fingers rapped on the glass conference door. It was Josie. "Matt, I booked your flight. It leaves tonight. You should go home and pack."

"Okay. Thanks," he said, thinking that was the end of her update. He turned his attention back to his phone, which now displayed Lola's ear.

"I booked a hotel room for you and Cadence near the convention center," Josie continued. "Your rental will be available at the airport—"

"Josie. I'm on the phone. Can you email me the info?"

Josie pursed her lips at him before leaving. He knew he was going to pay for his snippy reply later.

When Matt looked at his phone again, he was met with Lola's squinting eyes. Only her eyes. Lola needed to hold the phone farther away. "Who is Cadence and why are you sharing a room with her?"

"We're not sharing a room together. It's not what you think."

A single eyebrow arched on her face. "Are you bringing her to the party?"

"She's my coworker. That's it." Unfortunately. Regretfully.

"And? Does she like Filipino food?"

"Probably." Matt never encountered a free plate of food that Cadence didn't like.

"Good. Then I can't wait to see her at the party. Text me a picture!"

"She already has plans," he blurted, but she hung up before he could finish his sentence. For an old lady, she had quick fingers.

Damn it. How was he going to get himself out of this?

MATT STOOD NEAR a stall that sold snacks, headphones, and niche magazines he'd never heard of, looking at the silver lining to come out of his unlucky day. In the waiting area by gate 30A, Cadence was lost in a crossword puzzle, chewing on her pencil, alone on a long bench waiting for the same flight he was taking. Matt almost didn't recognize her, unaccustomed as he was to seeing her in anything but her work attire. This Cadence was dressed comfortably in an oversize red cable-knit cardigan, skinny jeans with rips at the knees, and dusty black Chuck Taylors. It was odd to see her head buried in something other than spreadsheets.

The strap from his messenger bag started to bite into his skin. It sunk in that they were about to spend two weeks together away from the office, outside the confines of their desks, and away from nosy coworkers. Suddenly, HR rules dictating office romances became a distant, inconvenient memory. Matt took a restless bounce on his toes and took off toward her. He didn't bother being discreet when he walked down the aisle of benches behind her. He leaned over her shoulder as she checked her phone.

"Are you cheating on a crossword puzzle?" he asked, startling her.

"Fuck!" Cadence gasped, drawing attention from passengers and airline staff alike. She turned around and huffed in annoyance when she saw it was him. When it was clear that Cadence was not a damsel in distress, nearby passengers looked back down at their phones and the sound of rolling suitcases going in every direction resumed.

"No, I don't think *fuck* is the right word for 11 Down." Matt smirked as he rested his forearms on the back of Cadence's seat. "Hmm. 'In present state.' I hate those vague clues. The Friday crosswords are tough."

Cadence's face paled. "Shit," she muttered, turning back around, sulking into her seat.

"Still not the right word," he joked.

Matt walked around the bench, dodging carry on bags in the aisle, and sat next to her. As he leaned forward to get a closer look at the unsolved clues, she backed away as much as her seat would allow.

She wrapped her cardigan tightly across herself. "Don't tell me we're on the same flight."

"Okay, Cady, I won't."

"Don't call me Cady."

Matt smiled to himself. Cadence didn't like being called Cady. She claimed it sounded too much like Sadie and didn't want to make it easier for people to confuse the two of them. Matt wasn't sure how that was possible. Sadie had to be in her late forties and consistently wore her jet-black hair in a bob like she was the Asian Anna Wintour in a pantsuit. Cadence, on the other hand, stupefied him with her mermaid hair and smart mouth, reducing him to immature tendencies.

"Okay, Lim Shady. Ooh! Ooh!" he nearly shouted from his sudden inspiration. "Lim *Cady*."

Cadence's nostrils flared as she inhaled deeply, which filled Matt with glee. This, of course, pissed her off.

"You are the worst," she hissed.

"I prefer acquired taste. Listen. I have a favor to ask."

"What kind of favor?" Cadence asked, wary.

"A week from tomorrow, my cousin is having a birthday party. Wanna come with me?"

"I don't think so." She balked, returning her attention to the crossword puzzle. "Don't you have a girlfriend for that?"

"If I had a girlfriend, I wouldn't be asking you."

Cadence's pencil slipped as she incorrectly guessed 11 Down. "The answer is still no," she said as she erased her mistake.

"Please? For your best friend?"

"I already have a best friend and her name is Maddie," she said dismissively.

Matt beamed. "Aw! Is that my new nickname?"

Cadence shoved Matt's shoulder. "What is wrong with you?"

"How about this?" Matt knew he was skating on thin ice, so he had to find a new way to convince her. He pointed at 11 Down. "If I tell you the answer, will you go with me?"

She peeked at him as she hid behind her shoulder. "Why would I agree to that? You don't even know the answer."

"If you're so sure, why don't you accept and then we'll see?" he challenged, tapping on the folded newspaper laid on her thigh. Cadence narrowed her eyes in defiance. His eyebrows arched, goading her to agree. She countered with a single unamused blink.

Matt was going to have to pull out all the stops. He bumped her shoulders, nudging her, and leaned back with a lazy smile that got him free toppings at the froyo place near his apartment. Cadence chewed on her pencil as she mulled it over, and it seemed like she was on the verge of agreeing until loud, squeaky feedback from the PA system interrupted her thoughts.

The airline staff announced that their gate was opening for first-class passengers and passengers who needed assistance, including passengers with young children. Cadence turned away to check the TV screen that displayed their flight information.

"So?" Matt asked, roping her back into their conversation.

She raked her hands into that mane of hers and flipped it to the right side. "Fine." She huffed. "What's the answer?"

"And if it's right, you'll go with me to the party?" Without looking at him, Cadence nodded like she couldn't believe she was agreeing to this.

"As is."

"What?"

"In present state. *As is.*"

Cadence scoffed, tentatively writing "AS IS" in capital letters. "Wipe that look off your face," she said of his smug smile.

"As you wish," he replied, though his expression remained the same. Cadence was running out of patience with him, so he jutted his chin toward the newspaper. "11 Across: E.g., In response to a princess's demand. *As you wish.*"

Cadence squinted at the newspaper. Once she lightly penciled in 11 Across, everything else fell into place. She quickly scribbled in the rest of the adjacent words when the theme revealed itself.

A nineties rom-com: *As Good as It Gets*. Will's play: *As You Like It*. Will's demise (or a 2000s metalcore band): *As I Lay Dying*. Cadence groaned in defeat.

"How did you know the answer?" she demanded.

Matt shrugged. "What? You don't think I'm smart enough to do crossword puzzles?" Ignoring her apparent doubt, he tapped the newspaper once again. "Where did you get this?"

"I found it on the seat. Why?"

"This is last Friday's paper."

"What?!" She lifted the newspaper up to her face, confirming the date. "That's not fair."

"What's not fair about it? You agreed to the terms presented. You had your chance to make modifications."

Cadence Level 8 glared at him, so Matt toned it down.

"Come on," he said, stretching out his arms, resting them behind the bench seats. "You're acting like I'm making you get a root canal or something. My family's fun and my aunt's a great cook. Is it so terrible to spend an afternoon with me?"

Cadence didn't reply. He was half joking when he asked the question. Had she caught the other half of it? The half that was worried that she'd brush him off like she usually did? This was stupid. Weren't they too old to play games? Matt was summoning the courage to tell her how he felt when a soft *ding* rang overhead.

A new announcement: The airline was now boarding the economy seats. Cadence shot up, blowing out a deep breath as she stretched her arms up.

"That's me." She stuffed the newspaper into her backpack and slipped on the straps. She reached for her carry-on, but Matt grabbed it first.

"I got it," he said, pulling the handle up with a click as he stood. "Go on. I'll follow you."

"Are we even in the same section?"

"Does it matter?" He rolled past her. "What are they going to do about it? Send me away?" He found the end of the line. While he waited, he removed his driver's license from his wallet and pulled up his boarding pass.

Cadence caught a glimpse of his phone. "We're not seated anywhere near each other."

"Don't worry. I'll handle it."

Cadence rolled her eyes at his confidence as she gathered her documents.

Matt didn't care. He walked ahead of her toward the counter and scanned his boarding pass. The flight attendant looked questioningly at him, but he flashed another signature smile. He tilted his head toward Cadence. "Helping her with her carry-on. She hurt herself training for Bay to Breakers." The flight attendant probably knew it was a lie, but with the long line behind them, she gestured them both into the gate.

Once they were in the jet bridge, Cadence elbowed him in the ribs. "So shameless," she scolded as she walked ahead of him, entering the plane. Why was she in such a rush to get to her seat? The plane was half full. Matt took measured steps, careful not to knock into the seats or roll over any personal items. Cadence was near the back of the plane when she stopped in her tracks.

"This is me." She pointed at the row behind Matt. "Row 27."

Matt pushed up his sleeves and lifted Cadence's carry-on into the open overhead compartment. She ducked underneath him and climbed into her seat by the window. "Thanks," she said as she removed earbuds from her pocket. "Wait, what are you doing?"

Matt tossed his messenger bag next to Cadence's suitcase and dropped himself in the middle seat beside her.

"Aren't you sitting on the other side of the plane?"

Matt buckled his seat belt. "Why can't I sit here? I'll leave if someone reserved this seat." He made himself comfortable, stretching his legs as much as space allowed and claiming his half of the armrest. "If no one comes, then I'll stay here." He flashed an innocent smile. "Oh, I forgot my headphones. Can I share with you?" He leaned in, pressing his arm into hers.

"You know what?" Cadence bent down and picked up her purse. "I'm feeling a little claustrophobic. I'll sit in the aisle seat instead."

He didn't understand what was freaking her out, but he obliged. He unbuckled his seat belt and started to get up when she impatiently tried to crab-walk over him. Her foot got caught under his leg, causing her to stumble. His arms flew out, wrapping them around her waist as he plopped back into his seat. Matt groaned in agony when Cadence landed on him, knocking the wind out of him. If the pain didn't kill him first, Cadence squirming on his lap would.

With her arms around his neck, she lifted her head as he looked down to see if she was okay. They both stopped when their noses aligned like the last number of a locker combination. Their faces were so close, it wouldn't have taken much for Matt to kiss Cadence's parted lips. All she had to do was give him the green light—a knowing glance through her lowered lashes, a directive to kiss her, her hand pulling his face toward hers. Any of the above would do. He pressed his fingers into her waist as insurance that he'd keep his distance while he waited. This backfired because she reflexively arched closer with a startling gasp and dug her nails into his shoulders. Matt willed himself not to groan again.

"Excuse me." A flight attendant stood over them with a strained professional smile. Life around them unmuted, from the dinging seat-belt sign to the hiss of the cabin pressurizing. "We're about to shut the door and taxi down the runway. Can you return to your seats and buckle your seat belts? Thanks," she said brightly, shutting their overhead bins before moving on to the guests behind them.

Cadence scrambled off Matt and sat in the aisle seat. She smoothed down her hair and cleared her throat, "I'm sorry."

Matt was sorry too. Sorry that there wasn't a subtle way to readjust his pants. He reached for the laminated safety protocol sheet and casually laid it on his lap, pretending to read up on emergency scenarios. Up ahead, another flight attendant closed the plane door.

"Guess you're stuck with me," Matt said.

"Lucky me," she muttered, ignoring him while she buckled her seat belt and put her phone on airplane mode. It was like he was watching her through an invisible partition. How could she pretend the last few minutes didn't happen?

Matt rested his head on her stiffened shoulder. "I forgot my pillow." He felt the rise and fall as she let out a resigned breath.

"The flight isn't that long, you know."

She didn't push him off, which he took as a good sign. He snuggled his head in and rested his eyes. "You're welcome, by the way."

"For what?"

"For saving your life right now. Catching you with these." With fisted hands, he flexed his exposed forearms.

"However did you bring those guns onto the plane?" she deadpanned. "You're so annoying sometimes," she muttered under her breath. "Like my brother."

Brother?! He'd much rather be associated with the *friend* label than be linked to her brother. Just when he thought he took a giant leap forward, he found himself two steps back.

"I didn't know you had a brother." As soon as Matt said it, he realized how little she ever spoke about her family. "What does your family do for your mom's death anniversary, if you don't mind me asking?"

Cadence tensed, so he sat up to give her some space. Watching Cadence stew on the question, Matt regretted how carelessly he broached the topic. She didn't seem so upset when Sadie brought it up.

"We visit her grave site and eat lunch," she finally said, careful and measured.

"How come you never told me?" It seemed simple enough. "I always assumed you were traveling somewhere. Doing your touristy thing."

The plane taxied to the runway. Cadence closed her eyes and gripped the armrests. "Vacations are supposed to be fun and relaxing," she spoke over the whirring engines. "Going home is the complete opposite."

CHAPTER 9
CADENCE

On Sunday morning, it took Cadence a minute to realize where she was. She hadn't acclimated to sleeping on a twin bed in the front house, made worse by the howling patrons of the Viet-Cajun crab shack across the street. The bedroom was filled with natural light, amplified by the sterile white walls. Unpacked boxes lined the opposite wall along with cases of Tristan's old photography gear. Cadence went to the kitchen in search of coffee, where she found Tristan in his pajamas, sitting by himself at the glass dining table, nursing a mug of hot water. He was looking every bit of his thirty-seven years of age with those bags under his eyes.

"When did you become Dad?" Cadence said as she sat across from Tristan. Dad regularly espoused the virtues of drinking hot water. It was the cure for most ailments—colds, cramps, teenage angst—you name it. Cadence never bought into it. Tristan kept a straight face as he ignored her. He punched a triangle opening into a can of condensed milk and made a smaller hole on the opposite side to vent. Tristan flooded his toast with sweetness from corner to corner. "You want some bread with that?"

Tristan took a crunchy bite, condensed milk dribbling off the edges. "We need to talk." Cadence didn't like the sound of that. Nothing good comes after the words *We need to talk.* Tristan pushed the plate of toast in front of her. "Want some?"

"Is it about Dad? How did he fall anyway?"

"He missed the last step on the stairs. He's fine, all things considered, but he's using a cane to be safe. That's why we moved into this house for now—no stairs." Tristan offered an infuriating nonchalant shrug.

"I wish you told me when it happened."

"There was too much going on with the move, so I forgot to text you. Sorry. I didn't think you'd show up." Cadence was ready to kick her insensitive brother under the table when he said, "That's not what I was going to tell you." Tristan took a deep breath and then whispered, "Linda is twelve weeks pregnant."

Seconds of uncomfortable silence dragged before Cadence followed up with a belated congratulations. "So are you guys engaged now or what?" She knew that wasn't the right thing to say, but she was flabbergasted by the news. Tristan and Linda had been on and off throughout their relationship. Cadence's parents had all but given up on the idea of the two of them getting married.

"We're still talking about it. Obviously, this was unplanned, but we're waiting until we make decisions before we tell our parents because you know how they'll get. They'll jump into wedding planning before the engagement ring hits her finger."

Cadence nodded. She didn't know about Linda's parents, but their dad was guaranteed to put in his two cents on their wedding. "What's holding you guys back?"

"Linda wants us to have our own place." *Without Dad.* Tristan didn't need to say it. "But we can't afford to move out on our own right now."

Cadence averted her eyes. That was supposed to be her cue to offer her assistance, but when she imagined her next move, home was nowhere on her list of potential locales. Tristan had lived with their parents ever since he'd dropped out after his second year at Yale, saying it wasn't his scene. He endured so much anger from Dad, who pushed Tristan and Cadence toward the Ivy League, but Mom played the peacekeeper. She was happy to have Tristan back so that he could deal with their affairs as needed.

Cadence was grateful for it, knowing that Tristan was home to take care of their parents as she pursued her career. This had been their norm for so long that Cadence assumed that Tristan would always take on the responsibility, but now that it was presented to her, Cadence wasn't sure if she was up for the challenge. It wouldn't be such a big deal if her prideful father would accept outside help.

For as long as Cadence could remember, her parents shared their expectations that Tristan and Cadence would take care of them in their old age. Filial piety and all that jazz. Under no circumstances would Dad ever agree to go into an assisted living facility. Cadence knew this was coming, but she'd hoped that it would come much later, perhaps when she was more settled in her life or at least when she had figured out how to keep a plant alive.

"Don't worry about it," Tristan said after he picked up on her hesitance. "Linda and I will figure something out. Just don't tell Dad yet."

Cadence glanced at Tristan's unfinished toast. She regretted not taking a bite before it became soggy. Shòu, the deity for longevity, graced the can of condensed milk. With his long white beard, he grinned while holding on to his cane and a lucky peach. What was he so happy about? Getting older didn't seem to do Cadence any favors. For her last birthday, Maddie sent her an entire skincare regimen that had more steps than her Fitbit. Now she had more important things to worry about than visible pores.

A loud stomp from the adjacent room startled Cadence. She could have sworn it caused the room to rattle, accented by the pitter-patter of rice falling into the bottom tray of the rice dispenser. Squeaky wheels preceded the source of all the noise.

"You made it," Dad said in Hakka, standing at the entryway to the kitchen with a white-knuckle grip on his cane.

Tristan looked up and greeted Dad with a nod. Cadence kept her head down in anticipation, reverting back to her daughter role in his presence. "Hi, Dad," she greeted him, continuing their conversation in Hakka since it was preferred in the house.

"It's good to see you." Dad said it like he meant it. He didn't follow it up with nagging, either. Cadence examined his face, which had sunk considerably since she saw him last year. Had time softened him?

Like clockwork, Tristan stood and helped Dad walk to the table. Once Dad was situated next to Cadence, Tristan went into the kitchen. Scooping a heaping ladle of brown rice porridge into a bowl, he placed it on a tray and set it in front of Dad before returning to the kitchen. Accompanying the bowl of brown rice porridge was a small bowl of thinly sliced omelet and a small side dish of preserved mustard greens. Tristan returned with a steaming-hot mug of Dad's favorite oolong tea.

"This is my lucky day," Dad announced, sounding pleased. "Your brother never gives me this," he said, tapping the side dish of preserved mustard greens with his wooden chopsticks.

"It has too much salt," Tristan explained. "I've been looking up heart-healthy alternatives to Dad's favorite dishes, but preserved vegetables are hard to replace. A little bit shouldn't hurt."

"It's the least you could do. This brown rice tastes like wet cardboard," Dad said mid-chew.

"I need to pick up the food," Tristan said as he wiped down the counter. "Make sure Dad takes his medicine after he eats. It's in the pillbox next to the electric kettle."

"How do I know which one he's supposed to take?" Cadence asked, slightly panicked. She couldn't remember what ailed her dad these days. High blood pressure? High cholesterol? Acid reflux?

"Everything in the Sunday AM compartment," Tristan said with a silent *duh* added at the end as he departed the kitchen.

Cadence wished she had her phone on her to take notes on Dad's diet and his medication. It would give her something to do besides feel inadequate. How could she take care of Dad when she was coming up short on conversation topics that wouldn't blow up into an argument? Rather than sit in awkward silence, Cadence excused herself to get dressed.

"SLOW DOWN! YOU'RE going to miss it again," Dad shouted at Tristan from the back seat. This was their second time driving through the windy path into the cemetery. Stoic, Tristan pressed on because he swore Mom's plot was underneath a big shady tree up the hill. Cadence didn't know how he could differentiate it from the other trees. They all looked the same to her, since she hadn't paid much attention to her surroundings on the day of Mom's funeral, which had been a blur between the tears and the stream of condolences from people she didn't know. Between the shouting and Tristan's driving, Cadence couldn't tell if the topsy-turvy feeling was from her pounding headache, her racing heart, or the knots in her stomach.

Tristan eventually found Mom's plot on a hill, high above the nearest tree. With no other road leading up there, they had to hike the rest of the way. Tristan and Cadence disagreed on the best route to take.

"You should have brought a wagon or something," Cadence said, surveying the ceremonial items and trays of Cantonese food in their trunk. "You help Dad walk up while I carry this."

"You help Dad. I can carry more stuff and make fewer trips." Tristan adjusted his tie. For Mom, he made an effort to look nice, wearing a long-sleeved white dress shirt and black slacks that looked like they were steam-pressed. He even popped out the plugs in his earlobes, since Mom never liked them. "You're going to take too long getting up there with those heels."

Cadence had only packed shoes that went with her work attire. It was either these black pumps or her ratty sneakers. The latter didn't pair well with her black suit, which she regretted wearing on this sunny day. Cadence forgot that there were no seasons in Southern California. "If you hadn't wasted so much time finding the place, we wouldn't have to rush."

"Let's get this over with," he said, stacking the foil trays of char siu and Peking duck.

Both of them slipped on their sunglasses and stepped away from the car like Secret Service agents. Tristan worked swiftly, packing items into boxes and making several trips up and down the hill. With her heels and his cane, Cadence and her dad punched the grass with each step. By the time she made it up there, Tristan had wiped Mom's black granite headstone clean and laid out the food around it.

"Did you guys clear out the garage or something?" Cadence folded a heaping pile of hell bank notes and gold joss paper, finding it strange that they were doing this at the cemetery. In the past, they burned this at home. Dad—not wanting to sit down—stood over her and supervised. "They let you guys burn this here?"

"Actually, they don't, so we have to act fast." Tristan threw a match and a handful of notes into the joss paper burner, which resembled a large red stockpot with blackened vents around the side. "Mom's about to get rich."

"Throw more in before they tell us to leave," Dad nagged. He kept a lookout, using his cabbie hat as his disguise.

"No, that will make it smoke more," Tristan argued.

Cadence blocked them out as she threw in her offering. She searched among the boxes, and of all things, they forgot a small incense burner. Cadence resorted to driving her sticks of incense into the dirt at the corner of her mom's granite headstone.

She was about to pray when she heard Tristan and Dad's argument escalate.

"Hurry, hurry, hurry!" Dad commanded.

In the distance, she spotted a security guard swerving toward them in a golf cart. In a moment of panic, Tristan threw a wad of paper money into the bucket. A dark plume of smoke polluted the air. Dad lost his balance from coughing, knocking the burner over with his cane. Cadence caught him in time, but she couldn't save the food from getting covered by black soot. Tristan kicked the burner back upright as the security officer approached him.

"Excuse me! You're not allowed to burn that on cemetery grounds!" the security guard reprimanded.

"Did you know that before coming here?" Cadence asked Tristan. She took stock of the guard. It was hard to take him seriously, with his baby face and bony arms.

Tristan shushed her. "Let me handle this. Hey, man," he said to the guard, "we'll put this out right now and be on our way."

"We only allow burning joss paper during Qingming, when we have fire safety on hand. Other days must be requested through the office." The security guard reached for his walkie-talkie. "I have to report you guys. This is a hazard."

Cadence wondered how to get out of this jam. Could she pay the security guard off? She didn't have any cash on her, but she was flush with hell notes.

Dad invaded the guard's personal space and squinted at his face.

Affronted, the guard took a step back and did a quick threat assessment of Dad. "Can I help you, sir?"

"Are you Mrs. Chan's grandson?" Dad asked in Cantonese.

Here we go again. Dad always knew somebody who knew somebody. He used to use his connections to get meals comped or to feel self-important. Cadence never imagined her father using his clout to evade cemetery security.

"Yeah . . ." the guard said, weirded out by Dad's familiarity.

"Ah! I thought I recognized you. It's me, Mr. Lim. I played mah-jongg with your grandma last month at your house."

"Oh. Hi, Mr. Lim." The security guard bowed awkwardly.

"She was telling me how you'll be going back to school. Good for you! Did she like the spice blend I gave her?"

The security guard sighed and returned his walkie-talkie back into his holster. He assessed the smoky, ashy mess before scanning the empty hillside. "Look, if you can put out the fire and clean this up, I'll let it go. Next time, please burn this at home. I saw the smoke from the front entrance." He turned a blind eye and clomped down to his golf cart.

Cadence patted ash off her suit. "What do we do now?"

"I'll put out the fire," Tristan said, fanning the smoke away from his face. "We'll have to toss the food."

"Not that. What about Mom?" Cadence knelt down and wiped her headstone. Her poor mom. She didn't deserve these idiots ruining her day.

"I'll drop you guys off at home. I'll pick up more food so we can do something at home," Tristan suggested. "Why don't you help Dad down to the car? I'll clean up."

Cadence hooked her dad's arm and they made their descent, carefully stepping around other headstones.

"Mom would have laughed," Dad said.

"She would have been mad about the wasted food."

"She would have been happy that you were here today. She always looked forward to your visits."

Cadence smiled somberly, remembering how her mom doted on her whenever she flew home from college.

"*When* you came home, that is," Dad added.

Cadence clenched her jaw. He always had to sprinkle extra salt on old wounds. She wished that for once, he would consider his part in making her visits home a test in diplomacy. What did he think he'd gain from that comment? Did he want her to open the books and show him how he ran his shop at a loss for months? That this forced Mom to work more at the garment factory to make ends meet?

Cadence held her tongue. It was Mom's day and Cadence didn't want to ruin it by fighting with her dad.

CHAPTER 10
MATT

On Saturday, Matt texted Cadence to check in, but she didn't reply until midafternoon, when she sent a concise message.

CADENCE: Sorry. Busy with family stuff.

By that time, Matt had spent a dull day alone, sitting in a stiff leather chair in his hotel room, answering emails and reaching out to his old L.A. contacts. It felt completely unproductive. On Sunday morning, he began to draft a text, but stopped himself from pressing send. He reread her last message. Busy with family stuff, meaning her mom's death anniversary. He decided to let her be.

A new email appeared in his inbox, sent from Josie on behalf of Sadie. Attached was a list of contacts she wanted him to reach out to. Matt picked up his phone, ready to dial the first number, when he reviewed the accompanying list of addresses. Rather than staying cooped up in his hotel on this gorgeous day, Matt went for a drive.

MATT PARALLEL PARKED in front of a small Spanish-style house on a street lined with well-maintained classic California bungalows and storybook homes. He could imagine these houses in flickering old film reels from a bygone Hollywood era, except Matt was far from Hollywood. He was east of Hollywood in the suburbs, but if he didn't know any better, he would have said he had traveled to the Far East.

Valley Boulevard, which cuts through San Gabriel's main commercial area, was stacked with Chinese signs. Besides its namesake mission, the towering Serbian Orthodox church, and the retro pizza joint, this section of San Gabriel was undeniably Asian. Except there was a new European-style mini mansion that stood out like a sore thumb. Who would want to build their home next to a Viet-Cajun crab shack? He wondered if the owners liked living in luxury and going to bed to the aroma of seafood doused in garlicky butter.

Matt's main destination was a small motel, creatively named Best Eastern. Professional real estate photos always made properties appear better than they were. His expectations were already low, but in broad daylight, Best Eastern looked downright shady, with its washed-out salmon-colored stucco and rusty, formerly white railings. All it had going for it was its location. It was situated in a high-traffic, high-density area, so there was potential for the right developer.

Matt was about to cross the street to get a closer look when he heard a door slam and yelling in Mandarin. Or was that Cantonese? He could never tell the difference. It came from the house right behind the motel's parking lot. At first it looked like the elderly man shuffling out of his front door was yelling to himself.

Pulling a lighter out of his black puffer vest, the old man lit a few sticks of incense and held them up to his forehead.

As the old man knelt down at the flowerbed in front of the large picture window, a woman yelled from inside the home. Matt stayed put, wanting to see the formidable Chinese grandma that was shouting at this stubborn man.

When the metal screen door swung open, the first thing Matt saw were legs. Pale long ones that belonged to a woman who wore track shorts underneath a faded gray University of Washington T-shirt. The woman (not a grandma) continued to scold the old man, holding him steady as he rose up with the help of his cane. Once he stood firmly on his two feet, the woman swiped the hair that escaped her loose bun away from her face. When they stepped away from the flowerbed, Matt finally saw what the fuss was all about. The old man had planted three sticks of incense into the ground.

The woman shooed the old man into the house, repeating her frustration at a more socially appropriate decibel level. Before she closed the door behind her, she turned around and looked around the neighborhood, as if to check if anybody had witnessed the commotion. When she spotted Matt standing across the street, she held up her hand to shield the sunlight and squinted.

"Shit!"

It was the third time Cadence had cursed at him this weekend.

CHAPTER 11

CADENCE

Cadence didn't intend to swear so loud, but standing outside her dad's house while Matt gawked at her "good for repainting your house" outfit broke the volume control on her voice. This weekend was getting worse by the minute.

Matt jogged across the street, stopping on the sidewalk at the end of the short paver walkway. She shifted her stance, trying to regain some balance as her worlds collided in front of her. Matt was only supposed to exist in San Francisco. Seeing him standing in her front yard, she felt like an underdog on her own turf. She crossed her arms to hide her old college T-shirt, but quickly uncrossed them since it was pointless.

"Fancy seeing you here," he said with an awkward smile, casually easing his hands into the front pockets of his tan chino pants.

Cadence tried not to notice how his short-sleeved button shirt looked like it was vacuum-sealed to his torso. How did Matt hide his toned arms all these years? His lean and tall frame made her assume he was scrawny underneath his suit. Cadence took in the burning incense, inhaling deeply, hoping it would clear her mind from imagining what else was underneath Matt's clothes.

"What? You just happened to be in the neighborhood or something?" Cadence tried to keep her tone light, but she was trying to figure out how to get rid of Matt before her dad noticed she was still outside. Given that her dad was a slow walker, Cadence figured she had about one, two minutes tops.

Matt shrugged with his hands still in his pockets. "Looks like it."

"Come on. What are you doing here?"

Matt bristled at her cool reception. "Have you read *any* of your emails?"

At this, Cadence crossed her arms in irritation. "I told you that I was busy with family stuff this weekend."

"I got a lead on that beauty over there," he said, pointing at the pink monstrosity next door.

Cadence didn't know that Best Eastern was up for sale. It was a miracle that it stayed in business as long as it did. There were better accommodations in the city that didn't come with a side of bedbugs.

"Who are you talking to?" her dad asked in Hakka through the screen door.

Cadence replied, "He's trying to get me to join his church. I told him I don't believe in Jehovah." Since she didn't know how to say Jehovah in Hakka and resorted to English, Matt caught on to her lie.

"Hi, Mr. Lim?" Matt yelled past Cadence. "I'm Cadence's friend. We work together," he said, flicking a pointed finger between him and Cadence.

"He's not deaf, you know," she said. Turning back to her dad, she said, "Ba, this is Matt."

"Oh! Welcome, Matt!" her dad said in English. "Cady, don't be rude. Invite him in!"

Matt's face lit up like he discovered a hidden treasure. "Yeah, *Cady*." He strutted down the walkway. "Don't be rude."

Cadence held up both her hands, causing Matt's catwalk to come to a screeching halt.

"But Ba! Tristan's on his way home. We're about to pray . . . and stuff."

"So what?" her dad said in Hakka, not wanting to offend Matt. "He's already here. Let him in. He can help us eat the food."

Cadence sighed at Matt, who was giving her the "Are you going to let me in or not?" look. She caved. The wall that divided her work and personal life was blown to smithereens. She moved aside and gestured toward the door.

"Come on in," she said with all the enthusiasm she could muster.

Once inside, Matt took in his surroundings, like he was cataloging every piece of furniture. Cadence didn't know what was so fascinating. The house was still in a bare-bones state after Tristan and Dad had downsized from the house in the back. Having Matt in her parents' home left her feeling more and more exposed, especially in her ugly home clothes. Cadence quickly diverted Matt's attention by giving a tour. It was wholly unnecessary since they could see the entire house from where they were standing. She gave him a rundown about their disaster morning at the cemetery as a way to explain her poor appearance.

"Cady! Where are your manners?" her dad said in English from the kitchen. "Offer your friend something to drink."

Instead of getting flustered at her dad's instruction, she took advantage of the situation.

"Oh, Matt!" she said, pulling out a seat for him at the dining table. "Come sit with my dad." She quickly filled a glass of water from the fridge and set it in front of Matt. "Ba. Tell Matt about the time you counseled Mr. Chou when his son ran away." To Matt, she said with fake excitement, "You gotta hear this. So amazing. Spoiler alert: his son came home." Her dad loved telling this story every chance he got. Cadence heard it so many times, she knew it word for word, which is how she knew she had exactly sixteen minutes to change her clothes and touch up her makeup. She couldn't look like a slob now that they were hosting a guest.

Cadence returned to the kitchen in her white sleeveless shirtdress—something she normally reserved for work—and found Tristan and Linda introducing themselves, saving Matt from another one of Dad's stories.

"What took you so long?" she asked while Tristan placed trays of food on the kitchen counter. Cadence gave Linda a quick hug, backing off when her belly made contact with the small baby bump hidden underneath Linda's empire-waist dress. They exchanged a secret look before Linda took a seat at the table.

"I went back to the barbecue place. There were no more plump-looking ducks hanging on the rack. Dad kept hounding me to get one with smooth skin."

"That's how you know it's fresh!" her dad interjected.

"Is that lechón?" Matt asked, drooling over the tray of crispy pork.

Cadence nodded as she gathered serving utensils and plates and placed them on the table. She shooed Matt away from the food and pointed at his seat. Cadence and Tristan busied themselves, plating some of the food for the altar. Dad directed them, helping them create a nice presentation in front of the portrait of her mother. Cadence divided three sticks of incense for her brother and dad. They took turns praying before returning to the kitchen.

Cadence went last. She brought her incense up to her forehead, closed her eyes, and silently prayed for her mom. For most other occasions, her prayers were bundled in an all-inclusive "good luck, good fortune, and good health" package. They were brief by design to finish before ashes fell on her hands. In this instance, she took her time and pictured the last happy memory she had with her mom, cooking for what would be their last Lunar New Year together. When Mom offered her a red envelope, Cadence refused. It was the polite thing to do, but also because Cadence was proud to be financially independent and wanted her mom to keep it. A week had passed before Cadence found the red envelope hidden in her coat pocket.

When she opened her eyes after she bowed, she saw Matt in her periphery. How long had he been standing there? Suddenly, she felt self-conscious to be in his gaze. He must have realized this because he turned his attention to the floor, to the furniture. Cadence shoved her incense in the burner in between candles and quickly squeegeed her tears away with her hands, trying to regroup before she faced him.

"I didn't mean to intrude," he said apologetically. "I was going to wash my hands." Matt stood taller, his expression warm with empathy. It changed the equilibrium between them, and Cadence wasn't sure how she felt about it. Normally, when she vented to him about work, he'd crack jokes to cheer her up. He was supposed to be the fun, shiny wrapping paper in their relationship, not the tape that held things together.

Cadence sniffled. "Let's eat," she said, pivoting past Matt and headed toward the dining table. She ate silently, stuffing her face with rice as Dad yammered on about people in his social circle. Tristan mirrored her, since he had probably heard it all before. To Matt's credit, he hung on to Dad's every word, nodding along even though he didn't know any of the people Dad was talking about. Still, she wished Matt hadn't shown up. Cadence could have powered through an awkward, silent meal to honor her mother. Instead, Matt had virgin ears to her dad's stories, and now she must suffer through the theatrics of the wizard of San Gabriel and how he gave the cowardly Mr. Lee the courage to seek medical assistance.

Tristan was the first to break. "Dad, I don't think Mr. Lee would want us to know about the rash on his leg."

"Ah! He don't care! He pulled up his pant leg to show me the other day from the sidewalk, when he was walking his yappy dog."

"Ba! Please." Tristan frowned with disgust. "We're trying to eat."

"Fine," Dad said. "Linda, how are you? How are your parents?"

Linda shrunk under the sudden attention. "They're fine."

Dad scratched his gray stubble. "I haven't seen them in a long time. Are they well?"

"They're fine," Tristan said with his mouth full. "She's fine. We're fine."

It was pretty obvious that things were not fine, but Cadence knew Tristan wouldn't say another word about it. Cadence chewed mindlessly, staring at the freebie tear-away supermarket calendar hanging on the wall. It was only day two and she was already counting the days before her flight back to San Francisco.

To her left, Matt tried to be subtle in getting her attention. He pretended to adjust his sitting position, knocking her knee with his in the process. This was his move when he needed her to help him during meetings, whether it was to fill him in on information he missed or to chime in with data to back up his arguments. She cast a quick sideways glance and shook her head, a quick one-two, like a bobblehead in a 1.3 earthquake. *I'll tell you later.*

He nodded back in the same fashion before he returned his attention back to eating. He clicked his chopsticks as he eyed the trays of glistening meat.

"Oh my god," Cadence muttered, knowing Matt was searching for a boneless piece. She selected a perfectly layered piece of crispy pork, cleanly pulled off the bone underneath, and placed it on Matt's plate. Matt tipped his head ever so slightly in gratitude and was about to pop the slice of meat into his mouth when she made a quick grab for the crackled golden-brown skin with her chopsticks.

"Hey!" he whined after getting shortchanged.

"Payment for my services," she teased, locking eyes with him as she chomped on the crunchy skin. She might as well have flipped him off. She knew this was a passive-aggressive way to exact revenge on Matt for barging in today, but she couldn't help it. It was too easy. Matt looked like he was near tears, causing the laugh that was bubbling up in Cadence to spill over. Before she could think it was mean of her, he bumped her shoulders, chuckling softly.

When they both turned their attention back to the table, they realized they had an audience.

"So what's the deal with you two?" Linda asked, waving her chopsticks between them like a needle on a polygraph machine. Cadence didn't think Linda should be the one asking questions like this, but she was pregnant, so Cadence gave her a pass.

"Nothing. We're coworkers." After years of office rumors, the reply came out like a reflex. She glanced at Matt, who carefully peeled the limp layer of fat off his pork. She felt bad because she knew it didn't fully describe their relationship. Matt would want and deserved more credit than that, so she added, "And . . . we're friends. Good friends."

She wished it didn't come out like a question. She wanted Tristan and her dad to have a good impression of Matt. She didn't know why that was important to her, but it was. She peeked at Matt to gauge his reaction.

Matt kept a straight face for a moment before it broke into a dazzling smile. "Best friends."

Just like that, Matt was back.

"Don't tell Maddie that," Dad said. "She'll fight you over Cady. They were always together. People used to ask if Maddie was my other daughter. How is she?"

"She's good. She sent me a new picture of the baby." Cadence whipped out her phone and showed Tristan and her dad a picture of James splashing in a pool. Tristan pounded his chest like he had heartburn. Linda coughed into her napkin. Dad nodded with mild interest.

"That could have been you, Cady," Dad said. "If you didn't work so much, you could have had a husband and baby by now."

Oh my god. "Not now, Ba."

"What do you think, Matt?"

Matt looked like a deer caught in the headlights. "What do I think about what?"

"Cady works too much. Always been that way."

Cadence stuffed her mouth to the brim. It was so hypocritical of Dad to say when he spent all day at his shop, hosting patrons who didn't bother to buy anything. If it wasn't for Mom, they wouldn't have been able to pay the bills. Now that Mom was gone, Cadence took over that responsibility. Dad wouldn't have been able to retire without her, but he seemed to have forgotten that.

"Uh . . . I'm probably not the best person to ask," Matt said. "I work on commission, so I'm always working. That reminds me," he said to Cadence, "when you're free, can you help me gather some data about the area?"

"You're here for work?" Dad asked, placing down his chopsticks.

Cadence thought the question was directed at Matt, but Dad was looking at her. She'd been waiting for the right time to tell him about her assignment, but so much for that.

Matt answered for the both of them. "The motel next door is looking to sell. We're one of the brokerages being considered for the listing."

"I wouldn't bother with the motel," Dad said dismissively while he scratched his stray whiskers. "They've tried to sell many times."

Matt cleared his throat. "With all due respect, we're the best that Prism has to offer. Not to mention, if I get this listing, it will help me secure a position here in L.A."

"I didn't know you could transfer locations," Dad said with re-newed interest.

"It's not a transfer," Cadence clarified, knowing the question was directed at her. "Matt's seeking a promotion for a new office location down here that hasn't opened yet."

"I see," Dad replied thoughtfully. "It must be a good opportu-nity if you're willing to relocate."

"It is." Matt finished his food before saying more. "I'll get to run my own staff and have a real stake in the company as part of their leadership team. But the biggest perk to the job is that it'll be closer to family."

"Family should always come first." Dad took a careful sip of his tea, making agreeable humming sounds. "Do you hear that, Cadence?"

"You're one to talk." Cadence was not in the mood for Dad's posturing. When had he put their family first? By going into debt? Never attending any of Cadence's tournaments when she'd taken up golf only at his insistence?

"Where are your manners?" Dad asked in Hakka. "We have guests." Cadence could have held her tongue until he added, "And we have more coming, so you need to behave."

"Who else is coming?" Everyone who was supposed to be there plus Matt was already sitting at the table.

"Mr. Lee. Some of your mom's friends from the factory. I in-vited them to help us eat the food. They are running late. They were supposed to bring noodl—where are you going?"

Cadence didn't know how her mom's death anniversary turned into a potluck party. What was all of Dad's griping about her coming home if it wasn't to spend time together? He could see his friends anytime. Cadence calmly stood up from her seat and cleaned up after herself. "I need to go. Come on, Matt."

"Hmm?" Matt stuffed one last bite into his mouth.

"You're here to pick me up, right?" Cadence gave him the same get-me-out-of-here eye slide that Matt used every time they were stuck in the elevator with one of his ex-flings.

"Oh . . . right." Matt got the signal and wiped the corners of his mouth with his napkin. "Thank you for lunch and . . . um. Sorry for your loss . . . ?" He stood and let himself out of this awkward exchange.

Cadence went into her room, threw her duffel bag on top of her carry-on, and wheeled it into the living room. Without a word, Matt slid her bag over his shoulder and the suitcase handle exchanged hands. His face zeroed in on hers, silently asking her questions that she was not ready to answer. Cadence opened the door and stepped aside for Matt. Fresh air rushed in, clearing the smoke from the incense. Over her shoulder, she took one last look at her mom's portrait and closed the door behind her.

CHAPTER 12

MATT

M att sat in the CVS parking lot, waiting for Cadence to pick up a few things. She left in such a rush that she forgot some "personal items." She didn't specify what that entailed, and Matt didn't ask, not after the long, quiet drive from her dad's house to Downtown. He had asked her if she wanted to talk about it, to which she replied with a resounding no.

The lunch was an eye-opening experience. Matt added more line items to the list of things he didn't know about Cadence before today. One, she wasn't afraid to throw him to the wolves. Her dad seemed nice, but damn, he talked a lot. Two, Cadence could get mad. Real mad in a silent, ticking-time-bomb kind of way. The Cadence that suffered through lunch was far from the Cadence who communicated her thoughts with authority. Matt couldn't fathom how this was the same person.

To kill time, Matt called Jack Shen, the owner of Best Eastern, and scheduled their meeting for Wednesday. When Cadence still hadn't reappeared, he replied to client emails, then a text came from his cousin AJ.

AJ: Jason, what time are you coming to drop off baby clothes?

AJ: Oops, wrong group chat.

Wrong group chat? There was another group chat?

Matt called AJ. "Hey! What's going on?"

"Matt!" AJ shouted over drilling noise. "Sorry, let me step out. There's so much going on."

"Yeah, what's this about baby clothes?"

"Oh! I was going to tell you at the party this weekend, but George and I are going to become foster parents!"

"Wow!" Matt replied. "Congrats. That's awesome."

"We're hoping it will lead to adoption, but one step at a time. There's a whole approval process," AJ said with an underlying *ugh*. "George and I are trying to get everything together, so I've been getting hand-me-downs from Jason. Celine is going to drop off some stuff too. She was gonna save it for you, but . . . you know."

"No, I know." Matt was nowhere close to kids. He wasn't going to hold it against his sister for donating her stuff already. So why was he feeling a little left out? "What am I supposed to do with a BabyBjörn?"

"Exactly!" AJ laughed, like he was relieved. "You get it."

Matt laughed it off like he did. "But what's this about another group chat?"

"Oh. Um, it's nothing. There's a group of us cousins who are parents, like Jason, Celine. Justine. Diane." Basically, every cousin over thirty. "They've been giving us tips on feeding and sleep training and different kinds of poops. You'd find it boring." A loud bang preceded Spanish curse words in the background. "I have to go," AJ whispered. "You know George isn't handy. I better go help them before they have a meltdown. See you Saturday!"

Matt hung up and stowed his phone in a cup holder. He was happy for AJ and George and to be an uncle to another kid, but the last thing he wanted to be was *that* uncle. The lifelong bachelor uncle that was always three beers too drunk and tried too hard to be cool. He honestly always thought his cousin Gerald would be that guy. He was loud, crass, and still lived at home with Auntie Patricia and Uncle Dennis. Despite Lola's persistent reminders, Matt hadn't put much consideration into settling down, but he was starting to wonder if he was running out of time.

Up ahead, Cadence walked out of the sliding doors. She had a bag nestled in her arms like she was carrying a baby. A baby that looked like a bottle of gin. She climbed into the passenger seat and set the bag down by her feet. Matt eyed her purchase and then chanced a look at Cadence.

"It's makeup, okay?" she said while she folded a dissertation of a receipt and stuffed it in her purse. "And face wash, a toothbrush, toothpaste, deodorant. Some snacks." Matt had opened his mouth to say something when she interjected: "I know what you're thinking. Sometimes I have a drink when I work. Don't judge!"

Matt held up his hands. "I didn't say anything!"

"You don't have to! You look at me with your big old eyes or you give me a nudge, waiting for me to fill in the blanks for you, and—and . . ." She released a deep breath. "I'm sorry. Things are complicated with my family, and I wish you hadn't been there to see that today."

He covered her hand with his while she stared out the windshield. "No, I'm sorry. I shouldn't have invited myself over." Since she didn't pull her hand away, he added, "Can I ask you something?"

"I'll tell you another time," she said, curling her fingers in.

"No, it's not about your family."

Cadence dipped her head, breaking her gaze from the windshield, bouncing it off the sight of their hands, and landed on Matt's face. "What then?"

"You really think my eyes are big?" He looked up toward the sunroof and batted his eyes. It probably looked like he had something in his eye.

Cadence withdrew her hand. "You're so stupid." He kept it up until she finally snickered. "Okay! Stop. Let's go."

IT WAS A surreal experience to walk into the hotel with Cadence. It was designed for extended stays and could have doubled as Prism's office. Everything was white, geometric, shiny, and modern. It was nice enough to impress clients, whether it was in one of the smart conference rooms, all equipped with state-of-the-art technology, or in their four-star restaurant on the top floor.

The lobby was bustling with professionals, coming in to start the workweek. Still, rolling up to the front desk with Cadence by his side unleashed his imagination in ways that were both exciting and anxiety-provoking. It was hard enough not to stare at her legs during the car ride here. Her dress seemed to inch up every time she moved. Why was it suddenly hot? He pinched the front of his shirt and hopelessly tugged it a few times out of habit.

"What is it? You got the meat sweats? I swear, I've never seen you eat so much." After Cadence brushed down his collar, her hand trailed off his shoulder, setting ablaze a path to his own personal Friend Zone hell. She probably thought nothing of this innocent gesture. It was pathetic, the way he looked forward to that all-too-brief contact every day.

"Welcome to Grand Park Suites. How may I assist you today?" Behind the front desk, a young clerk in a three-piece suit looked up from her computer monitor, beaming.

"Hi, uh . . . Araceli," Matt said after glancing at her name tag. "I have a second room under my reservation. Can I get a key?" He handed over his driver's license and credit card.

Araceli's fingers rapped on the counter when her smile pulled down into a frown. She began to click around, almost haphazardly. When another clerk walked behind her, she grabbed him and started whispering, followed by more frantic clicking and typing.

It was pretty clear what was happening, and Cadence wasn't having any of it.

"Are you telling me there isn't another room reserved?" she demanded. "I'm going to call Josie." She started angry scrolling on her phone in search of Josie's contact information.

"Araceli," Matt said with a gracious smile, "isn't there something you can do?"

"I'm sorry," Araceli squeaked as she batted her eyelashes over apologetic eyes and a small pout. "We don't have any available rooms."

Damn. He was counting on that to work. "When I checked in, I could have sworn I had two rooms."

Araceli winced. "You did, but it appears that we gave it up since you only checked in for one and we overbooked. Your suite does have two bedrooms, though."

"Oh hell no!" Cadence fumed, slamming her phone on the

counter. Forget the time bomb. Matt was dealing with a live grenade. "Forget this. I'm going to another hotel."

Araceli raised her index finger to interject. "There are three different conferences going on in the area. Every hotel within a five-mile radius is booked."

Cadence looked pissed and Matt needed to get her away before she went full Karen on Araceli.

"Thanks for your help. We'll figure something out," Matt said. He quickly dragged Cadence to the elevator by her elbow. When the elevator doors closed, Cadence unloaded her simmering rage.

"This is bullshit!" Matt opened his mouth, but Cadence kept ranting. "How could they just give away the other room? And why did you pull me away? I should have asked to speak to the manager. There has to be another room somewhere!"

"She did the best she could," Matt said gently.

"How can you even defend her? Was it because Araceli couldn't take her eyes off you?"

Really? Matt hadn't noticed. Was Cadence *jealous*? A hopeful feeling unfurled in his chest.

"I was just being nice like I always am." The elevator door opened, and he led her to the suite. "If you really don't want to stay here, we can look for another hotel, but check it out first."

He held up his hotel key to the sensor and opened the door. After she walked inside, he turned on all the lights, so that she could get the full effect.

"Jesus," she said under her breath, surveying the ultra-modern suite. There was a small kitchen with a marble island. The living room had a perfectly rectangular and terribly uncomfortable gray sofa that could easily seat five people. "This place is bigger than my apartment."

"That's not even the best part." Matt crossed the suite and pulled a remote control from the desk drawer. Slowly the curtains parted, revealing floor-to-ceiling windows and a view of the clear blue California sky hovering over turn-of-the-century brick buildings.

Cadence walked around with her mouth agape, stunned by her surroundings. Matt used this calm moment to lead her across the kitchen and into the small hallway. He made a quick left and gestured her into an immaculate bedroom with the same view of Downtown.

"If you stayed here, this would be your room. My room is past the bathroom," he said, pointing to the opposite end of the hallway. She stepped further inside the room, contemplating quietly.

Matt went all in. "Come on. Let's be honest here. We're working on a time crunch and this will make it a lot easier to get work done. So don't worry about finding another place. If you get tired of my face, you can hide in here. I won't be offended."

Hands on her hips, Cadence sighed. She didn't like the idea, but this was her version of relenting. She placed her bags on her dresser and rolled her luggage toward him, forcing him to walk backward out the doorway.

"What are you—?"

"I'll be out in one hour. Order a pizza and be ready to work."

Cadence shut the door in his face. It was like they had never left San Francisco.

CHAPTER 13

CADENCE

The suite is beautiful, she thought. *And free! Let's not forget that.* That was how Matt convinced her to stay, Cadence rationalized, though she never thought she'd ever fall for one of his sales pitches. He had been getting under her skin all day. She hated how easily he disarmed people with his cute smile and how his attentiveness could make you feel special. Cadence needed to get a grip. She was the one who almost kissed him on the plane, and afterward, he talked to her like nothing had happened. People fawning over him must be an everyday occurrence for him. If she was going to survive living with him for two weeks, she had to double her efforts to keep her guard up.

Cadence twisted the lid off her soda to a satisfying cracking sound. Sitting across from her at the glass dining table, Matt stared at her as she chugged her drink.

"What?" she said, wiping her mouth with the back of her hand.

"Uh." Matt paused, carefully considering his next words. His eyes slowly traveled down Cadence from head to toe. "I . . . I . . ." he stammered, rubbing the back of his neck. "I have never seen you like—I mean, is this how you are normally? Like, when you take

work home, does *this*"—he flicked an open palm at her outfit—
"work for you?"

Cadence wiggled her finger into the spiky bun sitting on top of
her head, loosening it so that it didn't hurt every time she blinked.
Then she patted it down, flattening it so that she could pull her
massive gray hoodie over her head. She crossed her legs into a
lotus pose and made herself comfortable.

"Don't question my process," she said, shoving a handful of
Skittles into her mouth. "This is how I graduated magna cum
laude—a twenty-ounce Coke, a sharing-size bag of Skittles, pizza,
and a celebratory gin and tonic."

Matt glanced at her high school sweatshirt. "Student govern-
ment, huh? What were you? Class treasurer?"

"How dare you?" She swiftly pointed at the embroidery above
her left boob. "I was class *president*."

Matt held his hands up. "Sorry! You like numbers, so I assumed."

She regretted her brusque reply, but she had lived long enough
in someone's shadow. Growing up, she was either Tristan's little
sister or Mr. Lim's daughter. Everyone in her life relegated her to
a sidekick role, except for Maddie, who helped her campaign for
her presidency by joining her ticket. Then there was Sadie. After her mom died, all Cadence wanted to do was hide, but Sadie
wouldn't let her sell herself short and made sure Cadence worked
on several high-profile transactions. If it hadn't been for Sadie,
everyone at Prism would still think Cadence was a quiet, meek
number cruncher.

She couldn't stay mad at Matt, though. He looked like a wounded
golden retriever.

"No, I'm sorry," Cadence said, closing her eyes as she rubbed her temples. "It's been a long day and I'm hangry and I'm working during my vacation."

"Do you want to talk about it?"

"Sure." She turned her laptop around. Matt frowned when he saw graphs and PivotTables. She knew it wasn't what he meant, but she'd rather discuss work than her family.

"When did you do this?"

She picked at the frayed edges around her cuffs. "Had a hard time sleeping last night. I browsed through market data near Silicon Beach."

Matt's eyebrows shot up as he nodded. He was duly impressed. "So, you're saying my job is done?" Matt checked the time at the bottom corner of her laptop. "I could head downstairs to the gym. They close in an hour."

The image of a shirtless Matt lifting weights, his toned arms glistening, flashed before her eyes. "Um, no. There's a shit ton to do."

Matt chuckled like he was laughing off her questionable inclination to work. "My apologies, Madam President." He flipped her laptop back around. "Is there anything else I can do for you?"

Cadence met his inviting brown eyes over her screen. His lips stretched into a kind smile, but not before an errant tongue stuck out, quickly swiping his bottom lip. Instantly, Cadence had a running list of things she wanted him to do *for* her and *to* her with that tongue. This was really bad. She shook her head and ducked behind her laptop. "No . . . nothing else."

She tried to concentrate on her work but had a few false starts. She wasn't used to having Matt within her view while she did her work. At the office, once the partition was drawn, he was out of sight, out of mind. In the suite, he was unavoidable. His every movement drew her attention, like when he reached over to steal her candy or absentmindedly spun his pen through his fingers as he read. She resorted to putting on her headphones to tune him out.

The pizza arrived twenty minutes later and they took a break to eat. She took another swig of her soda as Matt tossed another uneaten crust back into the pizza box.

"How come you're not eating your pizza bones?" What a waste of perfectly good pizza crust.

Matt arched an eyebrow, amused at her word choice. "Trying to cut carbs."

"If you wanted to do that, you shouldn't have eaten half of a large pepperoni pizza."

"Every little bit helps." He lifted up his shirt, insisting he needed to lose the obnoxious tiny pinch of pudge on his otherwise smooth and deliciously flat stomach. Cadence leaned forward over the table, hopelessly gawking while Matt unbuttoned his pants and rubbed his full belly.

"Why haven't you changed into something more comfortable?" she said, distracted by the taut black elastic band of his boxer briefs. When she looked up, she was met with Matt's amused face. When she realized what she had said, she covered her mouth with both hands. What she meant to ask was why he hadn't changed into his home clothes. He'd been wearing the same outfit since lunch. Growing up, the second she arrived home from school, she would immediately change out of her school clothes into something as uncool as it was comfortable. It was a habit she continued into her adulthood. There was nothing more satisfying than unzipping herself out of her constricting pencil skirts and pulling on something soft and stretchy for her curves to be curvy in.

Matt laughed nervously, catching his tongue in between his teeth to stop himself from smiling. He leaned back into his chair, hands in his pockets, his outstretched legs flanking hers. "Are you trying to get me out of my clothes?"

His voice was low and slow, daring her. With a weakened resolve, Cadence contemplated playing this game, fighting fire with fire to see how far they'd go. Then Matt's lips pulled into a mischievous smile, giving himself away. That jerk! She hated how much pleasure he found in pestering her.

"You know that wasn't what I meant." She ducked her head behind her laptop.

"Yeah, but I'm down for a pajama party. We can braid each other's hair and tell each other secrets." Matt gasped. "*Pillow fights.*"

Cadence threw a pizza crust like a ninja star and hit him square between the eyes. "You're impossible." While Matt dusted the crumbs off his face, Cadence gathered her laptop, soda, and candy, and plopped onto the sofa. Over her shoulder, she spoke to Matt. "Tell me when you come up with something. I'll finish this report."

Cadence expected him to reply with a comeback, but he stayed in his seat, his back facing her, nodding before hanging his head low. She wished she could see his face. She couldn't shake off the feeling like she'd done something wrong, even though Matt deserved the drive-by breading. It was the only way she knew how to get him to stop talking before she had a meltdown, imagining a sexy pillow fight with him.

After cleaning up, Matt sat at the dining table, quietly review-ing the files she sent him. He stayed out of her way, but she felt his presence everywhere. She was so flustered that she mixed up her Excel shortcuts and kept having to correct herself. She closed her eyes, trying to regain composure. Instead, a supercut of Matt's sexiest moments projected behind her eyelids. His swagger at the Prism Christmas party. Backing her up at the last pipeline meet-ing. His pushing up his sleeves and lifting her suitcase over his head like it was nothing. There was no escaping him. She couldn't work in the same room with him, so she flew off the couch. In doing so, she spilled her Skittles, causing them to clatter on the marble floors. Matt turned around to see what the commotion was about.

"Sorry. The couch is uncomfortable. I . . . I'm gonna work in my room."

For a split second, she was conflicted about leaving Skittles scattered across the living room floor, but she caught Matt's baf-fled face and she knew she had to go. She grabbed her laptop and dashed to her room. When she closed the door behind her, she threw herself into work and tried to forget who was on the oppo-site side of the wall. She sat at the slim glass desk in the corner of her room and spent hours importing and organizing data. When she hit a mental roadblock, she reached for her Coke and found none. She had left it on the coffee table. She contemplated not get-ting it, but she was starting to crash.

She quietly turned the knob. It was around eleven-thirty and she was hoping Matt was already asleep. Down the hall, the door to Matt's room was open. It was dark inside, much like the rest of the suite, except for the flickering glow coming from the TV in the living room.

She tiptoed toward the hallway entrance. With her back flushed against the wall, Cadence slowly stretched her neck to peek into the living room. Not a single Skittle was on the floor and whatever remained of her bag of candy was neatly bundled on the coffee table, next to the remote. Where was Matt, though? His laptop still sat on the dining table, but otherwise there was no sign of him anywhere.

The coast was clear. Cadence let out a tired sigh and went after her soda and candy. She was reaching for the remote to turn off the TV when a soft snore coming from the couch startled her. She covered her mouth with both hands, a redundant gesture for her silent scream. Situations like this reminded her that she would be the first person to die in a zombie apocalypse.

Why was she so jumpy? Of course the snore came from Matt. From the looks of it, he was out cold, hugging the pillow his face was resting on. His mouth hung open as though his jaw was un-hinged. She never understood how people found it romantic to watch another person sleep. *Is that what he sleeps in?* He was defi-nitely wearing home clothes, with his unspectacular sweatpants and a plain white tee.

She sat down at the end of the sofa, lowering herself slowly, careful not to disturb Matt. She wondered what he had watched earlier. It couldn't have been the advertisement that was playing on the TV. Who in the world would pay twenty dollars for a manual chopper? Matt shuffled next to her, drawing her attention to him. The first thing she noticed were his feet. They weren't Hobbit feet or anything, but they weren't great to look at, either. She took a mental picture so she could remember he at least had one unattractive trait.

"Why are you staring at my feet?" Matt said groggily.

Cadence gasped at his sudden consciousness. Her eyes shot up from his feet to his face, which was still semi-buried into his pillow. "I'm sorry! I didn't mean to wake you."

Matt grumbled as he sat up and patted his hair, trying to tamp down his bedhead. "What are you doing out here?" His sleepy eyes glanced at the TV. "You need an Easy Chopper? I'll get you one for your birthday."

She chuckled softly and held up her bag of Skittles. "I came out for sustenance."

"Ah." Matt stole a quick glance at her before he leaned forward, resting his elbows on his thighs. He covered his face with both hands, gently rubbing his eyes. He looked exhausted.

How many times had they sat next to each other like this? Countless times at the conference table, but he was usually talking or smiling or laughing. That Matt always had a spotlight on him and nothing could dull his shine. Obstacles always seemed to roll off his back, never slowing him down. Staring at his side profile, light blue from the TV's glow, she knew what she could do to get him out of this funk.

She knocked his knee with hers. "What do you want to know?"

"What?"

"You must have a million questions from today. Go ahead."

"Anything?" His eyes started to gleam as he considered his options. This scared Cadence to death.

"Three questions," she amended. "It's late, so short-answer questions, please."

"Aw, come on. That's hardly anything."

Cadence shrugged and unfurled her bun, shaking her hair out. "Take it or leave it."

"If I knew we were negotiating, I would have come more prepared." A wry smile broke out on Matt's face. "Let me think about it." When Matt finally decided, he angled his face toward her. "Okay. What's the deal with your family?"

That was a loaded question. "You gotta be more specific than that."

"Fine. What's your beef with Tristan? Or vice versa?"

"Nothing. We don't have *beef*," she said, gesturing air quotes. "Next question."

"Wait a minute. You don't get out of that one. There is clearly something, because you guys hardly talked at lunch."

"What do you want me to say? We are not like you. We don't talk incessantly."

"*Incessantly?* You think I talk incessantly?" he asked, wounded.

This was harder than she thought. "Sorry. Um . . . we're not very close. He's six years older than me and we don't have much in common. Tristan has lived the same life as he did in high school—working as a mechanic, driving the same car, same friends, same on-and-off girlfriend. I'm the one who finished school and built my career, and I haven't really been home since. And because he's lived at home, he naturally took care of my parents. Better him than me, though."

"Why do you say that?" Before she could answer, Matt clarified, "This is not my second question. You never said anything about follow-up questions."

Cadence narrowed her eyes at him. "No more after this."

"Deal."

"I don't know." Cadence leaned back, pulled her sleeves over her hands, and crossed her arms. To avoid his gaze, Cadence looked straight at the TV. "He's the oldest, so it was already an unspoken expectation that he would take care of them when they were older. And it was easier to let him. At least that's how it's always been, but now Linda is pregnant and Tristan wants me to help more with my dad, but I don't know if I can commit to it."

Cadence knew how bad that sounded, but Tristan never complained about it. The only time he would get frustrated was when he had to be the middleman between Dad and her. Now that he had asked for help, Cadence felt the sense of obligation tugging at her. It wasn't fair to Tristan to be the only one taking care of Dad, and Dad wasn't getting any younger.

"Why?"

Cadence let out a humorless laugh. "Where do I even start? Um . . . when my dad had his store, people would stop by during good times and bad. One time, a widow came in crying. As my dad would say, he didn't say anything out of the ordinary. He tried to comfort her, reassure her that things would get better. That woman must have found his words to be profound because then she told somebody who told somebody and so on and so forth. Next thing you know, people in the community are stopping by his store for advice. Everyone in San Gabriel knows my dad, from the mayor to the guy driving around picking up scrap metal. He was the person people called if their fortune-teller was unavailable.

"And as he became more popular, it became more and more important to him that Tristan and I also presented ourselves well because he saw us as extensions of him. He pushed us to do well in school and to join a bunch of extracurricular activities. There was a point where my mom's only job was to drive Tristan and me around. When Tristan dropped out of college, my dad was livid. I was in high school at the time and it scared me, seeing Tristan take so much heat. So I followed along with my dad's plan, not knowing that the store was declining. Nobody was buying anything when they stopped to talk to my dad. My mom was taking on extra work while my dad was shooting the breeze, going into debt over his ego. "

Matt nodded, processing her answer. He rubbed his neck, unsure if he should ask his next question, but she knew what he was thinking.

"Come on. Final question." Cadence steeled herself, anticipating the question she hated answering.

In a quiet, hesitant voice, Matt asked, "What happened with your mom?"

"She had a heart attack while she was at work." It was all Cadence could say about her mother, who let the limelight shine on Dad while she toiled behind her sewing machine to make ends meet. She thought that she could close the gap on their finances, believing Dad when he downplayed the drop in revenue. Cadence thought about the time her mom refused to let her quit golf and cello lessons to take a part-time job, citing how the extracurricular activities would help with college applications. How her mother protected Tristan from Dad's rant of disappointment when Tristan dropped out. Like the air they breathed, her mother was essential, operating in the background, and without her . . .

Cadence felt the weight of her sadness against her chest.

"I'm sorry. I'm not always like this," she said, dabbing a stray tear with her sleeve. She thought after going to therapy that she would cry less as she learned to cope. But feelings were complicated, harder to master than the analytical thinking she learned from her business courses. Emotions didn't neatly follow an "if x, then y" logic. They were immeasurable, amorphous. At times, insurmountable.

"I know you're not always like this," Matt said, but not in a reaffirming way. Concerned, if his face was any indication—it looked like all his thoughts gathered in the triangle between his eyebrows and the bridge of his nose. "I wish you'd told me. I wouldn't have—"

"It's okay."

"Don't do that," he said, not accepting her dismissive reply. "I'd hate it if you couldn't tell me if something bothered you. I know I talk a lot—incessantly, apparently—but I can listen too."

"I know," she said, not sure how the conversation turned around on them. "But I've talked about it plenty. To my therapist, to Maddie."

"You also have me," he said firmly, almost affronted. And then, as if he remembered himself, his face softened. "If you'll have me."

If you'll have me. Cadence tried to file this phrase and Matt's formality away as a joke, but there was an intensity behind his eyes that made her insides unravel. That's why she didn't put up a fight when Matt draped his arm around her sagging shoulders, letting him run his comforting hand up and down her arm. She gave in and rested her face on his solid shoulder. The pressure in her chest waned, her body slowly deflating onto his. It was cozy, so much so that she burrowed closer, inhaling the clean linen scent of his soft shirt. The way Matt's body stiffened, the sharp intake of his breath and its restrained release, Cadence was sure she went too far, smelling his shirt. But Matt continued to comfort her, not saying a word. She had no idea how long they sat together like this, but at some point Matt shut off the TV, leaving them in sheer darkness.

Cadence sat up, not wanting to overstay her welcome, and smoothed her hair. "Thanks."

"Anything for my best friend," Matt said with a tired smile. He laid his hand on top of hers, clasping her fingers in a princess hold. A respectful gesture. "You feel okay?"

He said it so warm and gentle, unlike anything she'd heard from him before. Then again, when had she ever let herself be vulnerable around him? Cadence nodded, hypnotized by his thumb gliding back and forth over the back of her hand. Their newfound intimacy was some kind of drug. Her eyes adjusted to where she could make out the outline of his chiseled face. It almost made the soft slope of his nose and the curve of his lips look out of place. She wondered what he could see of her, if he could sense her quickened breath and the gravitational pull that drew her face within an inch of his.

Cadence lightly pressed her lips on his. The tender kiss Matt returned was soft and sweet, but she saw the question mark on his face after. *What is this?* Cadence hated the ambiguity because she had imagined what it would be like to kiss him before. In each version, there was an exclamation point, whether the kiss was fueled by want or a way to shut him up. If this was going to be her chance to kiss him, then she had to kiss him the way she wanted to be kissed. So Cadence tried again, her right hand palming his smooth face while she let him get a taste of her candy-coated tongue, coaxing him to show her that his mouth wasn't all talk. Matt responded, much to her relief, with hungry, frenzied kisses that were somehow life-affirming while taking her breath away. She moaned into his mouth when his hands found their way under her hoodie, gliding up her back, making Cadence desperate to bring their bodies closer. She wrapped her arms around his neck for leverage and climbed onto his lap when Matt pulled back.

"Maybe this isn't a good idea," he said into the crook of her neck with a ragged breath.

"Oh." That was the last thing she expected him to say. The interruption sobered her and allowed blood to flow back up to her brain. She replayed the series of events.

1. Matt witnessed her family drama on the day of her mom's death anniversary.
2. She unloaded a bunch of sad shit on him.
3. Then she destroyed his face.

What was she thinking?

"Don't get me wrong." He ran his hands up and down her thighs. "This was very good—"

Very good? Kill me now. Just when she thought her day couldn't get any worse, she was about to get some consolation speech for a pity kiss. "Look, it's okay. You can save the 'I don't want to ruin our friendship' speech." She shot up from the couch and straightened her sweatshirt.

"Wait. I—" Matt scrambled to his feet.

Cadence cleared her throat to stop her voice from trembling. "I will see you in the morning and we can forget this ever happened."

She set her sights on her room to wallow in her embarrassment when Matt caught her wrist and twirled her back around. His other hand landed on her waist, stopping her momentum.

"Look. It's late and we should get some rest, but let me be clear. I've wanted to kiss you for a long time. I'm done pretending that I don't want to kiss you when you walk into the office, and I sure as hell am not going to forget that this happened. But I promise you, I'm not going to kiss you again until we're on the same page. And if we are, we're going to do a hell of a lot more than kiss."

CHAPTER 14

MATT

Matt checked his phone when he woke up and found boring work emails from Cadence sent at 3:24 in the morning. If he had known she was still up, he would have asked her if they could not sleep and not work together. Lord knows he couldn't fall asleep after tasting the rainbow on Cadence's lips. It was worth it, even though at the end of it, he found a case of blue balls instead of a pot of gold. If last night proved anything, it was that he wasn't the only one toeing the line of their friendship. If they were going to cross the lines and level up their relationship, he wanted Cadence to decide, clearheaded and without regrets.

By the time he joined Cadence at the opposite end of the dining table, her head was deep into her laptop. In her oversize decrepit sweatshirt with the hood draped over her headphones, she blatantly ignored him in plain sight. It was a bit anticlimactic, but he didn't let it deter him. He said his piece, so the ball was in her court. But as far as work went, he was going to let his presence be known. He opened his calendar on his laptop and sent individual invitations to all the meetings and work events he had scheduled for the week.

Monday

12:00 p.m. Lunch with Serj Abgaryan/South Bay
   International Realty

3:00 p.m. Meeting with Josh Klein/Ridgecrest Property
   Group

6:00 p.m. Young Real Estate Professionals—Los Angeles
   Mixer

Tuesday

2:00 p.m. Phone Call with Blake Hall/Quintara Development

Wednesday

4:00 p.m. Meeting with Thom Price/Price Property Partners

Thursday

10:00 a.m. Meeting with Jack Shen/Best Eastern

1:00 p.m. Meeting with Percy Ma/L.A. Convention Center

Friday

3:00 p.m. Prism L.A. Office Walk-Through

Saturday

4:00 p.m. Missy's Birthday Party

He peeked over his screen to see how she'd react to her inbox suddenly flooding. He was met with unamused eyes. Her response was an efficient email request to sync calendars. Matt accepted and let their lives electronically merge, though that was a romantic way to put it. Her calendar was entirely blank except for the meeting with Percy Ma, which was scheduled an hour before he headlined as the keynote speaker at TechXpo. Since Cadence didn't seem to be in the talking mood, he sent her a message over their Prism internal chat.

MATT: What do you think are the chances that Percy will open an office here in L.A.?

CADENCE: He should. Between Silicon Beach, the entertainment industry, and a bevy of influencers, iStan would be perfect in L.A.

CADENCE: I already gathered the data points together for a pitch.

MATT: Sweet. Thanks.

MATT: Speaking of pitches, i'm waiting for your response to mine. 🙃

"Are you crazy?" Cadence slipped off her headphones and shut her laptop. "IT archives the interoffice chats."

Was it awful that he found her flustered reaction adorable?

"Hi. Good morning," he said with an innocent smile. "I was thinking, if you're interested in my idea, I'd be happy to give you a formal presentation."

While he was tossing and turning last night, he thought about all the ways Cadence could have analyzed the prospect of their dating. He wouldn't be shocked if there was a spreadsheet on her laptop about him, listing the pros and cons. Hopefully, the former outnumbered and outweighed the latter. Cadence crossed her arms as Matt stood up. Akin to staging a home for sale, Matt needed to show off his best features to sell his potential. He smoothed down his fitted white dress shirt, which was tucked neatly into his snug gray chinos.

"Located conveniently in the same room as you, Matt is available right away for dates. As you already know, he makes an excellent professional partner and tells killer jokes."

"That's a matter of personal opinion," she muttered to herself.

Matt powered past her commentary. "At five-eleven, he is the ideal height for analysts that are five-seven—five-ten in heels. Amenities include these"—he gestured to his shoulders—"for leaning on or falling asleep against while watching movies." He displayed his hands. "And these, which can cook, open doors for you, carry things, and massage you anywhere you want," he continued conspiratorially. "I could go on, but feel free to interrupt me if you have questions."

"Look, this is very cute—"

"Thanks. Wait until you take the tour."

"But—"

"I have one of those too," he said. He turned around, hands on his hips, and shifted his weight to achieve maximum strain from his tiny ass. This was him working with what he had.

"Matt."

The firm but resigned tone in her voice made him spin on his heel. It was a warning to cut the shit. He grabbed the seat next to her to level with her. "Cadence, I meant every word I said last night. If you don't want to do this, we don't have to do this. All I'm asking for is a fair shot." He reminded himself to invite Cadence to his next poker game with the guys because she was giving nothing away. "What do you say?"

Cadence sighed. "I'm not going to lie and say I haven't thought about this before, but this is a lot to consider, Matt. Like, if you wanted this for a while, why now? The timing couldn't be worse. You're about to get a job down here."

"Let's not put the cart before the horse. Nothing is guaranteed."

Cadence shot him a disbelieving look. "Even so, we work together."

"So what? It's not like I'm your boss or anything. And HR will probably make us sign something. Don't tell me you're holding back over some paperwork."

Cadence chewed on her lip like she wasn't sure she should say what she was about to say. "I don't know how to break it to you, but I don't see you as boyfriend material."

Matt blanked out for a second, disoriented from being blindsided. "Excuse me?" He was smart, successful, attractive, and came from a good family. He was a catch! "What was last night, then?"

"A moment of weakness," she said under her breath. "Look, I know you. You're ambitious, and it's one of the things I like about you. But it also means that you work around the clock and I haven't seen you go past the third date with any one of the *many* women you've dated."

"If I knew you were interested, I wouldn't have even—" Matt leaned over and held his head between his knees. He had a feeling it boiled down to this, recalling her comment about Miki, but to hear her say it to his face was a real wake-up call. This was it. His do-or-die moment. He had to show Cadence that when it came to her, he wasn't fucking around.

Matt looked up at her and sandwiched her hand between his.

"Forget them. If I cared about any of them, I wouldn't be here asking you for a chance." If she couldn't tell how sincere he was, then he was shit out of luck.

He watched Cadence carefully consider his words. Slowly, her fortress laid down its defenses. Her eye contact broke first, traveling down Matt's face to their hands. Finally, her shoulders slouched, bringing her forward until she was face-to-face with him. "No one from work can know about this," she said in a low voice.

Matt bit his lip to stop his smile from spreading. "Absolutely."

"I know we're friends, but that doesn't mean you get to skip a bunch of steps. I want to take things slow."

"I agree." With the most serious face he could muster, he held up his hand. "Scout's honor." Adrenaline coursed through Matt's veins. He was ready to cross the *t*'s and dot the *i*'s on this and resume what they started last night.

"And work time has to be for work. No kissing, no flirting, et cetera."

"What?" It was as if she had dumped a bucketful of cold water on him. "Where's the fun in that?"

"We'd never get our work done."

"I couldn't care less about work right now . . ." Cadence cocked an eyebrow at him. "Point taken." Matt groaned in reluctance. "Fine, but can we seal the deal with a kiss?"

He brought her hand up to his lips and lightly kissed inside her wrist. With a slight hitch in her breath, Cadence began to lean in with parted lips, closing her eyes.

Oh, this was going to be more fun than he thought.

Matt shot up from his seat, nearly toppling Cadence off her chair. "I gotta run," he announced. "I have a lunch meeting right now with some guys from my old firm, and then I'm going to stop by to see some old clients. I'd kiss you goodbye, but you know. No kissing while we're on the clock."

Cadence had fire in her eyes. "You're a jerk, you know that?"

"I didn't make the rules. I just follow them." He winked at her before he made his way toward the door. "I'll be back to pick you up for the networking mixer tonight."

Cadence flipped her hood over her shaking head. "I'm not going to that."

She hated schmoozing, but Matt knew she'd do it if it benefited her somehow. "It'll be a good opportunity to introduce Prism to L.A. I know Sadie would appreciate it," he said, slipping his blazer on. He was out the door when he received a text from her.

CADENCE: Don't be late

Throughout his lunch and client meetings, Matt found himself anxious for things to wrap up. His old coworker, Serj, asked him if he was all right because Matt seemed distracted. That was a first. For his last meeting, Matt asked his client to switch their meeting to a phone call or else he would have been stuck in traffic coming from the Westside. He was hoping to get back to their suite early enough to catch Cadence on a break, but when he walked in, she was dressed in her blush-pink pantsuit, ready to go. Work Cadence didn't mess around. When Matt offered the crook of his arm to walk her out, she walked straight past him out the door. He didn't make things better for himself when he suggested walking to Gild, a bar inside a refurbished Art Deco building located three blocks away from their hotel.

"What is this mixer, anyway?" Cadence grumbled, stopping in front of their hotel to fix the strap on the back of one of her black open-toed heels. It was dark outside with a slight chill, which was the only indication of winter. A rash of red lights covered Grand Avenue's gridlocked lanes.

"It's by the Young Real Estate Professionals of Los Angeles, or YREPLA for short," he said, walking alongside her while a cool breeze refreshed the warm, smoggy air. "My friend John runs it."

"That explains how you got in."

"Are you trying to imply something?"

"I'm not trying to imply anything. I'm saying you're old." At the corner, Cadence pressed the crosswalk signal and waited next to a Latina who was setting up a jangling cart with condiments hanging off the side. There was a sheet pan laid on top where onions and hot dogs would be sizzling in a few hours. There had to be a game at the Staples Center.

"Hey! Their age cutoff is thirty-five."

"Thirty-five? That's a hop, skip, and jump away from middle age."

"Why are you so obsessed with aging?" Matt counted eight different skin-care products on their bathroom counter. Since when did one person need more than one cleanser and moisturizer? And what the hell was toner?

Cadence stepped off the curb when the crosswalk signal turned, picking up the pace with each step. "You're not a woman, so you don't get it. Guys get to be 'dignified' when they're old. Women get to be 'pretty young things' or 'sweet old grandmas.' There's nothing in between. The closest thing women like me are supposed to aspire to is 'girlboss.' *Girl.* Boss. So you can't blame me for wanting to hold on to my youth. My joints might be starting to creak, but damned if I'm not going to look good while I struggle to get out of bed."

Matt leaned in close to her ear. "I'd have you struggling to get out of bed for other reasons."

Cadence was a loss for words before she recovered. "What happened to following the rules?"

Matt shrugged. "Rules were meant to be broken."

When they walked into Gild, it was brimming with brokers, shouting over beers and bite-size appetizers. True to its name, gold accents gleamed from every corner of the bar, from the illuminated coffer ceiling tiles to the trellis-patterned mirrors that surrounded the liquor display.

"Do all your mixers look like the International House of Bros?"

Matt searched for the sarcasm in Cadence's voice, but he found none. Cadence was checking out the sausage-fest in awe, like she was having difficulty choosing between Swedish crepes or tres leches pancakes.

Matt cleared his throat. "I know mixers aren't your thing, so we don't have to stay if—"

"No, no," she said, indiscriminately patting his chest as she walked away. "This was your idea and I'm here to support you. Go get me a drink." She looked over her shoulder and winked at him. Great. Matt was suffering the consequences of his actions.

Matt weaved between brokers, rubbing elbows with his elbows and brushing butts with his butt on the way to the bar. He leaned over the counter to wave down the bartender.

"I had a feeling you'd show up."

Matt straightened up at the familiar voice.

Hunter squeezed himself into the bar and ordered three beers over other patrons. "I saw you walk in with Cadence. I thought she was supposed to be on vacation. Don't tell me you two have been banging this whole time or else I'm going to lose some money to Josie."

Matt wasn't going to dignify Hunter's inappropriate comment with a response. "What are you doing here?"

"I should be asking you that."

"I don't know what you're getting at, but I'm here to meet up with Percy, my client."

Hunter snorted. "Don't play dumb. If that's the case, why would you need to be here networking?"

"Reconnecting with some old friends. You know how it is. Networking mixers are an excuse to get drunk and pass it off as work."

"I bet Sadie would love hearing you say that." The bartender placed three IPAs in front of Hunter. "Don't worry, I got this. Give Cadence my regards. If you don't mind, I'll be making my rounds so people will recognize me when I get announced as Prism L.A.'s new director."

When Sadie had mentioned this opportunity, Matt knew he'd want the job. It was the natural next step in his career, but now he really wanted it, deep in his bones, if it meant wiping the floor with Hunter's entitled face. Matt picked up the beers and found Cadence near the jukebox, talking to some brunette woman whose back was turned toward him. When Cadence saw Matt from a distance, she flashed him a frosty look and returned a strained smile to the mystery woman. Matt wasn't sure if he was supposed to save Cadence or run for the hills. He took his chances and weaved through the sea of suits. Reaching past the woman, he handed Cadence her drink.

"Ah," Cadence said as she accepted her beer with both hands. "And here's Matt!" she announced with an edge to her enthusiasm.

Before he could turn around, he was suddenly accosted in a back hug. He shuddered from the contact as pink manicured hands trailed up his chest.

"Matt! It's me, Ashley!" She popped out from under his arm and hugged his waist.

Ashley? Oh, shit.

Matt froze and held his hands up, like an NBA player when a ball is about to bounce out of bounds. "Ashley!" he said, stepping out of her hold to stand next to Cadence. "Long time no see."

"I know, right?" she squealed. "When I saw Cadence, I practically ran over! Of all the places to bump into each other—at a mixer, like real colleagues. Your former intern's moving on up!"

Matt winced at her high-pitched voice. She was like a chipmunk on Red Bull.

Oblivious, Ashley continued talking. "Cadence was telling me how you're up for a promotion! Go you! Maybe you can hire me. I'd be happy to work under you again."

"*Oh?*" Cadence asked, swinging her head toward Matt with her interrogating eyes.

Matt gulped. He had no idea where Ashley was going with this. They had gone out a few times after she left Prism, and if he hadn't taken her to his family's Thanksgiving that year, she wouldn't be hanging on his arm, thinking that they could rekindle something that didn't exist.

"It was really good seeing you, Ashley, but I need to talk to Cadence alone."

"Yeah, sure." Ashley hugged Cadence goodbye. "It's so good to see you!" When she turned to hug Matt, he went on the offense and gave her a side hug, his hand on her shoulder. It was the most amount of physical contact that was still socially acceptable in this situation. "We can catch up later. Tell your lola I said hi! I still want her leche flan recipe. You still have my number, Matt."

Both of them watched Ashley disappear into the crowd, though they could still hear her. She had the kind of piercing voice that sounded like writing on whiteboard with a dry-erase marker. Matt knocked back his beer to give himself some time to think of what to say. Cadence, on the other hand, continued to babysit her IPA, twisting the bottle neck with her fingers.

Cadence broke the tension with her biting tone. "Wow . . . I have—"

"It's not what—"

"—*so* many questions." Cadence chugged her beer. "Blech! Why does anyone like this?" she said, frowning at the bitter taste as she walked away.

Matt caught her elbow. "I can explain. It's nothing to get upset over."

"I'm not upset," she insisted.

"Then why is your face so red?"

"Asian flush," she said dismissively. *After half a beer? Such a lightweight.* Cadence took another swig.

"We went on a couple of dates last year after she left the company. The last time I saw her was last year, when she relocated down here."

"Okay. Fine." It didn't sound convincing. "That was fun, but if you'll excuse me, I'm going to go mix and mingle," she said before she immersed herself in the fold. He cursed under his breath.

He hated that he was in the doghouse over a misunderstanding. As much as he wanted to wade through the crowd to find her, he knew if she chose to network over talking to him, he had to give her some space.

A couple hours later, Matt had sufficiently worked the room and run into his friends, Saurabh and John, who had to stay until the event ended. The crowd started to thin out; the remaining brokers dispersed across the room. Fortunately, Ashley cut out a while back, but not without sending Matt a dainty wave as she exited the bar. Matt spotted Cadence standing at a cocktail table with a few people. Based on her animated hand gestures as she spoke, she'd likely found her tribe of fellow analysts.

"This was fun, but you should come to the YREPLA golf tournament next week," John said. "That's where you'll meet the major players. Any excuse to tee up. I can add you to the registration list."

"Hmm? Yeah, I'll get back to you on that," Matt said noncommittally.

"Who are you checking out?" John asked, following Matt's line of sight. "If you're looking at who I think you're looking at, let me save you the trouble."

"Oh yeah?" Matt asked. He was curious what John thought of Cadence. "Why do you say that?"

"She's in town for a conference. I offered to show her around, but she didn't even take my business card. Can you believe that?"

"She shot him down cold," Saurabh chimed in.

Matt brought his bottle of beer up to his lips to cover up his laugh. Cadence would never go for someone like John. He was a cool guy to hang around with and he wasn't bad-looking, if you liked the former small-town high school quarterback type who still liked to talk about their former glory days.

"Oh, you think you can do better?" John challenged.

"Don't be a sore loser." Matt handed his beer to John, rendering him speechless. "She's just not that into you."

Matt buttoned his blazer and made his way to Cadence. He gently placed his hand on the back of her elbow so that she would be aware of his presence. Matt jumped right into introductions and shook everyone's hands. With the flow of conversation interrupted, everyone pulled out their phones to check the time. One guy decided to leave, which opened the door for the rest of them to go. They exchanged pleasantries and business cards with Cadence as they filed out one by one.

"You looked like you were having fun," he said, noting the two empty cocktail glasses on the table.

"I *was*," she drawled, flashing him a broad smile. Tipsy Cadence was in the house and she was feeling *very* good.

"I didn't mean to scare everyone away."

"Why are you whispering?" she asked, lowering her voice. Her hand shot out and grabbed Matt's arm when her feet wobbled. "Sorry. My shoes are starting to hurt."

"Can I ask you something?" he asked after she regained her balance.

"Anything." Her answer slipped out easily, velvet soft.

Two gin and tonics made her very agreeable. "Did a guy hit on you earlier?"

"You mean Tan Suit Guy with small dick energy?"

Matt held in a snort. "That was my buddy John. What did you say to him? He seemed pretty hurt."

"All I said was that I was seeing someone." Cadence toyed with his tie, tugging him a step forward, when she cinched it tighter. "Karl."

Matt choked out a laugh. "That guy again? Didn't you leave him in San Francisco?"

"Yeah. It was amicable, though." Cadence sipped on her melted ice. "The chemistry evaporated."

"I can't imagine, but I'm glad he's out of the picture." Matt slid his hand down Cadence's arm to lure her closer, but she flicked it off before it reached her elbow.

"Unlike some people, my exes don't tend to pop up out of nowhere."

Not this again. "I can explain, but not here." The truth was too embarrassing to admit when they were surrounded by colleagues.

Cadence shrugged like she didn't care, but her cold shoulder indicated otherwise. This was not how Matt wanted to start their budding romance, jumping into ex talk. In fact, if he was playing by Cadence's rules, he needed to start at the very beginning. He had to woo her.

"What did I tell you earlier? Don't worry about people I've dated. They're in the past. I'd much rather spend time with you." Matt tucked a stray strand of Cadence's hair behind her ear, letting his fingers lightly trail along her jaw. "Did you know that one of the first things I noticed about you is when you're stuck on a problem, you scrunch up your nose like you smell stinky cheese? It makes me laugh every time."

"That doesn't sound attractive." Cadence pursed those pretty lips of hers. Lips he very much wanted to kiss again.

"It is. Trust me." Matt leaned over her shoulder and whispered in her ear, "And don't get me started on your pencil skirts."

"What about them?"

"They always make me want to touch you here," he said, placing his hand on Cadence's waist, "and here." His palm slid around to the small of her back. Matt couldn't see her face to gauge her reaction, but she leaned in closer to proffer a secret of her own.

"If you would have told me, I might have let you."

Matt groaned at the thought and the feeling of her breath on his skin.

"I wanted to," Matt admitted, feeling naked in his transparency. "You are very hard to read."

"I see," she said, her voice dropping with understanding. She leaned back until their eyes met. Her deep brown eyes focused on him intently, like she was seeing him for the first time. Then they fluttered with a sharp inhale. "I'd stay and chat more, but I'm off the clock," she said, as if she had just remembered they were at a work function. Her hand snaked around his shoulder and palmed the back of his neck, bringing her lips to his ear once again. "You know what that means?"

As if he needed a reminder, Cadence brushed her lips against his cheek when she took a step back. It couldn't have lasted more than a second, but it lit his entire body on fire. If he hadn't been so stunned by it, he would have caught her lips with his, but by the time he could react, her face was already too far.

"Should we get out of here?"

Matt thought she'd never ask.

CHAPTER 15

CADENCE

M y feet are killing me." Cadence mused that she probably looked real sexy, knocking her knees as she walked like a foal taking its first steps. On top of that, she was hungry. In the midst of networking, Cadence had forgotten to eat something while she drank. Cadence held on to Matt's arm while she trudged along, determined to tough it out. They were one block from the hotel when she suddenly fell forward, landing on her hands. "What the fuck?"

Cadence pushed herself up and looked behind her. Her wobbly heels had gone head-to-head with a crack on the sidewalk. The sidewalk won, snapping her heel cleanly off.

"Here." Matt gathered her broken shoes and knelt in front of her, offering her a piggyback ride. "I'll carry you back."

It was chivalrous of him, but let's be real. "No, I'm too heavy."

"It's only a block away. Come on."

The hotel wasn't too far and the sidewalk looked grimy. A couple of men walked around them, minding their own business. One of them casually spat on the ground. Yeah, she was not going to walk in her bare feet on that. She gingerly climbed onto Matt's back, wrapping her arms around his neck and gripping her legs against him as he slowly got on his feet.

"Are you sure this is okay?"

Matt took deep breaths. "Don't talk. I gotta"—he clenched his jaw as he hefted her up higher—"I gotta focus." Matt grunted again as he tried to power walk the rest of the way.

"If it's any consolation, this is the best piggyback ride of my life."

"Not now," he gritted through his teeth. They made it into the lobby, catching plenty of puzzled looks, and took the elevator up to their suite.

By the time Matt got to their door, his breathing had become labored, accented with soft grunts. "I can't . . . get . . . the door."

"I got it." Cadence reached into her pocket and withdrew the key card. Matt's hands wrapped around Cadence's knees, gripping them apart, while he lowered himself. Cadence wrapped her arms around his neck, trying to keep up.

"Closer," she whined. "I'm so . . . so close."

"Hurry." He huffed. "I can't hold on much longer." Deep guttural sounds escaped as he started to lose control. "Come on, Cadence. Do it for me, please."

Cadence was running out of time. She dug her nails into his strong shoulders to reposition herself. Reaching down, she let her fingers explore, rubbing circles until she got what she was looking for.

A satisfying single click of their hotel door unlocking.

"Ahh," Matt and Cadence sighed in unison. Cadence reached as far as her arms would allow and pushed the door open without falling off Matt's back.

"I'm sorry." Cadence pouted into the crook of Matt's neck. Wow, he still smelled good.

"It's okay," he said through gritted teeth. Matt tumbled toward her room and unloaded her on her bed. With her weight off his shoulders, he sank to the floor beside the bed to catch his breath.

Cadence groaned when her body bounced on impact. She rolled her jelly body around until she lay sideways across the bed, facing Matt. He was an arm's length away, shuffling out of his blazer and wiping the sweat dripping off his forehead.

"You're like ridiculously good looking," she drawled. It was an unintelligent observation, but Cadence's mind was frazzled from the sensation of Matt's hands around her knees.

"Is that right?" Matt said while he wheezed. He nestled his head on the edge of the bed with vested interest, like it was the beginning of his bedtime story.

"Don't pretend like you don't know. It's annoying when hot people pretend that they don't know that they're hot." She squinted at the ceiling, repeating her words on her lips. "Did I say that right?"

"You're drunk."

"No, I'm not," she protested. As it turns out, holding on to a hot man for dear life made her very alert.

"It's the first time hearing you say it, so sue me for liking it." Matt's eyes shined with mirth. "I wasn't sure if you thought about me like that at all."

"Oh, please." She shot him a pointed look. "Have you seen yourself?"

"What stopped you from telling me?" His voice was more curious than accusatory.

"Because we're friends." Cadence shrugged lamely. "And whenever I considered it, you were dating someone, like Miki or *Ashley*."

Matt sighed. "I can explain."

"You've said that a lot this evening and I haven't heard any 'splainin'."

"Um . . . this is embarrassing." Matt leaned his back against the nightstand, resting his arms across his tented knees. "We did go out a couple times last year before she relocated down here. Then, around Thanksgiving, I thought it would be a good idea to take her to my family's Thanksgiving dinner and learned the hard way that people assume things must be really serious when you bring someone home for the holidays."

"Uh, yeah." Cadence laughed through her secondhand embarrassment. "Wow. You didn't think about that going in? How did Ashley react?"

"She loved my family and the attention. For what it's worth, she fooled nobody. What you saw today was nothing compared to how she acted in front of my family. My lola did not like her and my cousins knew right away that it was not going to last. They've given me plenty of grief about it."

"Why didn't you go solo?"

"I didn't want to be the only one without a date," he admitted. "You think I'm pathetic, don't you?"

Cadence shook her head. "Is that why you asked me to go to your cousin's birthday party?"

Matt nodded, letting his head hang on his chest. "Look, I love my family, but the idea of showing up for another family gathering alone *again* when everyone has a family or significant other already . . ." Matt sighed. "I know they mean well, but sometimes it makes me feel like there's something wrong with me. My lola *literally* asked me if there was something wrong with me."

"There's nothing wrong with you." The words came out of Cadence's mouth effortlessly, but not to flatter him. That feeling of being under a microscope hit close to home. Flashes from the past few weeks populated in her mind. The times Matt would try to make her laugh after her draining meetings with Bill. When "freebie" coffees started showing up on her desk on the days she ran late to work. How he'd make it a point to give her credit or back her up at meetings. Memories she once took for granted now painted a new picture. Cadence scrambled up on her elbows, getting a bird's-eye view of him. "How come you never told me how you felt about me?"

"You didn't seem interested, no matter how hard I tried to get your attention or tried to spend more time with you." Matt brushed her hair away from her face and tucked it behind her ear. "I ate that bland porridge and then you left me alone at Christmas!"

Cadence covered her face. "I know. I'm sorry. Would you forgive me if I told you I thought you were ridiculously good looking even when you were being such a baby?"

"Maybe." Matt grinned. "You can tell me more over dinner."

Matt's idea of dinner was ordering room service. That was fine by Cadence, who was in no shape to leave their suite. After she changed into her old UW T-shirt and shorts, she caught her reflection in the bathroom mirror. To her horror, she found herself looking like Two-Face. The makeup on the right side of her face had transferred onto Matt's suit jacket. It was beyond repair, so there was no point covering it back up. Cadence washed her face and joined Matt at the kitchen table. He ordered them both a hamburger and gave Cadence the plate that had more fries. Her butt wasn't fully on the seat of her chair when he bombarded her with questions of the self-absorbed variety.

"So did you think I was irresistible when we danced at the holiday party?"

"You do dance well," she replied, picking up a hot fry.

"Admit it. You loved my ugly Christmas sweater, didn't you?"

"No, that was horrendous. An insult to all sweaters."

"You are not one to critique clothing when you are wearing that."

Cadence looked down at her shabby outfit. "What? It's comfortable. You know, my mom used to sew clothes for a fast fashion brand, which sold their pieces for cheap, so that people wouldn't feel bad when they threw them away to buy into the next fashion trend. It seemed wasteful to me, so I don't spend money on clothes that nobody will see but me."

"Oh, I had no idea," Matt said. He picked up his burger and paused, staring at it with a thoughtful *hmm*.

"What?"

"Just when I think I know you, you keep surprising me. You're different than I expected."

"Sorry to disappoint you."

"I didn't mean it that way. I'm hardly one to judge." Matt put his burger down and wiped his hand on his napkin before he extended it to Cadence. "Pathetic bachelor with fake girlfriends. Nice to meet you."

"Charmed," she said, shaking his hand.

"And you are?"

"Um." Cadence threw out the first thing that came to mind. "Dense work wife with family drama?"

Matt released her hand with a smirk. "It doesn't quite roll off the tongue, but we'll work on it."

Cadence responded with a weak backhanded slap to his arm. After two sleepless nights, she didn't have any strength to throw behind it. Matt must have noticed, because after dinner he escorted her to the entrance of her room with good intentions.

"So, this is me," she joked, leaning her back against the door in a flamingo stance.

Matt's eyes crinkled with his crooked smile. "Get some sleep. I don't want to see three A.M. work emails from you." Cadence nodded. "Good night." His hand ambled up her bare, propped-up thigh, settling on the small of her back.

Cadence readied herself because she knew that this time there would be no fake-out, no accident, no interruptions. The wild thing was that Cadence felt nervous. How absurd was that? It wasn't like they'd returned from their first date. In the last few years, she'd conversed and eaten more meals with him than anyone, and their lives were getting more intertwined by the minute. Matt already met her family *and* they were presently cohabitating. Perhaps, she reasoned, for all their missed signs, they finally jumped both feet into this murky space—too close to be casually dating, but too early to be committed. For someone who liked to live in either black or white, Cadence found herself excited for once about the undefined.

Matt's fingers tightened at her waist one by one in a wave like a countdown as his soft mouth descended. It started innocently enough, with a slip of his tongue, testing hers. Cadence's hands roamed on his firm chest until they wrapped around his neck, pulling him closer, encouraging him to escalate his PG-13 kiss. Her enthusiasm caused Matt to lose his balance, and he latched on to her waist as he tripped forward, pressing her into the door. Oh, he was firm everywhere.

"Don't do that," he groaned, freeing his bottom lip from her teeth. "Don't make this harder for me."

Cadence hooked her leg around him, tempted to climb on top of him. "I think it's too late for that," she panted into his neck.

"You're drunk."

"Not anymore."

"What happened to not skipping steps?"

Oh. He was listening this morning. His question sounded sincere, but Matt gripped her shirt at her waist, struggling as he waited for her answer. His obvious want made her mind go blank, clearing way for her baser instincts. Cadence made a two-handed grab for his compact ass, keeping their bodies flush. "I made the rules, so I can change them."

"Good to know."

Matt's unrestrained kiss had Cadence fumbling to get the door open and the lights on, kicking off a clumsy, reckless effort between the two of them to get to the bed. They were like unleashed Black Friday shoppers at midnight, stumbling forward, grabbing everything in sight. Cadence teetered, gripping the front of Matt's shirt to keep his lips on her, which impeded him from hitching her up. They both switched focus and reached for his pants, turning themselves into a bad joke. How many horny hands does it take to unbuckle a belt? Not four.

"Wait," Matt said, peeling Cadence's hands away so he could unzip his pants.

No, she could not. She'd already waited too long for this. Cadence quickly disposed of her clothes. Matt stilled momentarily, studying Cadence's bare form like he wanted to set the curve. Soon his clothes were gone and his lean and streamlined figure held her steady, imprinting on her pliable body like a melted wax seal, walking her backward until she fell into bed.

Cadence lay on her side as Matt fished his wallet from his pants.

"You always carry condoms with you?" she asked. "Not that I'm complaining."

"Wishful thinking." Matt had the decency to look sheepish as he said this. When his eyes flicked up, there was a noticeable shift in the room. The music they had been dancing around their feelings to had switched to a slow dance. Years of wandering thoughts had finally become a reality. Cadence held her breath as Matt approached the bed and settled in between her legs.

Matt took his time without losing his sense of urgency, exploring every dip and turn, attentive to every reaction. Cadence was transfixed while he placed deliberate kisses—at the crook of her neck, on the swell of her breasts, and at the ticklish spot inside her knee—like he was documenting landmarks he wanted to revisit.

"Matt," she gasped, unable to hide the need in her voice. This was nice and all, but after all the pining and furtive glances, she could handle only so much teasing. If she hadn't thought it would be rude, Cadence would have bopped him on the head to get on with it.

Matt looked up with hooded eyes, telling her that he would not be rushed with a slow, lazy lick in between her thighs, treating her like a melting ice cream cone on a hot day. Cadence's head fell back with an involuntary deep moan. His self-satisfied smile pressed on her sensitive skin, proving that he didn't need words to instigate, daring her, asking her if she was ready for more. Cadence widened her legs, giving Matt full access, because when it came to him, she always rose to the occasion.

Luckily for her, so did Matt, who fervently took to his task, learning what she liked until her body trembled. Matt didn't even give her a chance to relax into the sated feeling. After he slipped on his condom, he thrust into her at a slow, torturous pace, keeping her on the precipice of another climax.

"Cadence. Look at me."

His voice cut through the haze. She almost didn't recognize it. Outside of his strained grunts, Matt hadn't spoken a word until now. His mouth had been very busy. Cadence whimpered as she pried her eyes open.

Matt's forehead dipped onto hers. "Are you okay?"

Couldn't he tell from her incoherent sounds that she'd been telling herself over and over how she'd been a fool to resist this for so long? Cadence nodded, having lost the ability to speak. She showed him how okay she was, grinding her body against his, chasing after that extra friction, climbing higher and higher until she came again. Matt followed soon after, collapsing onto his forearms.

"Fuck," he whispered into the valley between her breasts. That seemed to be the only word he was capable of saying for a while.

Out of breath, Cadence patted his back to share her sentiments. Matt withdrew from her, making her wonder if he mistook the complimentary gesture as a sign to leave. She didn't think about it too hard as she watched his cute butt saunter off to the bathroom, taking his place when he disappeared into his room. Cadence turned over in her bed and faced the window, wondering if every night would end in their going their separate ways. She tried not to read too much into it. Whatever this was, it was still new.

The side of the bed dipped as Matt climbed in. Arms scooped around her, pulling her backward until she found herself tucked into Matt, small spoon to his big spoon.

"You don't know how long I've wanted to do this." For a second, Cadence thought he was talking about the sex, which she was more than happy to repeat, but then his face nuzzled into her just-fucked hair. "It's even better than I imagined." Cadence couldn't help smiling, falling asleep wondering if she imagined the tender kisses on her shoulder.

SUNLIGHT PEEKED THROUGH the blackout curtains, shining right on Cadence's eyes. She didn't know what time it was, but it was too early. When she cracked her eyes open, she found herself lying on the left side of the bed. She must have untangled herself from Matt in their slumber, but not entirely, because Matt stirred behind her, on the opposite side of the bed, and the arm that draped over her body tightened around her waist.

"You're so far away," he said sleepily.

Cadence let Matt reel her in, rolling around until she found herself in a cozy cocoon of Matt and Egyptian-cotton sheets. She wasn't accustomed to sleeping with someone else in her bed and preferred having the bed all to herself, but with Matt's arms wrapped around her, she could be convinced otherwise.

Cadence woke up later that morning refreshed. Refreshed but alone. Matt wasn't too far away, based on the sound of running water from the hallway bathroom. She checked her phone for the time and found a text from Maddie instead.

MADDIE: Are you in town and didn't tell me?
CADENCE: Sorry! It's kind of a long story.

Maddie called right away.

"My mom heard from Mr. Lee that he saw you leaving your dad's house with a guy. So who is he? How long are you in town and when can I see you?"

"Ugh," Cadence groaned. Nothing escaped the neighborhood watch. "That was Matt. I'm here for two weeks. For work," she added. Cadence climbed out of bed to look for her clothes. "I might have some free time next week."

"Matt? Like *the* Matt? Any news on that front?"

Cadence pulled her T-shirt over her head and shimmied into her shorts. "That I've seen his front. And his back."

"You've seen his what and his what?" Maddie practically shouted. "Congratulations, Cady. You've been pining after that man for so long, it was about time you trapped him."

"I haven't been pining—why does this sound like you're practicing for your matron of honor speech?"

"Cady, I've been practicing for that speech since we first met in second grade wearing the same Chinatown tracksuit. Yes, you pined! Matt always comes up in conversation, like how irritating he is or how good he looks in coats. You get the point. So please, do me a favor and fall in love and don't deprive me of this."

Cadence rolled her eyes. "Yeah, I will do that for you."

"Can I pick out my own dress too? I think I look better in something strapless."

"Why don't you plan the whole thing while you're at it?"

"Hey, you're up." Matt appeared at the doorway, with his glistening chest still wet from the shower even though he possessed two towels—one slung low on his hips and another drying his damp hair. "I was thinking we should take the day off."

Cadence had to hand it to him. He really knew his audience.

"Is he there?" Maddie whispered. "Which are you looking at? His front or his back?"

"Goodbye, Maddie."

Cadence hung up the call and checked her calendar before tossing her phone aside. "We can't take the whole day off. We have an important meeting tomorrow." But relationships were about compromise, so she returned her clothes back to the floor. "We can start after lunch."

CHAPTER 16
MATT

Matt used to live for the challenge of breaking Cadence's focus. Now that he had it, he was woefully unprepared. When they finally left her room to get the day started, Matt knew whenever her eyes were on him. At first they'd dart back to her screen. Then they lingered a bit, usually paired with an easy smile, then transforming into a sly, I've-seen-you-naked smile. It was utterly distracting. Matt was starting to see the practicality of that ugly cubicle partition that he long despised, because he got nothing done that afternoon.

"How can you work here?" Matt sat next to Cadence on the couch, where she had her laptop balanced on her lap as she built a pro forma report from scratch. "And without a mouse?"

"Practice." Cadence shrugged like it was no big deal. "Are you ready for your meeting with Best Eastern tomorrow?"

Matt shut his laptop so Cadence wouldn't see that he fell deep into iStan's Gundam forum. It brought him back to his high school days when he'd go to the hobby store and spend all his money on model kits. Technically, it could be considered client research. "I think so, but I'm open to any insider, neighborly info that you may be privy to."

"Can't help you there. A gambling ring got busted there once, but other than that, I tried to ignore it as much as I could. It has been an eyesore for as long as I can remember. It has potential, though."

"I thought you hated that word—*potential*."

"Why do you say that?"

"Weren't you the one who said that *potential* is a nice way to say that something is falling short of expectations?"

"That's not always the case," she clarified. "Sometimes it means that there's enough evidence to hope for more."

Matt's ears perked up at her coy tone. "What is it today?"

The corners of her lips curled into a small smile. "There's hope for more."

Matt was mesmerized watching her arched fingers stretch and float across the keyboard. It was like watching a pianist in concert. "You're like the computer guy in the James Bond movies."

"Does that make you James Bond in this scenario?" Her hands paused while she stole a peek at him from the corner of her eye. "You *do* look good in suits, but I refuse to be the computer guy."

"I bet the computer guy didn't eat pizza over his keyboard." Matt picked out a crumb that was in between the worn-out + and *Enter* on her ten-key keypad. He always wondered what kind of remnants he'd find in her work keyboard. Whenever Matt threatened to shake her keyboard over her head, Cadence shot him a Level 8 glare. She was so territorial about her things, she even labeled her pens *Property of C. Lim.* "Then who do you want to be?"

Without skipping a beat, she replied, "I'm M."

Matt peeled her hand away from the keyboard and lifted it up to his lips. "Then I am at your service," he said in a haughty British accent that made Cadence cringe with laughter.

"Nice try." She tried to slip her hand out and resume work, but Matt stole her laptop and placed it on the coffee table. "Hey!"

"I think these need a break." Matt kissed each of Cadence's competent fingers. "It's not against the rules if it's a break, right?"

Cadence's eyes darkened in a flash when Matt scraped his teeth against the fleshy pad of her index finger. "No, but save the file first."

BEST EASTERN SHOULD have displayed a sign requiring guests to obtain a tetanus shot before entering. Matt kept his arms close to his body as he toured the building so he wouldn't accidentally scrape them on the peeling paint or rusted railings. During his meeting with owner Jack Shen, Matt spoke less of the building itself and more on positive aspects of the property and its prime location. It was a losing battle from the get-go. The air in Jack's office was stale with the smell of cigarettes and piles of yellowed paper. Matt was sweating bullets, trying to crack the impenetrable expression on Jack's greasy face.

Jack interrupted Matt before he could make his closing remarks. "That's enough. Thank you for coming." His nose crinkled with his sinus-clearing snort.

Matt swallowed down his anxiety over his abrupt dismissal. "Is there anything else I can answer for you before I go?"

Jack's mouth set in a grim line. "No. Everything you said, I've heard before from other brokers who have more experience in this area than you."

"I see. Nothing against local brokers, but if I may, Prism Realty can offer—"

"No need, Matt. I met with you because a friend of mine recommended Sadie, but if a local broker can't sell this place, I don't know how you can."

Matt rolled past Jack's curt tone. "I don't think I understand."

"I tried to sell a few years ago." Jack handed Matt a thick manila folder.

Matt thumbed through the paperwork. There was everything from old marketing flyers to rezoning documents and environmental reports. "What happened?"

"Too much red tape," Jack stated, running his hand through his matted unwashed hair. "Developers lost their investors. The property behind me refused to sell."

Cadence's house? "What do you mean?"

"Developers liked this location, but they wanted to build something bigger. The house behind us was open to selling, but then they backed out. I know I will have a better chance of selling if the house behind me sells too, but I haven't been able to reach them. I called. I knocked on their door. Nothing. So unless you can get them to sell too, I don't see why I should give you this listing." Jack pulled the manila folder out of Matt's hands.

"Wait. How long ago was this?"

Jack frowned, humming in thought. "About four or five years ago. And then I gave up on selling it for a few years, but I tried putting it back on the market about six months ago. I'm ready to retire."

What did Cadence know about this?

Matt shook Jack's hand as he stood. "Thanks for your time. Give me a week. Let me see what I can do."

"HOW DID IT GO?" Cadence greeted him the second he returned to their suite while preoccupying herself with the takeout he brought back from San Gabriel. There was nothing in the Downtown area that satisfied her craving for pan-fried pork buns.

"It was okay. I have a lot of competition," Matt replied. There was something off about this listing, so he broached the topic carefully. "Jack speculated that he'd probably get more interest if the lot was bigger."

"What does he expect?" Cadence released a small, disbelieving laugh, gesticulating with a half-eaten bun in her hand. "That you could magically extend his property line?"

It wasn't making sense to Cadence because she had no idea. The division in the Lim family ran deeper than Matt thought. "It doesn't matter. Jack made it clear that he preferred a local broker."

"Let me know if you think I can help," she offered sweetly. "I can try to play the neighbor card if needed."

How many times had Cadence helped him out, setting the ball up for Matt to spike? "What did I do to deserve you?"

"It'd be rude not to help my food supplier," she said, laughing off his earnest question. "Shit." Cadence stuffed her mouth with the last bite of her pork bun. "I have to get ready. Percy Ma waits for no one. I'll drive."

"Are you sure?"

"Yeah, you should rest." Cadence rubbed Matt's shoulder and gave him a peck on the cheek. "You're looking a little drained from this morning."

Matt looked down at the counter, withholding the questions that still filled his mind. It wouldn't be smart to bring up a sensitive topic with Cadence, distracting both of them before their meeting with Percy Ma. Blowing this meeting was not an option. Matt didn't know the entire Best Eastern situation himself, and the last thing he wanted to do was exacerbate the rift between Cadence and her family.

Cadence misread Matt's subdued expression. "Hey. Let's go out tonight and do something fun. Take your mind off work."

Matt caught the twinkle in her eyes, the excitement in her voice. It occurred to him that this would be the first time going out together, for no other reason than to enjoy each other's company. A real date. "Wanna go out for dinner? Somewhere nice?"

"Oh! Okay," she said brightly. Matt's heart ballooned at the sight of Cadence's unguarded smile. "I guess I'll dress up for the meeting." She scurried into her room to change.

"Percy better not get any wrong ideas," Matt said as he searched his phone for a restaurant.

"As if," she shouted from her room. "I only brought work clothes with me."

While Cadence stepped away to change, Matt sent a quick email to Kevin.

To: KLewis@prismrealty.com
From: MEscanilla@prismrealty.com
Date: January 13, 2022 12:09 P.M.
Subject: FW: Best Eastern

Kev,

See the email below from Sadie. Can you look into the sales history on this property for me and send it ASAP? Cadence and I are swamped, so anything you can find would be helpful. I'll owe you one.

Matt

Unlike Cadence, Matt trusted Kevin enough to handle this simple task. Matt would have done it himself, but with Cadence working so closely now, she would see it on his laptop before he had a chance to explain.

Cadence reappeared a few minutes later, slipping on a black blazer. She checked the waist of her fitted emerald-green pencil skirt, making sure her white blouse was neatly tucked in. Matt rarely used the word *chic*, but it suited Cadence and the ease in which she carried herself.

"You underestimate yourself," Matt said, kissing her forehead.

"It would look nicer if I had heels," she complained, slipping on pointy flats. "I need to get a new pair and pick up a dress for Saturday while I'm at it."

Oh, right. The birthday party. Matt was losing his mind. He

needed to hire an assistant. "You don't have to get a new dress for that."

"If you think I'm going to meet your family in my suit or my stained T-shirt, then you're sadly mistaken." Cadence flipped open her compact to check her makeup. "How do I look?"

"You look beautiful." Matt smoothed down her Peter Pan collar while she adjusted her earrings. She smiled like she was laughing at her own joke. "What's so funny?"

"I'm so used to doing that for you. It's nice to be on the receiving end." She snapped her compact closed and tucked it into her purse, which hung on the crook of her arm. "I hope you're ready for some first-date Q and A."

"What are you talking about? You already know that stuff— where I work and where I went to school. I have an older sister. I spend my spare time losing money in my family's fantasy football league. I'm a dog person, but cats are cool."

Cadence blinked at him. "Are those the kinds of questions you get on the first date?"

"Why? What kind of first dates have you been on?"

"Lately, questions I'd expect on a third or fourth date come up almost right away."

"Like what?" Matt wasn't keen on hearing about her dates with other men, but her reaction intrigued him.

"Some guys have asked me where I see myself in a few years. Not in terms of work, but if I see myself starting a family. If so, where? How religious I am . . ." Her voice trailed off.

Matt wasn't sure if Cadence felt self-conscious about her own answers to these questions or his. It could very well be him, because he found himself coming up short for the second time that day. It never occurred to him to ask any of the women he dated these types of questions. Come to think of it, when was the last time he made it to the third or fourth date?

She backpedaled before he could comment on it. "I mean, no pressure. I was giving you some examples. Let's see where the night takes us." Cadence grabbed her laptop. "We should head downstairs."

While Cadence drove, Matt mulled over these questions. What did it say about him that none of the women he'd dated had asked him these questions? He could chalk it up to his casual invitations for drinks. That usually set a low expectation for his dates, emphasizing the fact that he wasn't looking for anything serious. If they had asked him, what would he have said? Matt was approaching his late thirties. When his parents were his age, they had moved to a new country, settled in San Diego, and had two kids. Shit. What had Matt been doing with his time? And what about Cadence? What would she think if he moved to L.A. and she stayed in San Francisco? His head started pounding with more questions than answers.

CHAPTER 17

CADENCE

Walking would have been faster. Cadence's fingers drummed on the steering wheel as the car inched its way toward the Los Angeles Convention Center. TechXpo attracted a wide range of attendees—gamers, tech enthusiasts, bloggers, YouTubers, and the like—who all wanted to see the latest and greatest in technology. In recent years, this industry-specific conference turned into a vendor-oriented spectacle where Big Tech unveiled their next big (or small) shiny thing. A mass of lanyard-wearing pedestrians of every age clogged up the crosswalks, keeping Cadence and Matt stuck at the same intersection four long blocks away.

To pass the time, she reviewed pages of financial reports, market data, and due diligence in her mind. Meeting Percy Ma was an incredible opportunity and Cadence had to put her best foot forward. Self-doubt began to creep in.

"What am I doing at this meeting? The one-percenters of the world don't care about people like me," she mumbled.

"*Lim.*" Matt always called her by her last name whenever she needed a pep talk. "We went over this yesterday. If this meeting isn't enough for Percy, then it was a lost cause to begin with. And if anyone should be stressed out about this meeting, it should be me."

"I agree," she said, lifting her foot off the brake pad when traffic moved. "This is your area of expertise. Why do I need to be here?"

"Because we're a team and it's *your* expertise that got us this far. You should go for your broker's license."

Traffic stopped again. They moved half a block. On the sidewalk, a burly parking attendant rigorously waved an orange flag, trying to direct drivers into their parking garage. About twenty feet ahead, there was another attendant, employed by a different parking lot, twirling a large arrow. Cadence wondered what kind of relationship these two must have. It must be odd to work so close to your direct competition. Were they frenemies? Did they ignore each other while they shouted at the same cars to enter their lot?

"No thanks," Cadence eventually said. "After watching you make phone call after phone call, I am a hundred percent sure that I don't want to do what you do."

THE CONFERENCE ROOM above the bustling convention center floor was too big. Cadence and Matt sat at the corner of a table that was set up for thirty people. Two of Percy Ma's handlers greeted them, saying that Percy was running late. They then left Matt and Cadence alone and stood right outside the door, acting like security.

Cadence couldn't figure out the odd feeling in the atmosphere. To quell her nerves, she triple-checked her laptop connection to the projector. After ten minutes, the door swung open.

"Hello, hello," Percy said gruffly, announcing his presence. He strolled in with his entourage and a security guard, who stood by the door.

Cadence was expecting Percy to be taller, the same way she expected actors to be tall. Percy traded his signature gray zip-up hoodie for a gray knit sweater. This was him dressing up, though he kept it casual with his jeans and sneakers.

"Thank you for meeting with us, Percy." Matt greeted him with a handshake.

"This is my assistant, Ian," Percy said of the young man beside him, "and you've met Ms. Huang before." Percy and his team took their seats on the opposite side of the table. Ian whispered into Percy's ear and presented him with a leather padfolio. "I'm being reminded that I need to be onstage for my keynote speech in twenty minutes, so I must keep this short." Percy glanced at Cadence's presentation on the screen and held up his hand. "That won't be necessary."

Cadence's heart dropped. She'd never been cut off before a presentation started.

"Matt, you're very persistent," Percy continued, "but I'm going to tell you what I told Sadie. It doesn't make sense for us to invest in a building that is not suited for our company. More and more employees demand flexibility in their workday and don't want to bother with the long commute when they can work from home. The historic nature of the building alone limits our ability to make the space adaptable and accessible to how our employees prefer to work. I could set up our headquarters in the middle of nowhere and save the company some money."

Whatever despair Cadence had felt before evaporated in her

blistering anger. Percy agreed to this meeting only to break the news in person.

Matt kept his cool, unbuttoning his jacket as he leaned back in his seat. It was a power move to regain control of the meeting. "With all due respect, what kind of message do you think it would send to your competitors if you set up your headquarters in the middle of nowhere?"

"That we're forward-thinking and responsive to our employees' needs," Percy answered.

"How would they think that if they don't get to pass by you every day to witness your takeover of their market share?" Leave it to Matt to stroke an already big ego, but it was effective because Percy leaned in, entertaining the idea. "Think of the bigger picture, Percy. The San Francisco headquarters is your first introduction to the United States. It must make a mark. You can't go wrong when there is built-in talent in the Bay Area. You have plenty of opportunities to be creative with your future offices in places like Los Angeles, perhaps."

"Los Angeles is an obvious suggestion," Percy argued. "Sadie mentioned Prism's new office here."

Cadence interjected, sensing the meeting was getting sidetracked. "In regards to Sansome," she said, shooting from the hip, "yes, employees may like to work from home—I've done so myself— but it doesn't mean that they won't require their own workspace when they do come into the office. If an employee works outside of the office, say, twenty percent of the workweek, that doesn't mean the company can reduce their office space by twenty percent."

She pressed her clicker until she reached her slides. "We anticipated that you might be considering other spaces should more inventory became available this year. I analyzed the data in the most desirable sections of the Bay Area, and if you compare the fair market value of the Sansome building to other buildings with similar square footage, as well as its proximity to parking and mass transit, it's still the most ideal option. I presume as iStan continues to grow and monetize its services, there are office spaces near Sansome that you could expand into, should you want to build a small hub."

Percy, who had been listening intently with steepled fingers, huddled into a hushed conversation with Ms. Huang.

"Look, I respect your time and appreciate your efforts," Percy said to Matt and Cadence. "You've given me much to consider, but—"

"If you have any more time while you're in L.A., we are available to further discuss the lease," Matt added.

"All right, then." Percy snapped at his assistant. "We'll be in touch to set up a meeting with Ms. Huang and our legal counsel."

"Great," Matt said, relieved. He buttoned his blazer and stood to shake Percy's hand.

Percy remained seated, leaving Matt hanging. "Now if you don't mind, I'd like to speak to Cadence privately, please."

Matt and Cadence exchanged puzzled looks. "Sure," Matt said, shoving his hand into his pocket. "I'll be right outside."

Cadence anxiously watched Matt exit the room, feeling like she was on a trapeze without a safety net or a partner to hold on to. Meanwhile, Ian produced a tablet and slid it across the table. The iStan app refreshed on the screen.

"Cadence, have you used iStan before?" Percy asked, putting her on the spot.

Cadence chuckled nervously, hoping she wouldn't offend Percy with her answer. "I'm more of a casual user. Every so often, I might come across a viral video that originated from iStan." Last month, a clip of animals photoshopped onto popular book covers made its round on the internet, with appearances from Gossip Squirrel, Hens and Sensibility, and the Sloth Hero. Some people had too much time on their hands.

"What do you know about monetizing services?" Percy asked.

What was this? A pop quiz?

"Um, I've worked at a start-up before. It was nothing like iStan in terms of popularity, but I understand the general principles of how to monetize services when users expect everything to be free. Ads, of course, and in-app purchases. That would be ideal for iStan, now that I think of it." Cadence threw out the first idea that came to mind. "For instance, I heard that iStan has a forum where users share their handmade crafts over their favorite show or movie. Creating a marketplace for it within the platform where there is an existing audience for those products makes sense. That would open doors to partnerships or licensing."

Percy held up his hand, interrupting her snowballing ideas. "I'm not sure if you're aware of this, but we are hiring for our strategic analytics manager. We've had similar ideas, but we haven't been able to significantly increase our revenue. We're looking for a savvy person who can partner with our sales and strategy teams, and after seeing your work and now seeing your presentation skills, I think you would be an ideal candidate."

"Oh." Cadence gulped. Had she been inadvertently interviewing these last few weeks? "I . . . don't know what to say."

A high-handed smile appeared on Percy's face. "If I can give you some advice: say yes. I wouldn't have offered this job to you if I didn't think you could do it. Your analysis is consistently sharp and provides effective storytelling that would lend itself to our cross-functional teams. If you can speak Mandarin, I can recommend you to the lead analytics team in our Shenzhen office. But this offer is for the San Francisco office, wherever that will be. The starting salary is $125,000 plus perks and benefits." Cadence's lips began to chap from all her mouth-breathing. That was a lot more money than she was making at Prism. "I can see this is a lot to consider, so think about it. I'd like to know your decision by the end of the month, at the latest. If you have any questions, you may reach out to Ms. Huang."

Cadence nodded, unsure what to say. She came into the meeting nervous, debating whether she should ask Percy for a selfie, and here he was, offering her a job. Cadence deflected into small talk before she accepted the job on the spot. "What else do you have planned for your stay in L.A.? Will it be mostly business or leisure?"

"For business. We are meeting with investors. My assistant will also be helping me look for a house in the area. A few in Santa Monica and . . . where's the other one?" He turned to Ian. "San Marino?"

"Oh." Cadence assumed Percy would want an estate in Beverly Hills, but she could see the appeal of living near an Asian enclave. "Both are nice, but very different." And far apart. "If you'd like, I can send you some data on both neighborhoods."

"Thank you, but that's not necessary." Percy stood up when his assistant reminded him of the time. "Can I give you another piece of advice? Don't offer to work for free when someone is willing to pay for it."

"Of course," she said, embarrassed that she so easily suggested helping him with his house hunting. "You've probably hired an excellent broker already."

"No, I haven't chosen one yet. Many of the brokers I'm considering invited me to a golf tournament next week. YRE?" Percy squinted at the ceiling as he tried to recall the name.

"The Young Real Estate Professionals golf tournament?" Cadence asked.

"Yes! Such a long name. Anyway, it was a hard opportunity to turn down. I love golf, but I don't have much time to play these days."

"Same here. I used to play for many years." The words flew out of Cadence's mouth before she could catch them. She hadn't thought about golf in years. Her clubs were buried somewhere in her dad's garage, collecting dust.

"Why don't you come as my guest? It will give us a chance to talk more about this job. And who knows? If you accept, you can tell me if any of these L.A. brokers are worth my time."

"Yes, I'd love to join you." She'd be a fool not to, though it meant she'd have to pay another visit to Dad's to pick up her clubs. It was the only answer when she had to appease both her current and potentially future employer. "May I bring Matt?"

"Why not?" Percy conceded. "He would have found his way into the country club anyway."

After Percy and his team left, Cadence stayed in the room to gather her wits. Holy shit. Matt would flip out when she told him about the golf invitation she scored with Percy Ma. And the job! As the excitement waned, nagging details prodded her, reminding her that reality called. If she took on a new, bigger job in San Francisco, there was no way she could take over for Tristan. She could come down a weekend or two a month, but would that be enough? She'd have to ask him. Until then, she wanted to fantasize about nicer apartments with amenities like a washer and dryer.

Matt returned to the conference room. "That was weird. What's going on?"

Cadence assessed Matt's attire. He'd worn chinos earlier in the week, but his shirts were too tight for golf. "Do you have a polo shirt?"

"*What?*" It took him a while to realize it was a genuine question. "No."

Cadence packed up her laptop. "When is our dinner reservation?"

"Six o'clock. Why?"

"Let's go shopping."

CHAPTER 18
MATT

Matt's fingertips were turning purple from carrying Cadence's shopping bags. When Cadence mentioned going to the mall to kill time before their dinner reservation, he didn't imagine she'd go all *Pretty Woman* on him. *Big mistake, Matt. Big. Huge.* They hit the shoe store for replacement heels and a pair of sandals for the pale blue sundress that she took forever to decide on. She must have checked every hem and seam before buying it.

"Let's go in there." Cadence walked ahead of him, toward a store where he spotted lacy, strappy, and furry garments.

He floated toward the lingerie shop like a moth to a flame, quietly figuring out how he could casually draw her attention to the CHEEKS! CHEEKS! CHEEKS! two-for-one panty promo. Cadence liked a good bargain.

"Where are you going?" Cadence called after him, standing in front of the sporting goods store next door. Matt hung his head, dragging his feet toward her. She gave him a conciliatory pat on the back. "Wishful thinking again." Cadence ignored the large camping display at the store entrance and made a beeline toward the corner for racquet sports and golf. "What size are you?" The hangers clacked as she browsed through a rack of different-colored polo shirts. She held up a red one against his torso. "Very Tiger Woods on Sunday," she said to herself.

"What are we doing in here?"

She hung the shirt back on the rack. "I've been holding this in since we left the convention center." Cadence gripped both of his arms, giddy. "You're not going to believe this. You and I will be special guests of Percy Ma at the YREPLA golf tournament next week." She squealed into a happy dance. "Can. You. Believe? I can't! And I was there!"

Matt let his jaw hang as Cadence shook him with each word. He was still registering how easily YREPLA rolled off Cadence's tongue. She handed him a white polo with a black outline at the edge of the collar. "It might be hot, so a light color would be good." She gasped as an idea came to her. "You're going to need shoes." Cadence stalked off for her mission, leaving Matt hanging by the tennis rackets and golf clubs.

"Wait. Can you back up a little?" Matt trekked two aisles over.

"What about these?" Cadence held up a black-and-white pair of golf shoes with little spikes sprouting from the bottom. She knelt down and placed them by his feet, making him try them on. "Percy happened to mention that he'll be in town to look at homes and that he was meeting brokers at the golf tournament, so I asked if I could bring you."

"Thanks, but I haven't done residential in years." He unlaced his brown leather shoes and slipped on the golf shoes.

Cadence laughed as if he said something silly. "You wouldn't be helping him find a house. This is a chance to convince Percy Ma to lease Sansome over eighteen holes of golf."

"I see. There's a small problem, though."

Cadence tightened his laces and checked the fit. "What's that?"

"I don't know how to play golf."

"Oh. I do." She stood up like that was that, brushed off her skirt, and carried on shopping.

"I didn't know you played golf," he said, finding her going through the hat selection.

"How is that possible? I wear my UW golf shirt all the time."

Matt tried to picture her favorite T-shirt, which had spent more time on the floor than on her body lately. He recalled the faded purple *W* in block letter font that centered her shirt, but the letters underneath had peeled away into an indecipherable script. "You played golf for UW?"

"How did you think I got my scholarship?"

Matt thought he was going crazy. Was he supposed to know this? "I-I didn't think about it at all. You've never mentioned this before."

"Oh." Cadence shrugged, handing him a white visor. "See? We're learning things about each other on our first date." Picking up a few tops and skirts, she disappeared into a fitting room along the back wall.

Matt lifted the price tag for a set of golf clubs. "I don't know, Lim. This seems like a lot of money to spend to embarrass myself in front of a client."

"That's true."

"Thanks," he said sardonically. Matt sat down on a small bench near the fitting room door. He could see her feet step out of one skirt and into another. "How long have you played?"

"Um . . . since I was ten? My dad wanted his kids at the Ivies, so he essentially modeled us after preppy white trust-fund kids. That's how we ended up with names like Tristan and Cadence. I got golf. Tristan had violin lessons."

Matt tried to picture Tristan's calloused hands, nails darkened by auto grease, holding such a delicate instrument. "When was the last time you played golf?"

"Not since I quit sophomore year. Golf was more for my dad than it was for me. My clubs are still at his house."

Matt's ears perked up. This was it. Another possible segue into the Best Eastern listing. Cadence was in a good mood, so it seemed as good a time as any. "Speaking of—"

Cadence stepped out of the fitting room in a white tank top and pastel teal skirt that clung to her like a second skin. "I was thinking, what if you be my caddie and I'll play?" She looked over her shoulder, checking out her racerback top, pulling down at the hem that barely surpassed her round butt.

"Okay." Matt heard his stupid caveman voice. He would follow that ass anywhere. "Although I don't know anything about being a caddie, either."

"Sure you do." Cadence pointed at her shopping bags. "All you have to do is carry my golf bag and when I ask you for advice"— Cadence leaned down, bringing her lips to the shell of his ear— "you can whisper sweet nothings." She trailed a finger along his jaw while she backed away, nearly skipping toward the dressing room.

Wow. Matt wanted whatever Cadence was on.

"What did you talk to Percy about?" Matt knew how to charm his way into conversations, but chatting with Percy Ma over a round of golf was not within his usual skill set.

Cadence emerged from the fitting room in her own clothes. "I'll tell you at dinner," she said hurriedly, finalizing her purchases and grabbing the items that he was holding for her. "There's more to talk about, but not here," she said, lowering her voice.

Matt was suspicious of the quick smile she shot him before she lined up to check out. Percy was famously private, but that wasn't enough cause for Cadence to get jumpy all of a sudden. Matt couldn't wait until the restaurant to find out.

"Why did Percy want to meet with you?" he asked as soon as they were inside his car. He turned the key, letting it warm up.

"Um . . ." Cadence's secretive smile expanded into a grin. "I was offered a job."

"What?" Matt turned the car off to make sure he heard her correctly. "To do what?"

She told him how this opportunity came out of left field, but the more she explained, her voice grew louder—passionate even—at the thought of leading her own team. Her one concern was whether to sublet her studio or not. She said she wanted to think things through before deciding, but it sounded like she already had her answer.

"What do you think?" she asked, her doe eyes anticipating his answer.

What *could* he think? This was the exact thing he was afraid of from the moment she decided to look for a new job. How could he tell her that, when she had been nothing but supportive of his bid for a promotion from the very beginning? Who was he to get in her way if this was what she wanted? So he said the thing he thought he should say.

"I'm happy for you." Matt laced his fingers with hers. "Let's go celebrate over dinner."

This unintentionally opened the floodgates for Cadence's commentary about the meeting. Matt sank into his seat as she described how Percy's assistant gave her icy vibes and she wondered if she could adapt to a different workplace culture. She continued asking him questions that he didn't know how to answer.

"This is crazy, isn't it?"

"It's not like I have better job offers to entertain."

"Who knows if I'll ever get promoted at Prism?"

"What would you do if you were me?"

He'd gotten away with monosyllabic answers for the first three questions—*no, hmm, right*—but that last one was harder to pass off. He wanted to say, "It depends." Then he'd follow up with his own questions, like:

Where do you see yourself in a few years?

When do you see yourself settling down?

In this future life, who is with you?

But Matt couldn't say those things and ruin her electric mood. She deserved to celebrate this opportunity. "If it makes you this happy, you should take it."

CHAPTER 19

CADENCE

Matt chose a fine-dining restaurant on Melrose, claiming that it was on several top restaurant lists in L.A. At first Cadence found the dim lighting romantic, until they were seated and she realized she couldn't see much of Matt's face. The lighting was limited to the table to highlight the food. The waiter placed a lone oyster nestled on a bed of salt in front of her. She once took a dining etiquette class during college that covered silverware and glasses, but nothing about eating an oyster topped with a mountain of caviar.

Carpe diem. She tipped the oyster in her mouth and . . . was she supposed to chew this?

"It's good, isn't it?" Matt asked, eagerly awaiting her response.

"Mm-hmm." Cadence dabbed her mouth as she swallowed and washed it down with her water. "Um . . . it's salty?"

"You don't like it," he stated, sounding a bit discouraged.

"No, it's . . . I don't have a refined palate, I guess," she explained. "I'm a cheap date, remember?"

Another waiter appeared and removed their plates. There was a lull in their conversation as they waited for the next course on the tasting menu. When Cadence teased Matt about going on their first real date, she didn't mean to imply that they act like strangers. "Tell me more about your family. I want to know what I'm getting myself into with this birthday party on Saturday."

Matt swirled his wineglass. "There's my lola, who you've spoken to briefly. She thinks you're my girlfriend." Cadence held her breath, waiting for Matt to comment on that further, but he rolled past it. "My parents are retired and take care of my sister's kids. There's a whole slew of cousins, older and younger than me. There's Jason, who's the oldest. He used to wake me up to line up with him to get the latest Jordans. There's AJ, who is very sweet. You're going to love him. He's been trying to adopt a child with his husband, George. And then there's Gerry. He cracks a lot of jokes at my expense, but you can keep up with him."

"It must have been fun growing up with all your cousins." The next course arrived. There was a piece of seared fish the size of her palm garnished with three dots of a sauce that looked like ranch but was likely not ranch. Cadence forked off a bite.

"Yeah, it was. We are—or were—pretty close."

"Not anymore?"

"No, we are," he said in reversal, his voice uncharacteristically hushed as he reflected. "It's hard sometimes to stay connected when I'm the only one not living in the area. Then I missed Thanksgiving and Christmas, which never happened before. That's the main reason I want to move back here. I want to make memories with my family the same way I grew up. I feel like I'm missing out on so much, and now that my cousins all have kids, it's like there's a birthday party every week that I can't attend. And my parents and Lola aren't getting younger."

"I see." As soon as Cadence finished her plate, it was taken away and a new one appeared. A single scallop. At this rate, she hoped that there were still twenty courses to come.

"What about you?" Matt prompted after an awkward pause. "You never felt that way?"

"No." Cadence heard how flippant it sounded. "No," she repeated more gently. "Whenever I came home, I got a sense of nostalgia for the places I used to hang out with friends, but it wore off once my parents argued over money or when I'd find my living room full of my dad's friends. Then when my mom died, there weren't any arguments because nobody wanted to dredge up the past." In their collective grief, it was like there was a silent agreement that it didn't need to be addressed. Mom was gone and there wasn't anything they could do to change that. But now that Tristan, Dad, and Cadence had moved on in their own ways, a part of her worried that the bridges connecting them were weakening. "I should visit more to help Tristan out. I'll have to take a closer look at my job offer. See what I could negotiate. At least I can send more money if they need it."

Matt leaned forward enough for her to see his chin. "You send your dad money?"

"Yeah, it's not much, but it's the least I could do since I live far away. I didn't want my parents to suffer in debt. Now that my dad hasn't been renting out his house, it's probably coming in handy."

"Why doesn't he sell the house?"

"He would never." Cadence couldn't fathom the idea. "He's a pillar in the community and I can't see him moving when he receives so many visitors."

Their plates were exchanged as they progressed through the

meal. At first Cadence wondered if Matt wanted to savor his food because he was awfully quiet. But then they were served with dessert. Cadence waited for Matt to comment. He had to because they were presented with odds and ends of a cake, a tiny scoop of ice cream, and cookie crumbs meant to look like dirt. It looked like what her plate should look like after she'd eaten it. But he didn't say anything. He proceeded to finish it in two bites.

"Is everything okay? You seem distracted."

"Sorry. It's been a long day and I have a lot on my mind. If it's okay with you, I'm going to turn in early. I have clients to call in the morning before we check out the new office."

"Yeah, absolutely." Cadence felt terrible that she was so caught up in her own job offer that she'd forgotten about Matt's unsuccessful meetings. She reached across the table until their fingers met. "I'm so sorry. We could have gone out to dinner another time."

Matt kissed the back of her hand. "No, don't feel bad. I wanted to take you out. You should celebrate your accomplishments."

Matt said all the right things, but Cadence couldn't help but feel like there was more than he was letting on.

"DON'T LEAVE ANY detail out," Maddie whispered. Baby James fell asleep on her minutes before their phone call to get the scoop on Matt and Cadence's date the morning after. Cadence was open to rescheduling, but this was the only window of time Maddie had, so they kept it, so long as Cadence was willing to keep her voice down. "I'm living vicariously through your office romance."

"We had dinner, Maddie," Cadence whispered, looking over her shoulder from the couch to check that Matt's door was still closed. "It was fine."

"Uh-oh. How bad was it? Like he's-a-bad-tipper bad or he's-kind-of-a-sociopath bad? Do you need me to extract you from the room?" Maddie listened to one too many true crime podcasts.

"No, it was . . ." Cadence didn't know how to explain it. "Something was off."

"And what about today?"

"He's been working from his room." Cadence skipped the part when they returned to the hotel and Matt excused himself to his room, saying he needed to catch up on sleep after a long day. "He said he didn't want to bother me with his phone calls."

"I wonder . . ." Maddie hesitated. "Didn't you used to say that Matt's a casual dater? Do you think this is him playing it cool or do you think he's freaking out?"

"About what?" Cadence tried to pinpoint the moment when Matt started acting differently. Nothing jumped out at her except . . . "Yesterday I joked about interrogating him over dinner and he looked like he was about to shit his pants."

"What did you say you were going to ask him?"

"Nothing crazy," Cadence hedged, mumbling the rest. "Normal stuff like if he saw himself having kids."

"Cadence!" Maddie hissed, which caused James to whine. She shushed him until he quieted down.

"I threw that out as an example. I didn't think it would scare him."

"Why would you ask him about that?" Maddie accused. "*You* don't even want kids."

"You know that's not true." Cadence refused to rehash this conversation in a hushed environment. It wasn't that she didn't want kids. She just didn't want to have kids *yet*. After Cadence turned thirty, people would ask her if her biological clock was ticking. The only thing Cadence decided after thirty was that she was too old to crash on a friend's couch when traveling. No offense to her friends, but Cadence's back much preferred a bed with turndown service. "I can't think about kids when I might have a stubborn old man to take care of."

"No, no. Don't change the subject. You know you have no business asking Matt hard questions that you don't ask yourself."

"I do!" Cadence protested petulantly, probably giving baby James a run for his money.

"Okay then," Maddie said like she was about to give her some tough love. Cadence shut her eyes as if it would sufficiently guard her feelings. "Are you going to take the job or are you going to come home?"

"I'm still thinking about it. It's an important decision."

"What's there to think about? Your family needs you." Maddie wasn't shy about her opinions.

"I need to make a living too."

"Oh, I'm sorry. I forgot that there were no real estate jobs in L.A.," Maddie grumbled as James stirred. "I have to go. This is not the end of this conversation. Keep me posted if your man comes out of his cave."

Whenever that would be. Cadence hung up, wishing their conversations didn't always have a time limit. Cadence couldn't fault Maddie for fitting her in wherever she could, but there never seemed to be enough time for the two of them. But maybe Maddie was right. Cadence probably spooked him when she brought up serious topics. She assumed that because she and Matt were good friends, they would segue easily into this new phase of their relationship. The best thing to do was to slow things down. There was no need to add more pressure when they had enough of that from work.

Matt must have been swamped with phone calls because he didn't emerge from his office until the afternoon, when they had to stop by the Prism Realty L.A. office in Santa Monica. After some delays, renovations for the L.A. office were finally nearing completion. Per Josie's email, Matt was tasked with completing a walk-through of the office space, accounting for all the furniture and equipment. Matt entered the security code and pushed the doors open, instantly switching on all the white lights overhead.

"Whoa." Cadence maneuvered around the ladder next to the reception desk and stepped over a paint tray to stand in the middle aisle that separated two rows of cubicles. "It's bigger than our current office."

Bigger. Newer. Brighter. The office, which took up the entire fifth floor, was white with light wood finishes and mid-century modern furniture. The style was similar to that of the flagship office, but this space had a warmer ambience. The broker offices that lined the perimeter had glass walls to take advantage of the natural light brought in from the wide exterior windows. On the west-facing side, there was a break room with benches and small tables, where people could sit and enjoy the partially obstructed view of the ocean. Well, they could once the plastic wrap on the furniture was removed.

"Eight thousand square feet, big enough for fifty employees,"

Matt recalled from Josie's email. "I have a list of things to check on, but I shouldn't be long."

"I'll help you."

Cadence hung close to Matt as he diligently went through Josie's list, taking inventory of every chair, rug, and phone. She waited for him to break the ice, cut the tension with one of his stupid jokes, but he took a singular focus to the task, making his way through each office. Cadence knew this move. She invented this move! Something was up and she was going to get to the bottom of it.

"It's going to be nice to get back on the golf course," she said.

"Cool." *That's it? Cool?*

"I can't wait get my clubs back . . . run my hands along the shaft."

Not even a snicker.

"What are you doing?" Matt asked when Cadence palmed his forehead.

"You don't have a temperature, so you can't be sick." Cadence dropped her hand. "Did you hear anything I've said? What's going on with you? You're acting weird."

Matt clenched his jaw. "I spoke with Mr. Shen and things didn't work out the way I wanted, so I need to close the iStan deal if I still want a shot at the promotion."

"Oh." If Cadence had known that Best Eastern could have a significant impact on his promotion, she would have accompanied him to the meeting in the first place. She didn't initially suggest it because what she knew about Jack Shen was through her father, and he found Jack bothersome for some reason. "But your sales record should be enough, and you have Sadie on your side."

"With Hunter on my back, I want to make a solid case for my-self for the executive board."

Matt was the perpetual optimist. When things didn't go his way, he pivoted and made his own path toward his goals. He was agile in ways that Cadence was not. She had never seen him this dis-tressed, so she cut him some slack.

"You really want this, don't you?"

"Yeah," he said, sighing. "Overall, business has been good, and as it has grown, I'm working harder and longer. I anticipated see-ing my family less and less, but now I've started to feel like I'm getting left behind. My cousins have a separate group chat to talk about parenting, and here I am—I don't even have a girlfriend."

Cadence was *not* going to read into that comment. She was not.

"I know what you mean about feeling left behind. Every time I call Maddie now, it gets cut short because she's busy with her baby. Sometimes I worry if Maddie's outgrown me, but what am I sup-posed to do? That's her life now, and I have mine."

"Maddie," Matt repeated with feigned distaste. "The other best friend."

Cadence laughed. "Don't be jealous."

She waited for Matt's snarky remark, but he gazed at her with those rich brown eyes and reached for her hand, bringing her into a hug. "For what it's worth, speaking as your other best friend," he said, "I don't think I'll ever outgrow you."

Cadence tamped down the urge to ask him if that meant what she thought it meant. "Obviously. It's near impossible when you have chicken legs and an insane metabolism." Because Cadence and Matt were temple to temple, cheek to cheek, his mouth by her ear, she heard the soft groan for her bad joke. Old habits die hard, but she tried to rectify things with moral support. "You'll get this job. You'll see."

"Oh yeah? I didn't know you could look into the future."

"Projections point to a positive outcome." Cadence didn't need time to think of encouraging words. After all, she had been the recipient of Matt's cheerleading for years, so she learned from the best. She pulled back so he could see that she wasn't just humoring him. "You have sharp business acumen and the sales record to prove it. You put in the time, the blood, sweat, and tears. There's no better person for the job than you."

"What else?"

"What else what?" Was that not Matt-level flattery?

"What else do you foresee in my future?"

What version did Matt want to hear? The fantasy version where Matt and Cadence had gotten their heads out of their asses and begun their relationship years ago, ending their dates around San Francisco with a scoop of Bi-Rite ice cream, fighting over how much closet space she was going to need in their apartment? Or the more likely version, which would be Matt's moving to L.A. to be with his family and Cadence's starting over at iStan? It wasn't a job she anticipated, but it would be a fresh slate. One that didn't require moving out of her apartment for.

Cadence inched back to give herself some breathing room. Their conversation was treading dangerously close to deep waters. "Another date," she blurted like it was a shot in the dark, this hope to make up for lost time. "Something to take our minds off work. No phones, no shop talk."

Matt pursed his lips into a tight line as he exhaled and stared out the window. It made Cadence second-guess her answer. He was probably not in the mood to go out. How did she not notice the dark circles underneath his eyes? Cadence was ready to retract her suggestion when the corners of Matt's mouth curled up.

"I know exactly where we should go."

M att spent the morning reviewing the documents Kevin sent him. Best Eastern was a bigger headache than he anticipated. The sales history flip-flopped more than a nervous politician. With the small parcel of land it sat on, the property left much to be desired for developers. Best Eastern itself was not up to code, but it managed to get grandfathered in whenever city codes were updated. That wouldn't be the case for any new development. If Jack wanted a chance at getting any offers, Mr. Lim had to be willing to sell his house.

As things stood, Matt decided that the right thing to do was to step away from the property. Despite how much it would help him make a case for his promotion, he didn't want to get involved with Cadence's delicate family situation.

To: SChan@prismrealty.com, KLewis@prismrealty.com
From: MEscanilla@prismrealty.com
Date: January 14, 2022 11:47 a.m.
Subject: Re: Re: FW: Best Eastern

Sadie,

Location's great, but there are too many variables, too risky.
See attached property data (Thanks Kevin!). Owner prefers a
local broker anyway.

Matt

Matt didn't like resorting to excuses, but he had to provide
Sadie with enough reasons why he was letting go of the listing.
Withholding the secret from Cadence compounded the feeling
that he had failed. He knew he should have told her, but selfishly,
he wasn't ready to let reality break their bubble. Cadence must
have felt the same way or else they wouldn't be at the Santa Monica Pier, playing games.

With one eye closed, Cadence lined up her shot.

"Cad—"

"Shhhh!" Cadence remained steadfast, keeping her eye on the
target. "I promised this was the last time I was going to play, so I
have to win."

She said that two attempts ago. Miguel, the booth attendant,
exchanged a skeptical look with Matt. This had to be her last turn
because she was starting to scare the children and concerned parents seated around her.

"On your mark. Get set. Go," Miguel said with half the enthusiasm from the previous four attempts.

Once the bell rang, Cadence gripped the trigger on the water
gun. Slowly her elusive prize—a not-very-big plush Pikachu—rose
as the stream of water hit the target. It was a little scary (and sad)

how competitive she was for a toy she could have bought for much less. Matt watched with bated breath, praying she would win so they could make it farther down the boardwalk. When an orange flashing light appeared underneath Cadence's Pikachu and sirens rang, Matt sighed in relief.

"Yes!" Cadence muttered through gritted teeth, with a clenched fist. Catching Matt's stunned expression, she explained, "I play to win."

"I can see that."

Cadence graciously accepted her prize from Miguel, who offered his congratulations. "Where to next?" She slipped on her sunglasses as she stood and stretched after sitting for so long. "Ooh! Is that Whac-A-Mole?"

"Nope." Matt was not going to go through another round of games. He grabbed her hand and followed the smell of greasy food. "You hungry?"

Sitting at the edge of the pier, Cadence asked all her first-date questions over tacos. "So your family's in Eagle Rock? Is that where you grew up?"

"In San Diego. That's where most of my dad's side of the family lives. A lot of them worked at the naval base there. When I was in middle school, we moved to Glendale to be closer to my mom's side of the family."

"That's the side I'll be meeting tomorrow?"

"Yup," he replied, taking a bite of his corn dog. Matt had his family tree on the tip of his tongue, ready to brief Cadence on each of his relatives, when she breezed into the next question.

"What's your favorite movie?"

"*The Fast and the Furious: Tokyo Drift.*"

Cadence smirked as she drenched her tacos in salsa verde. "That is very specific. Not *2 Fast 2 Furious*?"

"You don't seem to appreciate the finer details of men driving fast cars in front of scantily clad women."

"Actually, I'm quite familiar with it."

"You've seen the movie?"

"No, it's how Tristan and Linda met."

"Racing cars in Tokyo while getting entangled with the Yakuza?"

Cadence laughed. "No. Back in the day, Tristan was in a racing crew—though they never raced. It was more of an excuse to show off their cars at meets."

"You know what this calls for?" Matt wiped his mouth with napkin. "A *Fast and Furious* marathon."

"No thanks," she protested. She quickly changed the subject. "What do you do in your free time? When you're home on the weekends?"

Matt took note of the softball questions Cadence was asking him. "Running errands most of the time. I'm not out and about like you, taking sourdough baking classes or visiting the Exploratorium."

"I chose those activities because I found coupons for them," Cadence admitted, ducking her head to hide her rosy cheeks. "But I do like sightseeing. When I lived in Chicago and New York, people used to ask me for recommendations and I never had a good answer because I hardly went outside of my own neighborhood or my commute to work. That's why I kind of love this date. I haven't been to the pier in a long time."

"Kind of? That won't do." Matt stood up and gathered their

empty trays to throw in the trash. Along the pier, the colorful storefronts began to light up as the sky darkened. An *ooh* arose from the crowd when hot pink and blue lights radiated from the Ferris wheel.

"Are you thinking what I'm thinking?"

Matt vigorously shook his head. "Me and heights don't mix." His phone pinged, saving him from Cadence, who looked like she was about to call him a chicken.

JOSIE: Heads-up: Hunter found out about the golf
tournament. He asked me if the registration fee could be
reimbursed

"Shit," he said under his breath. Matt knew it was a matter of time before Hunter found out. There was no way he would let Matt take this promotion without a fight.

"What is it?" Cadence popped up under his arm and leaned in to catch a glimpse of his phone.

Matt slipped his phone back into his pocket. "Josie texted me about the tournament. Looks like Hunter will be joining us."

"I wouldn't worry. I play to win, remember?" Cadence reached around him for a reassuring side hug. "But you are in violation of the 'no checking work messages' rule. As such, I dare you to go on the Ferris wheel with me."

Matt shuddered at the thought of being suspended in a dangling open-air basket. "I don't think you want to see a grown man cry."

"Crying is okay. Toxic masculinity is *so* yesterday."

"Is that right?" It took a week for her Valley Girl accent to come out. "If it's okay by you, I'd like to keep some dignity tonight."

"Fine," she agreed reluctantly. "I have another idea."

Cadence grabbed his hand and he followed her to the end of the boardwalk, where a band played covers of Buena Vista Social Club. Matt and Cadence joined the growing crowd that surrounded the musicians as they transitioned to an up-tempo song. Matt was stepping back as the crowd made room for a makeshift dance floor when Cadence tugged his arm.

"Come on. Let's dance."

"I don't know how to dance to this," he shouted over the trumpets and catchy conga beats.

"I've seen you dance," she said, pulling him into the center among other couples who effortlessly swayed their hips with each step. "You'll pick it up in no time."

Matt tried to emulate the other dancers. Cadence started dancing with simple back-and-forth steps, waiting for him to catch on.

"I took a beginner salsa class a while ago," she said at his curious expression. "I'm a little rusty."

"I wouldn't have known," he said, both about her dance skills and of her taking a class.

"I had a coupon," she added. Of course she did. "And I thought, *Why not?* What if I get challenged to a dance-off?" She grabbed his hands to attempt a twirl that went horribly wrong. Their grip was awkward and Matt huffed salty air when they crashed after they unintentionally spun into each other.

Cadence laughed it off, not seeming to mind that they were by far the worst dancers on the pier. "Let's keep it simple." She wrapped one arm around his right shoulder and clasped his left hand in a ballroom dance pose. Matt followed her lead, mirroring her as she took softer steps. "Your goal is to keep me close." That Matt could do, splaying his fingers on the small of her back. Once they found their rhythm, Cadence detached herself from his hold, twirling outward.

Instinctively, Matt caught her hand before she was out of reach and she spun back, returning to his arms with a sly quirk on her lips. It was the beginning of a flirtatious cat-and-mouse game. Matt was up for the chase, his heart thudding with anticipation. Each time she turned away, he found a new way to call her back. A lingering caress of her arm when he reached for her, his arm hooked around her waist, until she let go of the ruse, dancing face-to-face with a contagious smile. When the song ended, Matt and Cadence clapped with the crowd. Cadence turned and dipped her head in appreciation at the band, while Matt was breathlessly happy.

They wandered down to the beach. Matt held on to her prized Pikachu while she wiggled her feet out of her flats and folded up her jeans. Hand in hand, they walked along the beach where the water met the sand.

"Is there anything else you want to see?"

She shook her head. "No."

"Did you have a good time?"

"I did," she said coyly.

"Still kinda love it?" he prodded, fishing for a compliment.

"No. I love it, love it," she said simply, stopping to let a small wave roll into her ankles.

Her feet sank deeper and deeper into the sand, and as he watched,

Matt wondered what it would take to keep those feet planted in L.A. For all that time spent keeping things (mostly) professional, he finally had the chance to see all the sides of Cadence—raw and emotional, focused and driven, fun and carefree. He'd only begun to scratch the surface, but he gathered enough to know that if she'd let him, he could easily love her, love her.

CHAPTER 21

CADENCE

O ne more time."

Cadence zoomed in on Matt's phone, scrolling to the left of his family's group photo from Christmas. Starting from the back row, Matt recited everyone's names.

"That's Auntie Luz, my mom's older sister, and her husband, Uncle Rey. That's Auntie Patricia and Uncle Dennis. This is their house and they host every family party. If they are around, your drink will be magically refilled. Next to them are my cousins Gerald and Missy. It's her birthday party. That's her boyfriend, Kyle."

Cadence repeated all their names. "Okay, got it. Next row."

"Under Auntie Luz is my auntie Connie. That's my cousin Diane and her husband, Mike, holding their twins." Matt must have taken a discreet rapper's breath because he impatiently spat out the rest of the names. "That's Ilene. Her boyfriend, Jesse. AJ and George. Jason, Justine, and Jessica, and their spouses Maleena, Mark, and Bryan. That's my sister, Celine, my brother-in-law, Will, my mom, my dad, Lola. And then all these little guys—"

"I'm never going to remember all of this." Cadence had counted, and there were ten children and twenty-five adults, not including her and Matt. In some countries, they would qualify as a small- to medium-size enterprise.

"Don't worry. You'll get a chance to meet everyone. Half of them haven't even shown up yet. I told you we came too early." Matt checked his hair in the rearview mirror. "If anything, all my cousins with kids will be too busy running after them to talk to you."

"It might help if you'd show me other pictures." With so many people squished into one photo, she could barely make out anyone's faces. "What did you tell your family about me?" Cadence asked, handing the phone back to him. "Like . . . who I am to you. So that we have our stories straight."

She reminded herself, no matter how he answered, not to put too much meaning into it. There were zero expectations on her part. Sure, she couldn't have predicted the way their relationship had unfolded over the past week. But she couldn't tamp down the feeling that after all this time, their separate lives had finally intersected on the same x-axis and y-axis only for their paths to diverge once again.

Matt wanted to come back to L.A. and he didn't blink an eye when he found out about her iStan job offer. She was thrilled that he understood what an amazing opportunity it was, that he was never threatened by it. But what did that mean for them as a couple, if she could call them that?

"I told them that you're my coworker," he confessed, his voice low and wary.

"Oh." She managed to keep her voice light, but she couldn't school her face into a neutral expression.

"My very beautiful, funny, smart coworker," Matt added a little too late. "I asked you to come before we . . . if you don't want to come in, I'll take you back to the hotel. The party will still be going on. Nobody will know the difference."

That's right. He asked her when they were still just coworkers. She supposed she couldn't fault him for that. "No, you don't have to do that. I was thinking, if I'm here to show your family that you're capable of dating someone, then I can be that person. I *am* that person."

"I'm not saying you aren't, but meeting them is a big undertaking and I'm giving you an out."

"And I'm telling you that I don't want it. If Ashley can handle your family, then I can too."

Matt held her hand. "This is not a competition."

Obviously not. Cadence knew between her and Ashley, there was really no comparison. The fact that he felt the need to say that was offensive.

"I'm not being competitive. My point is, you've gone to great lengths to bring me here, so I'm here. I'm in it to—" She stopped herself from saying "to win it" before she canceled her own self. "I came to help, so let me help you."

Cadence pushed the car door open and stretched her arms to loosen up, the way she used to before teeing up.

Matt's hands landed on her shoulders, kneading out the knots. "Easy, tiger. You're looking at this all wrong."

She swatted him away and continued stretching. "What do you mean?"

"My family will like you because *I* like you," he explained. Cadence knew this already, but she couldn't help the flutter inside her chest. "They will welcome you, feed you, and make you feel like part of the family right away," he continued. "So the objective is not to win them over. The trick is, once they make you feel like family, that's when you stay light on your toes."

Cadence dropped her arms. "What do you mean?"

"They're going to wait until you let your guard down and then say or do things to test your reaction to see if you'd fit in. Sometimes it's real obvious, but sometimes it's not. That's why Ashley still thinks my family likes her, but there's a reason why she doesn't have Lola's leche flan recipe."

Fuck. Cadence liked questions because she usually had answers. Winging it was not in her vocabulary. "So what am I supposed to do?"

"Relax. Everything will be fine for the first hour or so. Once you feel suspicious, stay close to me. Got it?"

Cadence nodded. When he put it that way, it didn't give her much of a choice. These would have been important details to mention before she turned down going back to the hotel. If this was Matt's idea of prep, then he relied on his looks more than she thought. Matt gave her hand an encouraging squeeze and led her toward the front door.

The first test came right away when his uncle Dennis opened the door.

"Matt! Come, come! Everyone's out in the back." Dennis's eyes darted to Cadence for a quick appraising look, hitting all the major stops. Her face. Their joined hands. Matt's face. "And who's this?" he asked with singsong curiosity.

"This is Cadence," Matt replied.

"Hi. I'm Dennis, Matt's uncle," he said, inviting them in.

Matt and Cadence walked into the living room. The walls were plastered with picture frames. There were old sepia-toned family photos from the Philippines with what looked like Matt's grandparents surrounded by his aunts and uncles dressed in their barongs. Gerald's and Missy's school portraits from every school year lined the walls, ending with their college graduation photos near the ornate decorative mirror above the mantel. In between, there were framed collages with photos of extended family arranged in various circular cutout formations. It was like a museum exhibit featuring a detailed timeline of their family history. "Thank you for having me. You have a lovely home."

"Oh, thank you. Any girlfriend of Matt's is welcome here."

Any. Girlfriend.

The instant those words entered the atmosphere, Matt reflexively squeezed Cadence's hand, but he didn't correct his uncle, letting those words hang between them. There went their playbook for the party.

Cadence tried not to let it bother her. If anything, it was freeing to put a title on it, whether it was real or not. This way, she didn't have to worry about whether she was showing too little or too much affection as a "coworker." She changed gears into full-girlfriend mode. Since Dennis was the "party uncle," judging by his festive tropical shirt, Cadence figured she could have a little fun with this.

"Oh, that's good to hear," she said with an extra-sweet smile. "I was afraid there was a max on Matt's girlfriends."

"Oh ho ho," Dennis chuckled toward Matt. "I like her already." Dennis offered Cadence the crook of his arm. "What's your poison?"

"Gin and tonic, if you have it." She hooked her arm into his while Matt followed them through the kitchen into the balloon-filled backyard.

"Of course! We have everything. I'll be right back with it." Uncle Dennis let her go to head to their outdoor bar. Across the patio, Matt's cousin Jason was bumping party hits from his turntables to appease this multigenerational crowd, mixing in dance tracks with "September" by Earth, Wind & Fire.

"Nicely played," Matt said, joining her at her side. "Don't forget to smile," he said through his grin. "Everyone's looking at us."

If Cadence had the wherewithal to do the math earlier, then she would have realized that half of a nearly forty-person party was roughly twenty people. Those twenty people sat around a long outdoor dining table and immediately erupted with greetings, shouting after Matt. He waved at them but stayed beside Cadence.

"There's someone I have to introduce to you first," he said, gently pushing her from the small of her back toward the group of ladies sitting in Adirondack chairs, absorbed in their own conversation.

"Mano po," Matt greeted Lola as he bent down, lifting her hand to his forehead. The act of deference pleased Lola, who smiled at him lovingly, but she quickly brushed him aside to see Cadence. With her shimmery silver hair and diminutive frame, wearing a matching cardigan over a plumeria-pink sundress, Lola emanated a warm maternal aura that Cadence hadn't felt in a long time. She instantly gravitated toward Lola, like she would protect this precious woman with her life. Going clockwise, Matt introduced Cadence to his grandmother, his aunts, and his mom, all of whom welcomed her with ever-growing smiles.

Lola's strong hand tugged at Cadence's, signaling to lower herself for closer inspection.

"It's so nice to meet you. I've heard wonderful things about you," Cadence said, crouching down to meet Lola at eye level.

Lola tilted her petite face to assess Cadence through her bifocals. "She's the one," Lola announced.

"Excuse me?" Cadence looked up over her shoulder at Matt, wondering if this was a test. Was she the chosen one, and what was she getting chosen for? Matt was useless, returning an awkward blank stare.

"The one on the phone," Lola clarified.

"Oh," Matt said, relieved, to an audience of tittering aunties. "You have a good memory, Lola."

"Are you sure?" Auntie Patricia directed the question to Auntie Connie and Auntie Luz, lifting up her Coach visor to get a better look at Cadence. "Wasn't his last girlfriend a white girl?"

Cadence ignored the reference to Ashley and kept her attention on Lola, who had a twinkle in her eye like this was their inside joke. Lola patted the top of Cadence's hand, releasing her from further examination. "It's nice to meet you too, Ca-dence," Lola said, enunciating each syllable. "Go eat! There's plenty of food."

This began a wave of attention that Cadence wasn't used to. Uncle Dennis returned to hand her a gin and tonic filled to the brim; it smelled lethal at arm's length. "Yes, please eat!" He shooed Matt and Cadence along.

"Let me help you." Matt's mom scurried to dote on Cadence. "Your hands are full."

"It's okay, Mrs.—"

Matt's mom tutted. "Please. Call me Mom."

Cadence shot a wide-eyed look at Matt, who again replied with a dumbass look on his face she couldn't read. Was he sorry, scared shitless, or completely inept? Oblivious, Matt's mom made her way down the buffet, lifting the lid on every steaming-hot chafing dish, neatly assembling a heaped-up plate full of pancit palabok, steamed rice, simmering kare kare, and crispy lechón, topping it with two grilled meat skewers and lumpia.

"Everything looks delicious . . . M-mom," she said, pushing the word out of her mouth, testing it. She'd never called anyone "Mom" other than her own mother. Cadence's chest constricted at the passing bittersweet thought. Damn. This was going to be harder than she thought. Cadence knew how to handle Chinese aunties who picked apart her appearance and pried about her salary. But this—getting the red-carpet treatment and being fussed over—was another animal. Cadence suppressed her gut instinct to reject it with modesty and heeded Matt's advice. *Just go with it!*

"There's enough for seconds or thirds," Matt's mom said. "And there's sinigang in the kitchen."

"What about me?" Matt whined like he was somehow forgotten.

"Hay naku." His mom's eyes darted up and down, like she didn't know what stupid part of her son to look at. "You have hands. Use them," she snapped. Cadence hid her snort behind her glass. Mom's magenta-red lips rebounded into a polite smile. "Come sit!"

Matt gripped Cadence's elbow to hold her back for a brief huddle. "You're doing great," he whispered.

"No thanks to you," Cadence hissed.

"Trust me. You're knocking it out of the park right now. I can't explain." Matt must have drawn his mom's ire because he nudged Cadence toward the dining table. "Keep it up!"

Cadence had no idea what she was doing that needed to be kept up, but she was glad she was clearing all the hurdles presented so far. She took a small, blinding sip of her drink as she approached the big table like she was headed for the gauntlet, twenty avid pairs of eyes tracking her every move.

CHAPTER 22

MATT

Matt caught up to the woman of the hour and handed Missy her present.

"Happy birthday," he said, giving her a hug.

"Thank you." She tipped up her glass of rosé. "Cadence seems nice."

After introductions, Cadence made her rounds, chatting with everyone. She won his cousins over with a spot-on impression of Matt. After she finished her second plate, much to Auntie Patricia's delight, Cadence went into the kitchen to watch her fry another batch of lumpia. She even indulged some of his nieces and nephews and blew bubbles with them. The way Cadence seamlessly fit in with his family made Matt feel helpless, like catching up to his runaway heart was a fool's errand.

"Though you could have brought her another time and not stolen my thunder," Missy said, half joking, nudging her elbow into his rib.

"Nobody's going to forget that this is your party." Matt pointed at the huge vinyl poster of Missy's ginormous portrait with a *Happy 21st Birthday Missy!* message that stretched across the pergola. Laughter roared from the table, where Celine, AJ, and Gerald turned their eyes away once Matt caught them looking at him. "What's happening over there?"

"You better go." Missy stepped aside. "Cadence asked them for all your embarrassing stories."

"Oh shit." By the time he sat next to Cadence, she was wiping away tears from ugly laughing. He had a bad feeling about this. "What did I miss?"

"AJ showed Cadence the picture of the four of you in your wannabe high school boy band," Celine said in between snickers.

Damn. His family came locked and loaded with evidence today. How did AJ still have that picture? It was close to twenty years old, and there was much to regret about how he presented himself then. The long spiky hair that was orange from too much Sun-In. The coordinated oversize yellow Nautica T-shirts and cargo shorts accessorized with a white puka-shell necklace and K-Swiss shoes.

"That was the style back then. We looked cool," Matt insisted, ignoring Diane's and George's dissenting looks. "Gerald was the 'bad boy' because he has tattoos. Jason and AJ sang lead vocals and I danced. We were a hit at all the debuts."

"I have follow-up questions," Cadence said. "Number one: Why? Number two: What was your group name? Number three: Why? And Number four: Is there video?"

Matt pushed Cadence's drink away, assuming that was the cause of her louder than usual voice. "No. No video." Thank god. Those days were pre-smartphone and pre–social media.

"We need Jason. Jason!" AJ waved him over.

Aw, crap. Matt hadn't done this in a long time. He sipped on some water to clear his throat.

"What's up?" Jason slapped Matt's back. "What are we doing?"

"Cadence wants to know our boy-band group name, so on three," AJ commanded. "One, two, three."

"We are," the four of them harmonized, "Three Plus One!"

"See? We still got it!" Matt claimed.

Jason crinkled his nose while he scratched his goatee. "You were a little flat on the last note, bro."

"One?" Matt sang the last note again. AJ winced while he shook his head, pointing a finger up. Matt tried again, elongating the note and adjusting the pitch until AJ gave him the thumbs-up.

"Oh, it's too good," Cadence said, giggling. With the back of her hand, Cadence patted her flushed face, overheated from laughing at his expense. It was worth it.

"Having fun over here?"

Matt's shoulders squared at the sound of his dad's brusque voice. Coming from a military family, Dad was a stick-in-the-mud compared to his mom's side of the family. Dad liked to think that he has loosened up since retirement, but he was the one wearing a stuffy green-and-white-striped polo shirt tucked into his belted khakis while everyone else was in casual attire. The wonder was how his dad had transformed into a big softy once he became a grandparent. The way he spoiled Celine's kids was the complete opposite of his own rigid parenting style.

Matt pushed his chair back and stood up to greet him with a hug, which his dad tolerated. "Dad, where have you been?"

"Your mom made me go pick up the cake."

"Dad, this is—"

"Cadence. I know. Your mother told me," he said dismissively.

Dad turned to Cadence with a polite but stoic expression. "Pleased to make your acquaintance."

Cadence must have picked up on the formality because she stood from her seat with stick-straight posture and dipped her head demurely. If Matt hadn't known any better, he might have thought Cadence would curtsy.

"I hear you and Matt are colleagues," Dad said.

"That's right," Cadence replied. "We've worked together for a few years now." She paused and eyed Dad's shirt where the little *V* logo was embroidered. "We're in town to meet with a high-profile client over a round of golf."

"Really?" Dad asked, intrigued, though he side-eyed Matt curiously. "I've taken up golf recently."

"You have?" It was Matt's turn to be incredulous. "Since when?"

"Since your father's been bored sitting around the house," Mom added. She had come to drag Dad away. She must have guessed (correctly) that Dad was killing the vibe. "Now all he does is watch YouTube videos on golf."

"Maybe the next time we're in town, we can hit the driving range," Cadence suggested. "I played in college."

"Oh?" Dad said with renewed interest, freeing his arm from Mom's hold. "What's your handicap?"

"During my best season, it was five." Matt had no idea what that meant, but Dad was blown away. "But it's been a long time since I last played."

"Let them eat," Mom scolded, tugging Dad's arm once again. "You can bother them later."

Matt gave his mom a thankful look before she pulled his dad

back toward the bar, where the elders had congregated. Matt briefly caught Lola's eyes; she had been observing them from afar.

"Wow," Celine said. "I've never seen Dad warm up to anyone so fast."

"Oh, it's nothing," Cadence said as she returned to her seat. "I saw the Callaway logo on his shirt and figured we could talk golf."

"Still. Will and I have been married, what? Nine years, and Dad barely started smiling at him last year."

"It's true," Will chimed in, finally finished with feeding their kids. "My guess is because we gave him grandchildren. So, Cadence, if he likes you this much already, wait until you start popping out babies."

What the fuck, Will? What possessed him to bring up popping out babies to Cadence, who was practically a stranger to him? Matt ran interference before Cadence felt that she needed to reply. "Speaking of babies, how are things going for you two?" he asked AJ and George.

George let out a resigned sigh, swirling the red wine in their glass. "It's going. It's been a journey, to say the least, but it's going."

AJ and George described their lengthy application process, the required training sessions, CPR and first aid certifications, and the evaluation of their home by a caseworker. The process was quite rigorous, and there was no telling when they would receive a placement or whom it would be, even though there were thousands and thousands of children who needed homes. When AJ discussed the possibility of their future foster kids going back to their biological parents, it broke Matt's heart. He hadn't considered how complicated the process would be or the emotional roller coaster

AJ and George were about to embark on. AJ and George would make great parents; any kid would be lucky to have them.

Matt glanced at Cadence, who was engrossed in their story. She had never once talked about wanting children. It would never have come up anyway. Cadence kept their conversation on superficial topics the night before. Matt told himself that he was just following her lead, letting her let loose after a rough week, but he was starting to wonder if he'd done enough to show Cadence that he was capable of more than casual dates.

Of course, once the topic of babies came up, it was all anyone could talk about. Ilene launched into a diatribe about how "sleeping when the baby is sleeping" is a sham because there was so much to do before they woke up. Picking up Ilene's baton, Celine ranted that the kids had sucked her youth and her boobs away. Matt didn't need to know this. Jason chimed in about his swaddling techniques and emailed AJ organic baby food recipes.

"Dude, who *are* you, and what have you done with Jason?" Matt asked. It still boggled his mind that Jason had become so domesticated.

"What?" Jason pushed his hands at Matt, like he was throwing back the disrespect. "I'm still me. Let me show you." Jason pushed his son's stroller around the table and pointed at the red Supreme bumper sticker affixed to the bottom basket. "See? I'm a cool dad," he insisted. Nobody around the table disagreed with him, but nobody agreed, either. "You know who thinks I'm cool?" Jason whipped out his phone and shoved it in Matt's face. "Look how many people follow my SoundCloud."

Nearly a thousand people followed Jay's Music Productions, which was pretty remarkable for the year he'd been in business.

When Jason started deejaying again, his wife, Maleena, said it was Jason's midlife crisis side hustle. "It's not for the money. I think he wants to relive a bit of his youth." It seemed important to him, which was why she supported the venture, even though it took his Friday and Saturday evenings away.

Matt thumbed through the list of followers and found that a significant number of them consisted of their extended family. The rest were prospective couples looking to hire Jason for their wedding, since he preferred wedding gigs to raging house parties. Matt stopped scrolling when he came across a familiar face. "Hey," Matt said, tilting the phone toward Cadence. "Is that your brother?"

Cadence narrowed her eyes at the screen. "It is," she replied, somewhat spooked at the coincidence. "How do you know Tristan?"

"Tristan's your brother?" Jason said as he did a double take at Cadence. If he was looking for any resemblance, there was hardly any between the Lim siblings. "I've bumped into him at bridal conventions. You know, where a bunch of vendors set up for couples and wedding planners? His photography booth was across from mine. Tristan's a cool guy. He hooked it up when I replaced my tires."

"What a small world," Cadence said, shifting in her seat. "I didn't know he was shooting weddings."

Hushed voices traveled down the table. Heads turned slightly, leaving one ear on their side conversation and one ear toward theirs. Shit. Why did Cadence have to say that so loud? There were few things that would turn off his tight-knit family quicker than someone who didn't value family as much as they did. Nobody's family is perfect, they knew that, but Cadence's comment raised a red flag. One that his family would dissect if she didn't pivot quickly. Matt couldn't answer for Cadence on this one, so he did the next best thing and draped a protective arm around her shoulders.

"You don't know what your brother does?" Celine tried to make her question sound as nonchalant as possible, but she skidded on the landing.

"Well," Cadence started to say. "I don't keep track of every—" All other conversations came to a full stop with a thud, courtesy of AJ's half-eaten lumpia slipping through his greasy fingers and falling onto his plate. Cadence paused as she registered all the eyes and ears pointed in her direction.

Matt kept an encouraging smile on his face, but he hoped he could transmit a warning signal to steer clear from this path. He could see his family group chat blowing up with speculation on the horizon.

Cadence cleared her throat, trying to recover. To Celine, she asked, "I mean, you don't know everything Matt does, right?" She laughed nervously. "Not that it would be all that exciting. Gosh, his idea of adventure is eating baby back ribs."

Okay. Cadence went with the let's-clown-on-Matt strategy. It was an admirable move, but risky. There was a precarious second of silence before Jason broke the silence with a snort.

"Bro, I thought you got over that already." Jason picked up a rib from his plate and waved it in Matt's face. Matt cowardly ducked behind Cadence, exaggerating a bit for laughs.

"Good job," he whispered inside the cave of her hair. His breath must have tickled a sensitive part of her neck because an unexpected giggle escaped her lips as she shrugged into her cheek.

Cadence playfully crinkled her nose at him, annoyed that he had elicited such a reaction from her in front of everyone. Matt didn't care. He didn't even notice them anymore. Not when a heart-stopping shy smile appeared on her face. Not when a magnetic force kept their gazes locked on each other for an arguably long time.

"Ahem!"

The volume turned up as everyone resumed their side conversations. Matt reluctantly turned his attention back to Jason, who waved a rib between Cadence and him.

"So what's the deal with you two?" he asked, arching an eyebrow. "How did you guys meet?"

"At work," Cadence and Matt said in unison.

"Ugh," AJ said. "They even talk at the same time."

"No, but like *how*?" Celine probed. "When?"

"*Why*?" Gerald sneered, eliciting laughs from around the table.

Cadence and Matt turned to each other. Their eyes dared the other to start first. Of all things, how did they forget to craft their origin story before arriving?

Cadence took one for the team. "Because he genuinely cares about the people around him. He has a way of reminding me not to take life too seriously. Even when he's annoying, I can't help but laugh and I hate it." Cadence chuckled. She bit her lip, her amber brown eyes shining at Matt. "He's my best friend," she confessed.

After weeks of getting shot down, Matt almost didn't believe his ears. He waited to see if a sly smirk appeared on her face or a hint of sarcasm, but it never came. When it sank in that she meant it, Matt's smile nearly broke his face.

A swell of *aaw*s came from all corners of the party. Even Missy's sour face melted a little at the scene-stealing moment. It was heady stuff, Cadence making declarations in front of the most important people in his life. Did someone record it?

"Seriously, guys. Get a room or something." Gerald gagged. "There are children around."

As if on cue, Diane's eight-month-old twins, Amelia and Bella, woke up crying after taking a nap in their double stroller.

"It's around their feeding time," Diane said, glancing around the backyard for her husband, Mike. Diane let out a frustrated sigh when she spotted him getting sloshed with Uncle Dennis and Uncle Rey.

"Do you need any help?" Cadence asked.

Diane draped a breastfeeding cover around her and one of the twins. "Do you mind holding Amelia while I feed Bella?"

"Yeah, of course." Cadence knelt by the stroller and picked up Amelia, gently rocking her once she stood. Soon after, Amelia fell back asleep in Cadence's arms.

"Oh, you have the magic touch," Diane said, with a pointed look directed at Matt. When he surveyed the table, he found more of the same looks from his other cousins. Great.

Cadence didn't notice, since she kept her gaze fixed on Amelia's angelic face.

"Hardly," Cadence said softly. "Amelia is a sweetheart."

Matt had to admit that he always found it hard to envision himself as a parent, but seeing Cadence hold Amelia so naturally was making him feel a certain kind of way.

"Matt!" Lola gestured for him to come over to the elders' table. "Hoy! *Sssst!*"

Matt excused himself and crossed the yard to Lola. "Yes, po?"

Lola yanked on his arm to sit down. "I like this one," she said, referring to Cadence. "When are you two getting married?"

"Married?" Auntie Connie piped up. "Who's getting married?"

"Nobody's getting married," Matt said. He had to squash this before it spread like wildfire.

"What are you waiting for?" Lola asked. "I don't know how much time I have left—"

"Lola." Matt stopped her from going down that road. Guilt trips were one thing. Invoking death for the sake of argument was plain morbid.

"Do you love her?"

Damn. She was not playing around.

Matt hesitated. Truth be told, he was falling for Cadence, but he wasn't going to tell his lola that before he told Cadence.

They both turned and watched Cadence stand and bounce Amelia, who started fussing again. "That baby sure looks good on her."

"Lola," he said, exasperated.

"Women her age want a sign of commitment, Matt. If she doesn't think you're being serious, she's going to go find it somewhere else," she warned.

Matt didn't need the reminder that Cadence would leave for greener pastures. They hadn't talked about her job offer since Thursday, but it was the elephant in their suite.

Lola must have sensed the change in Matt's mood because her voice softened. She patted Matt's hand. "I want you to be happy like everyone else. Our family is everything, Matthew. We celebrate the good times together and we show up for each other when things are bad. Your problem is our problem. Why do you think I call you so much? You think I like wasting my minutes on this?"

Matt thought she was serious, but the crinkle at the corner of her eyes revealed she was teasing him. Though he suspected that she wasn't joking about the minutes. Didn't Lola know that she was on the unlimited family plan? He probably shouldn't tell her or else she'd start calling even more.

Some commotion broke out from the table, with Gerald's cackle rising above the noise. Whatever he was laughing at, Cadence was not in on the joke. Her face was beet red.

"You better go save her," Lola said, reading Matt's mind.

Damn it. He should have known better than to leave her alone with them. It was going so well. Too well, he realized in retrospect. His cousins were merely waiting for the right moment to pounce.

CHAPTER 23

CADENCE

When Lola summoned Matt, Cadence held in her panicked whimper as she lost her second line of defense. The second he was out of earshot, Gerald launched the first question.

"So, what was your first impression of Matt? Or did I miss that story?"

"Oh, um . . . I thought he was kind of cocky. Schmoozy like all the other brokers." A bunch of the guys snickered. "What's so funny?"

"Trying to picture Matt being like that," Jason said. "Matt is a huge nerd. Ask him how many lonely nights he spent assembling Gundam model kits during high school."

"That was a long time ago," Cadence said, feeling defensive on Matt's behalf. "People change. He's definitely not like that at work."

"That's because of us. Being part of Three Plus One got him out of his shell. Remember when he finally had the guts to ask out . . . what was her name?" Gerald snapped his fingers as he tried to jog his memory. "Brenda?"

"Brenda Rincon," AJ confirmed.

"Brenda Rincon!" Gerald practically jumped up from his seat. "Dude was so nervous that he sat on the same side of the booth as her so he didn't have to make eye contact."

"How do you know?" Celine asked.

"Matt told us!" Gerald claimed. "That boy choked so hard. He's always been that way when he really likes someone. It's a miracle that he gets laid at all."

Cadence stood still because she didn't know how to react. What was she supposed to say about Matt's dismal teenage dating life other than it sounded pretty normal? Cadence's arms were starting to feel like jelly from rocking Amelia, and the constant chatter was wearing her down. Gerald, the family's loudmouth, was starting to grate on her nerves. How could his girlfriend stand him? Cadence had hidden in the kitchen with Auntie Patricia when Gerald started an inappropriate conversation about whether anyone thought their parents still had sex. What the hell with the TMI? Was that considered typical party conversation in this family? Cadence wasn't going to add fuel to the fire with her two cents.

"Please excuse my brother," Missy said to Cadence. "That's his way of saying that we like you."

Really? Was that what Gerald meant? Nothing in this family made sense to Cadence. First, they filled your well with attention and then they dunked your head in it. Everyone in this family smiled like it was their default setting, so it was hard to tell if they were merely being polite or if they genuinely liked her (apparently Matt had a genetic predisposition to this). Getting the positive feedback finally allowed Cadence to breathe a sigh of relief. Unfortunately, her relaxed stance caused Amelia to stir and whine.

"Here." Diane fished a teal pacifier from the diaper bag and handed it to Cadence. "Try this. I'm almost done feeding Bella, so I can take Amelia from you in a bit." Cadence tried to put the pacifier in Amelia's mouth, but it made her fussier.

"This is really good practice for your future kids," Gerald said, egging her on.

Preoccupied with a now-crying baby rejecting her pacifier, Cadence muttered, "You're skipping a few steps." She started bouncing Amelia again to calm her down. "Marriage. A house," she listed absentmindedly.

"Oooh, you guys talked about marriage already?" Gerald clutched his porkpie hat to his head as he threw himself back into a cackle. "Will we have a wedding next year?"

Blood rushed into Cadence's face. She walked right into baby and marriage questions, and she couldn't come up with any plausible or evasive answers. Amelia's cries made it hard to think or breathe. Some people around the table like Celine, Missy, and most of the in-laws had sympathetic looks on their faces, while Gerald and Jason eagerly awaited her response. Fortunately, Diane finished feeding Bella and took Amelia from Cadence. With her arms free, Cadence dabbed her sweaty forehead with the back of her hand.

"Hey, what's going on?" Matt's concerned voice said from behind her. The skirt of her sundress floated as she spun around full circle to look for him. He was not there. Did she imagine his voice? How much booze was in her drink?

At the table, she found widened eyes, followed by gasps. What the hell was going on?

"Were you looking for this?" Matt knelt down and held up the pacifier from its ringlike handle . . . on one freaking knee!

Cadence stumbled back as a cacophony of reactions arose from swirling, shocked faces at every turn as if she were in her very own house of mirrors.

"Ooooh, what?!" Jason covered his mouth as he laughed in disbelief.

"Is this for real?" Celine and Missy asked, the former out of confusion and the latter in exasperation.

"Susmariosep!" Lola exclaimed. "I didn't think you'd propose right away!"

"Propose?!" Matt yelped while his face paled as if he had seen a ghost.

"I knew it! I called this shit!" Gerald howled. "Yo, Matt, can I be your best man?"

"SHUT UP, GERRY!"

Cadence slapped her hands over her mouth. She couldn't believe she said that out loud and neither could everyone else. Mouths gaped without a single sound escaping from them, giving Jason the perfect opportunity to play "Marry You" by Bruno Mars from his laptop.

"I . . . I-I-I," Cadence stammered, dabbing her burning face. "I need to get some air," she said, which she realized was a stupid thing to say because they were already outside. "I mean . . ." She turned around without finishing her sentence, dipped her chin, and let her sheer mortification fuel her feet. Surely, this public disaster could carry her all the way back to San Francisco, where she wouldn't have to face every member of Matt's family again.

She made it inside the empty house, not knowing where to go from there, when a hand gripped her elbow.

"Follow me." Matt didn't give her much of a choice, dragging her across the kitchen. Cadence couldn't read Matt's stony expression, his clenched jaw accentuating the angles of his face. Was he upset or embarrassed? Either way, she had screwed up any goodwill she'd earned.

Matt pulled her into a room at the end of the hallway. Immediately, she was hit with the scent of clean linens. The laundry room? "What are we doing in here?"

"It's the last place they'll look," he said, keeping his voice low while he closed the door behind him. "I'm sorry. I shouldn't have left you alone with those guys."

"No, it's . . ." Cadence palmed her forehead, still feeling disoriented. Matt gripped her waist and grunted softly as he picked her up and propped her on top of the dryer.

"Here." Matt handed her a bottle of water that he must have grabbed from the bar. "Are you okay?"

Cadence sipped her water, partly to collect herself and partly to stall. She crossed her ankles and smoothed down her dress, connecting the eyelet dots with her fingers. "I'm sorry," she said eventually.

"For what?" Matt leaned closer, flanking her with his hands on opposite corners of the dryer, giving her no room to hide.

"For blowing it. I was in over my head today. Your family is a tough crowd." Cadence couldn't bring herself to meet his eyes. "They must hate me."

"Why? Because you told Gerry to shut up? Telling Gerry to shut up is a rite of passage in this family."

"Matt." Cadence wasn't in the mood for his jokes. Closing her eyes, she let out a defeated sigh. "Maybe this was a mistake."

Matt straightened up. "What do you mean?"

Cadence felt guilty over the tension that flooded Matt's face. She meant it when she said that he was her best friend. She wanted to free him of worry the same way he freed her, but the uncertainty jumbled her brain. This past week, Cadence allowed herself to get swept up in Matt's presence, tucked away from their real life, but this was temporary. In a week, they would return to San Francisco. Back to their separate lives. Back to their separate professional goals that were taking them in different directions. But now they were tangled together, like the knots in her stomach.

"What was I thinking? I should have known better than to bring up marriage and kids. I hope I didn't give your family the wrong idea."

"And what would that be?"

"That we're . . ." Cadence was hoping Matt supply his own answer here, but he waited. He was going to make her finish the sentence. "This—what we're doing—is very new and things accelerated very quickly. Living together. Meeting your family. But I should have known that they would ask me questions about marriage and kids."

"Is that the reason why you're freaking out? Because we can clear this up right now."

"How? After the scene we made?" Hadn't Matt suffered enough humiliation? His fake girlfriend ran away from his accidental proposal in front of his entire family.

"Easy. What are your thoughts on the institution of marriage?" How could Matt be so glib?

"Do you see yourself having kids?" he plowed on.

"Are you proposing now? Because that pacifier doesn't cut it for me." Matt seemed undeterred by her sarcasm. His dark eyes bore into her, expecting an answer. Cadence wished there were a ladylike way to flap the skirt of her dress, because it was getting uncomfortably muggy in the laundry room. "Yeah," she admitted. "I have thought that I might get married or have kids someday." Someday, in a far distant future.

"I want those things too."

Cadence's ears were burning hot. Goose bumps rippled across her skin when Matt ran his hands down her arms, like his touch was a magnet to her skin. Matt swallowed hard. Maybe this conversation was too fast, too serious for him too.

"Not right at this minute and not all at the same time," he added, "but . . ." Matt's lips pressed into a straight line, hesitating. "If there's the slightest possibility that you could see us going down that road together, let's figure it out. What do you say, Lim?"

The what-ifs spinning in Cadence's head made her dizzy. Her hands slipped and gripped the front edge of the dryer. Matt grabbed her shoulders to keep her upright as a gentle classical song emitted from below. She must have pressed a button. The never-ending tune bounced along for a full minute, chipping away at the tension one beep at a time. Matt closed his eyes as he groaned, defeated, leaning forward until his face rested on her lap.

"I can't believe I'm discussing this with you . . . in this"—his hand flicked upward—"*fucking* laundry room."

Cadence's body shook with laughter. She hoped Matt didn't take it the wrong way. It stemmed from the relief that came from knowing that the weight in the air when they were together was not one-sided. She felt it all the time, even when he was pushy and annoying. If she wasn't already doing so, she would tell herself to sit down.

"At least you had the guts to look me in the eye and say it to my face," she gently teased him, letting her fingers play with his hair.

Matt growled. "Who told you about Brenda? Was it Gerry?" He didn't wait for her answer because he already knew. "I'm going to kill him."

Matt pushed himself up, but Cadence caught his face with both her hands before he could leave.

"Do you really mean it?" she asked. Matt met her gaze and nodded. "There's a lot of stuff to figure out, you know."

"Oh, I know." His arms wrapped around her, pulling her closer toward the edge. "I'm ready."

"Yeah?" she challenged. "You in it to win it?"

He unleashed a dazzling smile. "Yeah."

Cadence's breath hitched. Oh that smile. It blinded that small, nagging, anxious voice in her into forgetting its concerns.

"Okay," she said, nodding. "Good." She angled his face as her lips descended on his for a soft, enduring kiss. One of his hands separated her knees as he leaned forward until their bodies were flush, making it easy for her legs to wrap around him.

"But," she continued when they broke apart and the no-fun part of her brain switched on, "can we go now? Before we end up having sex in the laundry room?"

"You say that like it's a bad thing." Matt kissed her again, letting his hand roam underneath her dress, making her forget why she brought it up in the first place.

"Matt?" a voice called out, followed by a knock on the door.

Cadence shooed Matt out from under her skirt, panicking at the sound of his mom's lilting voice and the rattling doorknob. Thankfully, it was locked.

"Oh my god. What are you doing in there?" Mom said, exasperated. "I packed a plate for you to take back. I will tell everyone that you two left. It's on the kitchen counter. Call you later, okay? Hope to see you again, Cadence."

Cadence waited a few moments before she spoke again, giving Matt's mom enough time to walk away. "Next time, you need to pick a different hiding spot," she scolded as she pushed Matt away and squeezed her frustrated thighs together.

Matt helped her down and stole a quick kiss. "As long as there's a next time . . ."

CHAPTER 24
MATT

Other than sending off a quick reply to all the apologetic messages in his family's group chat, Matt kept his hand on Cadence during the ride home. They were patient but frequent gestures. A kiss to the back of her hand. A light pat on her stomach—which earned him a stinging slap on the wrist—when she complained about eating too much. Replacing the strap on her shoulder to confirm her tan line on her sun-kissed skin. He couldn't stop touching her, as if letting go would break the electricity running between them.

Once they were back in the suite, Cadence started her arriving-home ritual. First she kicked off her shoes and lined them side by side near the door. Then she tied her hair up in a messy bun with an elastic hair band that always seemed to appear out of nowhere.

"I need to get out of this dress," she mumbled to herself, arching her back while her fingers reached behind her for the finicky hook and eye. Her fingers froze and she remained in a figure skater pose when Matt planted a light kiss at the nape of her neck.

"I can help you with that." Matt unhooked the clasp, then let his hands smooth down the curve of her waist.

"So corny," she teased, but the words died on her lips when his hands traveled up to cup her breasts and his thumbs grazed over the fabric on her pebbled nipples.

"I could stop," he murmured, slowly unzipping her dress. She answered by slipping the thin straps off her shoulders. His eyes followed her dress's descent, gazing down her exquisite naked body, except for those . . . plain ugly granny panties.

"What's wrong with these?" she asked, affronted, turning around to face him. He cursed at himself for saying that out loud. "They're very practical," she continued, referring to her underwear, which matched her skin. "You wouldn't know because you don't have to worry about panty lines or see-through fabric. Any other color and my underwear would have shown through my dress."

"Or you could have not worn any underwear at all," he suggested. What he wanted to tell her was that practicality was not sexy, but now was not the time. He could make a better case with a return trip to the lingerie shop, armed with the coupon for ten percent off he'd get after signing up for the store's emails.

"It's not like I planned to seduce you on this trip."

"That's disappointing," he grumbled under his breath.

"But you know," she said, stripping off the offensive piece of clothing, "plans change." Her doe eyes didn't look so innocent anymore.

Matt couldn't get his clothes off fast enough. Not when her hand reached under his boxers and grabbed his junk. Matt was convinced that Cadence was going to end him after the way she took the condom out of his hand, ripping the wrapper open with her teeth. He would have been fine lying back and letting her have at it. But when Cadence placed both of her hands on his chest, balancing herself as she slowly lowered onto him, tipping her head back as she savored the feeling, he didn't want to be a bystander anymore.

Matt pushed himself up, holding her close while she rolled her hips. Cadence liked to note that the only time he was quiet was when they had sex, but how could he speak when she ran her fingers through his hair, tugging it, directing him to trace the line of her neck with his lips and landing at the sensitive spot behind her ear? Why would he use his mouth to form words when he could taste the salt on her skin while she moaned into his shoulder as she shuddered in pleasure?

After Matt came, he pulled her down for an appreciative kiss. "You want to take a shower together?"

"No thanks." Cadence rolled off and pulled the covers up to her chin. "That's not for me, but you go ahead if you want." Since when did she get so shy? Matt didn't argue with her. If she didn't want to do it against the shower tiles, there were other surfaces in the suite that they had yet to explore.

While he was lathering up, Cadence walked in—clothed, to his dismay—with her hair pulled back and began to wash her face.

"Is that why you're not in here?" he asked as she rubbed a foamy cleanser on her cheeks and her forehead.

She splashed her face. "There's nothing sexy about seeing my makeup melt under the shower," she answered, dabbing her face with a towel.

"There's nothing sexy about that thing, either," he said, referring to the adhesive strip she carefully placed across her nose.

"You have ugly feet, but you don't hear me complaining about them," Cadence countered, which made Matt glance down. He wiggled his toes. What was so hideous about them?

On the other side of the sink, she lowered the lid on the toilet and took a seat.

Matt suddenly had an audience. "Are you just going to sit there and watch?"

"Mm-hmm," she said, her eyes sweeping unabashedly across his body as she wiped her face with a cotton pad. "Do you know how hard it was to ignore you at work? Show me the goods," she instructed, twirling her finger at him.

"I feel objectified." He smirked, obliging with a slow turn while he lathered his chest. "So are you saying I can finally knock down that cheap-ass partition in the office?"

Cadence hummed as she thought. "That depends on if you're even coming back to the office," she replied. Glancing down, she began to shred the cotton pad with her nails. "And you never know who will occupy your desk afterward."

Or her desk. She left that part out.

"What if my new cubicle mate is more annoying than you?" she said, chuckling nervously. "Ooh! Or what if he's hot? Maybe you *should* take it down."

Matt crushed the contents of the tiny bottle of hotel shampoo into his palm and worked it into his hair. He never considered himself the jealous type, but the thought of another (hot) man irked him more than the times he'd overheard her vent about her bad dates.

Matt quickly rinsed himself and grabbed a towel, drying himself before wrapping it around his waist. "Let's talk about this when I'm not so naked." Matt rushed out to his room to get dressed. He had put on a white T-shirt and a pair of boxers when he saw Cadence standing in the doorway, sans nose strip.

Cadence crossed her arms, watching her own feet shift. "What do you think about long-distance relationships?"

Her tentative question was injected with a forced casualness. If her opening idea wasn't even a feasible option, then this didn't bode well for Matt.

He leaned on his dresser, waiting for Cadence to look at him. She stayed put at the door, keeping herself at an infuriating distance. Matt ran his hand through his damp hair, trying to keep his cool.

"I'm sure it works great for some people, but I don't think I can, Lim," he said when she finally met his eyes. "I'd like to be able to see you every day. I know it's only been a week, but call me spoiled. I like waking up and seeing you in the morning. I want to keep seeing this version of you. The one that's not actively avoiding me most of the time. You can't see yourself coming to L.A.?"

Cadence glanced back down at her feet. "What's there to stay for?" she scoffed. She didn't catch herself until it was too late. "I mean—"

"Oh, that's great."

"You're not included when I say that," she rushed, talking over him.

"That's not much better."

"Matt." Cadence crossed the threshold into his room and sat on the corner of his bed. "My job is in San Francisco, and if I move back, I'd have to stay with my dad."

"A job that you've been ready to leave," he countered. "And it's not like you'd have to see your family all the time."

Cadence sighed. "Yes, I would. If Tristan wants to move out—which he's free to do—and if I came back, my dad would want me to move in with him. I just know it's not going to work out. I'm not like Tristan. He knows how to let certain things go, but I can't. I don't know how I'm supposed to take care of someone who didn't take care of me."

If Tristan wanted to move out and nobody wanted to live in their family home, then they should sell it, Matt thought. What was the point in staying? Her dad wouldn't be able to maintain both homes by himself. He could hardly take care of himself.

"How are you so sure that he'd want you to live with him? Is it about the money? They could sell it and get top dollar for it." Matt was about to mention how much the house could fetch if it sold with Best Eastern, but Cadence's eyes held a sharp stare.

"He'd never sell the house," she balked. "And he would definitely want me to live with him. He wouldn't have anyone else to take care of him besides me or Tristan."

"How are you so sure?" Matt chanced asking the question, knowing it might upset her further.

Exasperated, she said, "Trust me. I know. Which is why I'm suggesting we try long distance."

Matt rubbed the back of his neck. Their conversation went full circle.

"What about me?" he asked, taking a seat next to her. Where did she see him fitting into all of this? He held her limp hand, waiting for her answer.

Cadence kept her pensive eyes ahead, refusing to look at him. "I've tried to look at this in a lot of different ways," she said, her voice soft but clear. "Every time, I don't come up with an answer that you'll like."

Was this her way of sorting shit out? Because it sucked. Every project they'd ever worked on together, she always came with answers. Of all the times to come up short, why this time? "Then give me your best projection, Lim."

His request gave Cadence pause. "We should revisit this conversation after Thursday."

"Why Thursday?"

"The golf tournament?" she reminded him. "That's when we'll find out if you get the promotion."

"And what about you?" Matt was tired of her giving him the runaround. "Have you decided about iStan?"

"I'm still reading through the fine print and I'm trying to schedule a call with HR to discuss the terms of the offer. I can't say that I'm not tempted by it, if that's what you want to know. If I don't take it, I'd still be in San Francisco, so I don't know why it matters to you if I take the job or not," she reasoned.

Matt didn't think the conversation would go down this path, so he said the alternative that seemed obvious to him. "If I get the promotion, you should look for a job here in L.A."

Cadence let out a humorless laugh and crossed her arms. "Let me ask you this. Let's say the situation was reversed. Would you move to L.A. for me, with no other job offer in hand?" Matt opened his mouth, but nothing came out except for hot air. Now he really wished he had pants on. He stood from the bed and searched his dresser. He couldn't get himself to admit his answer, so she said it for him. "Don't put me in the position to adjust my whole life around you if you wouldn't do it for me."

"That's not what I'm trying to do."

"That's what it feels like and it's unfair. You asked for my most optimistic outlook and I gave it to you. Unless something changes, I don't know what else to say other than to try long distance or . . . maybe this isn't the right time for us. Maybe we should try again later."

Since when did her reasoning come from a Magic 8-Ball? Was this how they were making major life decisions now?

"What good would that do?" Matt slammed his dresser and stepped into sweatpants.

"Matt." Cadence stood beside him and held his hand. "If I'm being really honest, I've seen you flirt with other women, but I kind of knew that things were different between us. As much as I hoped it meant something, I also knew it would come down to this. That's why I never said anything." Cadence reached up smoothed his damp hair until both of them cooled down. "So can we revisit this on Thursday?"

Matt reluctantly agreed for the time being. This conversation had reached a stalemate. "When do you want to pick up your clubs?"

"Tomorrow, I guess," she said, cupping his face. "I'll try to get as much practice as I can."

"Or don't," he suggested. "Isn't it customary to let the client win?"

Cadence quirked an eyebrow and took a step back as she replied, "Let Percy win? It's like you don't know me at all."

Matt couldn't help his wry smile. "Is this your plan to keep me in San Francisco?"

"No . . . yes!" Cadence stomped her feet in her confusion. "That's a trick question!"

Matt chuckled even though he found her answer unsatisfactory, but what could he say when they were at an impasse? He kissed her forehead. "Do your best."

He tightened his arms around her, nuzzling his nose into her hair. It still had the faint lavender smell of hotel shampoo that smelled better on her than it did on him. How could he give this up? No FaceTime call could replicate this. One way or another, he'd show her how much better this was. Maybe then he could tip the scales in his favor.

CHAPTER 25

CADENCE

Sunlight shone between the crack in the curtains, waking Cadence up the next morning promptly at seven. With eyes still closed, she rolled over into cool sheets. Instead of Matt, Cadence found a note on his pillow, written on the hotel stationery.

Wait here.

xoxo, Matt
(unless you have to pee, then by all means)

Cadence laughed but found the note very suspicious. If there was one good thing to take away from this, it was that Matt still retained his sense of humor. She was afraid their talk yesterday had strained their relationship.

An email notification flashed on her phone. Josie had set up a call for Cadence with Sadie later that afternoon, which Cadence accepted. It was probably a check-in call, one that Cadence would keep brief. She didn't have much to report as far as professional matters went.

Matt knocked softly on the door before peeking in. "Oh, good. You're awake."

Cadence pushed herself up and sat against her pillows as Matt carefully backed into the room. He gently set a room-service tray on the desk adjacent to the bed, settling the clinking glasses and silverware. Cadence shielded her eyes when he pulled back the curtains. Matt unfurled a white cloth napkin with a snap before tying it around her neck. This man was so extra.

"What are you doing?" she asked, redirecting her wary eye from his face to the tray of delicious things that he propped over her lap.

"I woke up early this morning, hoping to make breakfast for you. Problem is, there's only a lousy electric griddle in the cupboard. So now the fridge is stocked with drinks and food I can't cook." He pointed at each item on the tray. "The coffee and waffles are from the café around the corner. Strawberries sliced by me. Orange juice freshly poured by me too."

"Very nice presentation," she said, cutting into the crunchy waffle. Cadence unapologetically moaned when she took her first bite.

"Ahem. There's Nutella on the side," he interrupted, pointing at the little sauce cup next to her plate.

Cadence forgot about Matt for a second there. She cleared her throat and took a sip of her coffee. "Thank you."

Matt smirked. "When you're done, this will be waiting for you." He handed her the newspaper, opened to the Sunday crossword puzzle. "It's today's paper, in case you're wondering."

This was all very thoughtful, but Cadence knew Matt. It wasn't like he was incapable of giving her something without anything in return, but she knew a bribe when she saw one. "This is very nice of you."

"So why are you looking at me like that?"

Cadence relaxed her suspicious face. "What is all of this for?"

"I'm giving you the Matt treatment. If you had stayed over at my place, I would have made you breakfast." Matt climbed onto his side of the bed. "Imagine if I made you breakfast every day."

Ah, so that's what this was. "You shouldn't overpromise," she warned, but she did appreciate it, so she added, "Thank you. I'll gladly eat it. Do you want some?"

"I thought you'd never ask." Matt popped a strawberry slice in his mouth. "MMMMM!" He exaggerated his imitation of Cadence, dramatically rolling his eyes back.

"Jerk!" Cadence swatted him with the newspaper, while he bowled over, laughing at himself.

He held up both hands to call a truce. When she lowered the newspaper, he sat up and gave her a quick peck on the cheek. A promise that he would be on his best behavior. As she ate, he read through the clues. By 10 Across, she wished he did have the answers. The Sunday crossword was hard! But she let him carry on, talking through possible answers, because as much as she'd hate to admit it, when he wasn't so busy being annoying, he was sweet.

THAT AFTERNOON, THEY stopped by Dad's house to pick up her clubs. They had to be in the garage in the main house. After a quick, albeit tense hello, Dad handed over the garage door keys with no further comment. Perhaps Dad had swept their last interaction under the rug. Cadence unlocked the dead bolt, gripped the garage door handle, and lifted it up. Matt offered to help, but there was a specific way to do it or the rickety door would come crashing down.

"I still got it," Cadence said, dusting off her hands. When she took her first step forward, she felt a pinch in her lower back. She winced as she massaged it. "Maybe not."

Matt whistled at the dusty boxes of junk piled everywhere in the garage. "What's all this stuff?"

"Damn it," Cadence said under her breath as she tied her hair into a ponytail. Despite burning a box of joss paper, the garage was still full of inventory from Dad's old shop. The people who leased the space after Dad didn't want any of the merchandise because they converted the store into one of those liquid nitrogen ice cream shops. What use did they have for stacks of old red envelopes, incense of every size, and good luck charms? Tristan cleaned out the whole store, leaving one 福 poster behind, at Dad's request.

"Someone should have good fortune here," Dad said at the time.

Where was Cadence's good fortune when she needed it? It was going to take forever to move all these unmarked boxes to dig up her clubs. When she texted Tristan to ask about her clubs' whereabouts, all he replied with was "*I dunno. In the garage probably.*" Typical.

"Here," Cadence said, handing Matt a box of miniature gold Buddha statues, "I think my clubs are on the shelf behind all these boxes."

Matt seemed so fascinated by all the trinkets and ceremonial items that he peeped into each box before moving them. It was slowing down their progress.

"Why do you guys have a whole box of red lightbulbs?"

"They go with the altar lamps," Cadence explained. She handed him the box of lamps so he stopped asking more questions. "Come on," she hurried him. "I wanna get out of here already."

"So are you pretty religious?" he asked as he moved more boxes.

Oh. A third-date question. It was fair, she supposed, given their current task.

"No, not really." Cadence picked up the next box with ease. From the rattling sound, she could tell it contained red plastic teacups the size of her thumb. "What about you?"

"I'm Catholic, but I don't go to church every Sunday. Don't tell my lola that, though."

"Okay." Cadence had no idea what to do with that information. It wasn't that big a deal for her, but she understood that it was for other people.

"Um . . ." Matt started to say.

Cadence was relieved that neither of them knew how to move the conversation from there. She looked over her shoulder to find Matt, ashen-faced, peering into another box. When she glanced inside, her heart sank. The box was full of remnants of her mom's funeral. There were leftover programs, a guestbook, and scattered photos that some uncle who wasn't really her uncle took from that day. Cadence caught a glimpse of the photo on top that captured Dad, Tristan, and her, all dressed in mourning white, greeting guests next to her mom's adorned casket.

Cadence folded the flaps, shutting the cardboard box, scraping Matt's nose in the process.

"Sorry," she said to Matt's scratched nose. She couldn't bring herself to look higher or else the tears forming in her eyes would surely fall. "Sorry you had to see that. I don't know why some people think it's okay to take pictures at funerals." Cadence didn't remember every aspect of that day, but she remembered enough not to need mementos.

"Hey." Her face met Matt's chest as he embraced her. There was something about his comforting voice and his soft T-shirt that pricked her eyes to an unexpected wave of sobs.

"No, I'm sorry. I shouldn't have looked." Matt rubbed her back, letting her cry. "I lost my lolo a few years ago, but he lived a long life. I can't imagine losing my mom. Do you want to talk about it?"

Cadence shook her head, wrinkling his damp shirt. "I need a second," she said, hiccuping as she tried to regain composure. She sniffled, turning her head to face the shelf.

"Damn it," she whispered.

Matt followed her line of sight. "What is it?"

"The clubs aren't even there." They were too big to be hidden behind any of the boxes that remained.

"Do you want to rent clubs?" Matt suggested.

"No. They have to be in the house somewhere," she replied, cleaning her dusty hands on her jeans before she wiped her face. "Let me run up to my old room. Maybe the clubs are there."

Matt nodded. "Do you mind if I use the restroom?"

Cadence avoided looking at his tearstained shirt. "I don't know if the water is on in this house. Would you be okay going into the front house? Don't feel obligated to talk to my dad for a long time."

"Yeah, that's fine. Don't worry. I'll meet you back here."

Cadence waited until Dad opened the creaky back door for Matt before she entered her childhood home. It still smelled of musty incense, but worse, since it had been weeks since anyone opened the windows or occupied the house, for that matter. The living room was half empty—some of the furniture had been moved to the front house.

Cadence jogged up the stairs to her room. To her surprise, someone—likely Tristan—had packed her things. They weren't anything of value. If they had been, she wouldn't have left them here for all these years. She rummaged through one box that contained her old college textbooks and binders. Another had her old golf clothes, none of which she could fit into anymore. She opened her closet and, to her relief, found her clubs standing upright in their black bag. Her Harry the Husky plush headcover, a gift from her former coach, still protected her driver. As she accounted for them all, her phone rang. It was Sadie.

Shit. Cadence lost track of time. She answered with her professional voice. "Hi, Sadie."

"Cadence. How are things going?"

"Good," she said out of habit.

"Hope you've had a chance to take a break this week."

"Can't say that I have," Cadence said, scanning her empty closet. All of her old clothes were taken off the hangers and thrown into trash bags. What possessed Tristan to do that? Were they planning on using her room for an office or gym? She wondered if he had thrown any of her things away.

"Make sure that you do because there will be assignments waiting for you when you return."

"Great. Looking forward to it," Cadence lied.

"I also wanted to warn you. Matt may have told you that Hunter signed up for that golf tournament. Josie learned that Hunter was able to get the tee time right after your group, so he won't be far behind."

"Thanks. That's helpful." Matt wasn't going to like the sound of that.

"Cadence. Be careful. With Hunter around, anything you and Matt do will travel back up to the office."

"What's that supposed to mean?" Where was this coming from? Cadence didn't think Sadie believed the office gossip.

"Hunter will not hesitate to use anything against Matt to get this promotion, and I don't want you to be collateral damage. I know you and Bill don't exactly mesh. Why? What did you think I meant?"

"Nothing!" Cadence cleared her throat. Smooth, Cadence. Smooth. "Thank you for letting me know."

Sadie paused so long that Cadence thought she had hung up on her.

"Riiiiight," Sadie finally replied. "Keep me posted. And, Cadence?"

"Hmm?"

"Thank you for all your hard work. It doesn't go unnoticed."

If that was the case, where was her bonus, then?

"Thank you, Sadie," Cadence replied before Sadie hung up. She threw her golf bag over her shoulder and hauled it downstairs to meet Matt.

CHAPTER 26

MATT

Matt washed his hands at the kitchen sink, and somehow Cadence's dad managed to rope him into a conversation about the new high-fiber diet he was on. Matt tuned out quickly, nodding along to be polite, because there was only so much information about Mr. Lim's digestive issues he could stomach (pun intended).

"Ah! Where are my manners? Would you like some water?" Mr. Lim extended a shaky finger at the damp spot on Matt's shirt. "It must be hot out there."

"No, it's okay," Matt said as he dried his hands. "I don't want you to get up."

"Why?" Mr. Lim asked defiantly, refusing assistance as he slowly stood up from the dining table. "See? I'm fine." He took small steps toward the kitchen, keeping a hand out in case he needed to grab on to something.

For peace of mind, Matt followed behind the stubborn old man. As Mr. Lim poured out a glass of water, an envelope on the counter caught Matt's eye. It was addressed to Mr. Lim from Best Eastern.

Matt kept an eye out the window to see if Cadence had returned. The garage was still empty. For now.

Without preamble, Matt asked, "Why didn't you sell the house before?"

Mr. Lim set the pitcher back upright, ushering silence in the room. His lips pressed into a hard line. Gone was the friendly Mr. Lim.

"How do you know about that?" he asked, his voice stern.

"Jack Shen told me when I met with him a few days ago. So what changed your mind?" Matt pressed, knowing his time was running short.

With a curt sigh, Mr. Lim slid the glass of water in front of Matt. "Everything seemed to happen at once. Years ago, I mortgaged the house to keep my business open. After I closed the store, our old renters left. Without renters, I couldn't afford this lot on my own. When my wife died, Jack approached us about selling. At the time, it didn't make sense to keep that big house, but then Cadence offered to send money, so we stayed. When Jack decided to sell again earlier this year, I considered it. Tristan had been talking about finding his own place with Linda, but then they broke up for a while." Mr. Lim threw up his hands with sigh. "So we decided to keep it for now. I told Tristan he could live in the back house, but he said it was up to Linda."

"Are you going to sell now?" Mr. Lim didn't respond, so Matt presented what he knew. "I made some calls and I can tell you that a developer would pay twice its worth if it meant getting the entire corner of this block. You wouldn't have to worry about money for a while. Even for a fixer-upper, the comps in this area are really good."

Mr. Lim considered Matt's words, but eventually shook his head. "No. It's bad luck to move with the baby coming."

"Oh?" Tristan and Linda's baby. Matt hesitated, unsure if he should play dumb, but Mr. Lim gave him a knowing look. "You found out about it?"

"Ah!" Mr. Lim swatted the air. "Who do they think they're fooling?" He made a circle with his arms around his belly. "Linda is out to here now. My phone wouldn't stop ringing when people saw her grocery shopping."

"Have they told you yet?"

"No, but they know I know."

This family and their secrets. From a distance, Matt heard a door shut. He glanced out the window and saw Cadence setting down her clubs to rearrange the boxes back along the shelf.

"Look," Matt said, cutting to the quick. "Bad luck or not, financially speaking, it's a good time to sell. Who knows? It could be a new beginning for everyone. You. Tristan. Linda. The baby."

"And what about Cadence?"

Matt didn't know how to respond to that. The new beginning Matt wanted for her was with him.

"What about me?"

The screen door squeaked behind Matt. Cadence stood outside the doorway, her eyes darting between Matt and her dad. "Are you going to give me a hand?" Cadence's eyes widened, signaling that she was offering him an out. "The sooner we move things back, we can be on our way."

"Wait. Before you go . . ." Mr. Lim shuffled to the overflowing mail organizer on the wall and lifted a set of keys from a hook below. "Tristan needs you to drive his car to the body shop. He said someone was interested in buying it."

"What? He's selling it?" Cadence was floored.

Matt accepted the keys from Mr. Lim and discreetly exchanged them with his business card. "Always good chatting with you, Mr. Lim. Hope to talk again soon," Matt said brightly, which got no reaction from Cadence's dad. Matt turned around and jiggled the keys as he made his way toward Cadence.

"I NEVER THOUGHT I'd see the day . . ."

Sitting in the passenger seat, Cadence smoothed her hand over the dashboard, stopping short of the rectangular air freshener that hovered over the vents. It had a fruity, new car smell. Matt suggested following Cadence to the body shop where Tristan worked, but she was afraid to drive Tristan's '97 Integra. According to her, the car was Tristan's first baby. When Matt offered to drive instead, Cadence insisted on riding along with him, knowing that Tristan would be pissed if Cadence let someone outside their family drive his precious car unsupervised. It wasn't a hard sell on Matt. Tristan kept his car in pristine condition, reminding Matt of the days he used to flip through car magazines with those hot import models. They had well-written articles, he presumed.

Cadence seemed to have a mild heart attack watching him back out of the driveway. Because the car was lowered, she refused to get in the car until he pulled up to the curb, reminding him that Tristan would know if there was the tiniest scratch on its waxed and polished surface. As he merged onto the main thoroughfare, heading east, she gripped the handle above her window like she was holding on for dear life over this ten-minute drive. Cadence needed to chill out and live a little.

When the traffic light turned green, Matt stepped on the gas. "Yeah!" Matt he shouted over the roaring exhaust, living out his *Fast and Furious* dreams.

"Stop! There's a—"

Whoop. Blue and red lights flashed in the extra-wide rearview mirror.

Cadence groaned. "I was trying to warn you. Cops like to hide in small residential streets to catch people speeding. If Tristan finds out we got a ticket, he'll kill us."

In the side mirror, Matt watched the police officer—a bald Asian dude with an average build—approach the car. The cop knocked on the dark-tinted window, towering over Matt since the car was so low.

"Oh shit," Cadence said, sinking into her seat while Matt rolled down the window. What was she so worried about? He wasn't driving over the speed limit (by much). If Matt played his cards right, he could talk his way out of a ticket.

"License and regi—" The cop paused once he noticed Matt's face. "You're not Tristan." Leaning his arm against the roof, the cop stuck his head into the car. "Cadence?" he asked with shock and awe.

Cadence reluctantly leaned forward in her seat. "Hi, Brandon," she greeted with a cutesy wave that Matt had never seen her do before. Suddenly he felt like he was caught in the middle of something.

Officer Brandon apparently thought so too, because he walked around to the passenger side to speak to Cadence directly. "Oh my god. Cadence! I haven't seen you—"

"In a long time. I know." Cadence laughed nervously as she demurely tucked her hair behind her ear.

"You look the same," he said, giving her the once-over. "What brings you back home?"

"I'm in town for business. This is my coworker, Matt."

Demoted back to coworker. Great.

Matt greeted Brandon with a head nod. "Sup?"

Brandon did the same. "Hope I didn't scare you guys. It's been a while since I pulled Tristan over. I wanted to give him a hard time. I gave him a warning about these windows months ago. They're too dark. Crazy about him and Linda, right? It's about time. And you," he said to Cadence, "you're going to be an aunt!"

"Yup. How 'bout that?" Cadence laughed awkwardly. "We'll keep the windows down when we drive," she said, trying to wrap up the conversation.

Brandon didn't get the hint. "So, what are you doing later?"

"Working," Matt interjected. "If you don't mind, we must get going. You know how it is. Time is money." Matt had never said that phrase before in his life. "Thanks, man."

If Cadence hadn't been there, Matt wouldn't have been so bold as to brush off a police officer. It didn't stop Brandon from writing his number for her on the back of a voided ticket.

Before Matt could ask, Cadence filled him in. "Brandon is Tristan's friend. No, we never dated because he's, like, way older than me. He always treated me like Tristan's kid sister. Not sure where this came from. I guess he's still single."

Matt tried not to take too much pleasure in watching Cadence tear up the ticket. "So, you really do know everyone in town."

"More like everyone knows me. I'm telling you. My dad is well-known around these parts."

"Do you know that lady?" Matt pointed at a random auntie carrying a tray of boba.

"She works at the pharmacy that my dad goes to. That was a coincidence."

"What about those Asian guys with the popular YouTube channel?"

"I saw them once in a Target, but I never met them. They're not exactly part of my dad's social circle."

Matt continued to quiz her while he drove. Cadence didn't want to play along, but every so often, she'd point out someone she recognized. Most of the people she identified were people she remembered visiting her house. Her dad really did seem to know everyone in town. Cadence shrugged it off as she instructed Matt to make a left turn, exiting San Gabriel and into the industrial part of the neighboring city of El Monte, where the warehouses and auto shops that lined the dusty, barren street had faded under the sun.

They spotted Tristan pacing along the sidewalk, anxiously awaiting their arrival. Matt suspected that Tristan didn't want him to pull the car into the parking lot, which had piles of cars waiting to be repaired. Matt parked the Integra on the street, leaving it running for Tristan.

"I can't believe you're selling it," Cadence said as she climbed out.

"Can't fit a car seat in here," Tristan said dryly while he waited for Matt to get out of the driver's seat.

"I heard you were getting back into photography," she said casually, shutting the door ever so gently. "I looked you up. Nice website."

Tristan shrugged. "Couldn't hurt to have some extra cash with a baby on the way. Thanks, man," he said to Matt before he got in and slowly swerved his car, inching his way up into the auto shop's parking lot.

"He really is a man of few words, isn't he?" Matt asked as he swiped his phone, searching for a ride back.

"Mm-hmm," she replied like it was an afterthought. Cadence stared at a nondescript warehouse across the street that had a narrow strip of cloudy windows near the roof.

"What is that place?" There were no signs along the brick building, except for one that read NO TRESPASSING on the parking lot gate.

"That's where my mom last worked. She used to sew clothes that you could buy for ten bucks when she was paid half that per hour. I didn't find out until after she died that she skipped her doctor's appointments." Her eyes fell to the sidewalk. Matt turned toward her, intending to comfort her, but she folded into her crossed arms, pivoting away from him. "She always said she was fine, that there was no reason to take time off and go to the doctor when she felt healthy."

Cadence's voice began to tremble, but her eyes were dry. "I thought with time the grief would go away, but it doesn't. Sometimes it slides in with a small memory, like . . . you know the tag on the back of your shirt? They used to print those in a big perforated sheet and my mom used to pay me a quarter to tear them apart." The corners of her lips lifted, but not quite into a smile.

"And other times"—she glanced at the warehouse—"it stares at you in the face like it wants to crush you."

Matt remembered the profound loss he felt when Lolo passed away, but his family rallied together as they grieved. He wanted to hold Cadence and tell her that what she was feeling was normal, that she had him to lean on. But the way Cadence continued to stare at the building with steely eyes, in her hardened stance, made him keep his distance. It seemed like the only thing he was supposed to do—or could do—was listen. "What was she like?"

"My mom was a fixer. There wasn't any problem that couldn't be resolved. She was stubborn in that way. Once I needed a new dress for a school recital, and instead of buying a new one, she took a dress from the factory that had a crooked seam. It was going to get thrown out anyway. It was black, so the seam wasn't that noticeable from far away, but I was embarrassed wearing it to school." Cadence worked her jaw, reflecting. "There was a brief period where my dad's business was doing okay. She quit working at the factory and it was like my mom transformed from this bone-tired woman into this soccer mom. Except instead of soccer, she shuttled Tristan to tutoring and me to the golf course. She watched all my tournaments. The local ones, I mean. She was too scared to drive on the freeway."

Cadence chuckled into a sniffle. "We were her world and she wanted big things for us. She pushed us because she wanted us to do our best, not to uphold some aspirational reputation like my dad. But I don't think she realized that meant us leaving. Dad was livid when Tristan came home to pursue his auto tech degree, but Mom liked having Tristan home. She hoped the same would happen with me. That I'd come home someday." Cadence's hands curled into fists. "I know death is a part of life and that parents die before their children. That's the natural order of things. I get that part. But she didn't leave. She was taken from me. From Tristan. From my dad. That's the part I can't reconcile."

Their ride came, prematurely ending their conversation. Cadence stayed silent during the drive back to her dad's house. Her disclosure was an anomaly. After Cadence loaded her golf clubs into Matt's rental, she spent the ride to the hotel peering at her phone, reviewing the course at Rolling Vista Country Club, where the YREPLA golf tournament was taking place.

Once they returned to their hotel suite, Cadence spent the rest of the day on golf. As much as he liked watching her whip the air with her swing, Matt couldn't help feeling guilty. This trip was supposed to be her vacation time and she spent most of it helping him. It didn't seem right to ask any more of her than she'd already given, so as promised, he didn't bring up her job offer or continue talks about their five-year projections. In the days leading up to the golf tournament, Matt worked around Cadence and tried not to add more to her plate if he could avoid it.

THURSDAY MORNING CAME too soon. Matt woke up early, anxious about the day. So much was at stake. Cadence felt it too, insisting that she sleep alone to get a good night's rest, claiming it was something she did before every match. He suspected that was maybe half true because she avoided his eyes when she said it.

Matt attempted to make breakfast with the electric griddle but made the mistake of crowding the pan. The eggs bled into the bacon, creating a mutant face. He set two glasses on the counter and started pouring orange juice when he heard Cadence's door click open. If this was Cadence on a good night's sleep, he must stop keeping her up at night.

She had her game face on, tightening her long ponytail over her white visor. The sunlight beamed in through the windows behind her, illuminating her heroine's walk toward the kitchen island. In her white tank top and teal skirt, she swayed her hips like there was a guitar solo from an eighties hair band playing in the background. She stopped at the island and bent down to readjust the tongues on her golf shoes. As she straightened up, her kohl-lined eyes glanced up at him through her eyelashes, conjuring vivid memories of that same look on her face two nights ago when she was down on both knees.

"Matt! You're spilling juice everywhere!"

Matt snapped out of his explicit thoughts and jumped back at the OJ cascading off the quartz countertop. He didn't feel the latent chill until he glanced down at his splattered pants.

"Shit." He set the carton down and stopped Cadence from walking around the island. "Don't come back here or else you'll end up drenched like me."

"Stop being dramatic. I don't see any . . ." Her voice disappeared as her eyes scanned down, stopping where his wet khakis clung to his thighs. He might have enjoyed Cadence staring at his crotch if it didn't look like he had pissed himself.

"You know," Matt said matter-of-factly, "they say you shouldn't look directly at it."

Cadence's head snapped up with a disapproving look. "Are you really comparing your dick to the sun?"

"Well, if you're not careful, it could hurt your eyes."

Cadence pursed her lips and threw a towel at him. "Go change already. You're lucky you didn't get juice on your new shirt."

When Matt returned wearing a fresh pair of gray chinos and his miraculously unspoiled white polo, Cadence unfortunately had finished her stretches.

"How do I look?" Matt gave her a quick spin.

Cadence smirked. "Like you're ready to carry my bag. Let's go before we miss tee time."

CHAPTER 27

CADENCE

Cadence dreamed of playing at places like the Rolling Vista Country Club when she was a junior golfer. The château-style clubhouse was surrounded by roses and manicured topiaries. It was a stark contrast to the municipal golf courses she had practiced at after school.

Cadence and Matt walked past preppy ladies who were on their way to the tennis court and onto the back deck, where the lush golf course began. Under the shade of a jacaranda tree, people they knew from last week's YREPLA mixer checked Cadence and Matt in at the tournament registration table.

"So *you're* Percy's guests." John greeted Matt with a fist bump and a touch of jealousy. "He reserved a golf cart for your party. Please silence your cell phones—clubhouse rules. Last but not least, please tee off on time. There are several groups teeing off after yours, and we want to keep the pace moving."

Cadence collected her scorecard, glad to see that there weren't any hard feelings. "Thanks, John. Has Percy checked in yet?"

"He's been warming up with someone for the last twenty minutes. Claimed he was a colleague of yours."

Damn it. How did Hunter get here so early? Did he sleep on the fairway?

"Thanks." Cadence started down on the winding pathway leading toward the practice area. "Come on. We have to hurry," she said to Matt. To her, twenty minutes with Hunter felt like an eternity. Who knew what kind of bullshit Hunter subjected Percy to this morning?

"We'll be fine," Matt said, following behind. He began to massage Cadence's shoulders, bringing her to a halt.

Cadence turned around and stepped out of his hold. "No. Stop that." She looked around to make sure no one was watching them. "This is a work event. No flirting, no touching. Nothing. The only thing I want Hunter to see today is us kicking his ass. Got it?"

Matt shrank back like a wilted daisy. "Got it." He tentatively extended his arm up like he was about to smooth her hair.

"I said no touching," Cadence hissed. She thought she was pretty clear about that.

"I just was getting this." He lowered his arm to reveal a single lavender bloom between his pinched fingers. "It was on your visor."

Was it possible to swoon and feel guilty at the same time? That's what Matt's puppy-dog eyes were doing to Cadence. She could never let Matt know about this or else he'd use it to get away with everything.

"Sorry. I don't want to cause any gossip and I don't want to mess this up for you." However the day unfolded, whether it was cause for celebration or not, she and Matt were destined to have the conversation about their future. As much as she tried to get a good night's rest, she couldn't stop thinking about it.

"You won't, Lim. You can't," Matt reassured her. "It's not yours to mess up."

"Okay." Cadence nodded, hoping the smell of fresh-cut grass would soothe her like old times, but she was running purely on anxiety at this point. The best she could offer to relieve Matt's concerned face was a small, apologetic smile. "Not bad for your first-time caddying job," she said, patting her golf bag, which he'd slung over his shoulder. "Keep it up."

At the practice area, they found Hunter and Percy chatting over long putts with Percy's assistant, Ian, standing by.

Percy spotted them first, waving them over. "Cadence. Matt. Glad you can join us. Hunter here was letting me test out his new putter."

Cadence greeted Percy with a handshake. "We should head over to the course," she said, trying to remove Hunter from this scenario. Percy handed back Hunter's club as Ian started up the golf cart. Matt loaded Cadence's bag next to Percy's in the cargo bed.

"You're not playing, Matt?" Hunter said, pointing at the one set of clubs between them. "I should join you guys. Up to four players per group."

"We wouldn't want to mess up the tournament schedule," Cadence shouted as she climbed in the back seat. As they drove off, Cadence reminded herself not to take too much time with each shot. Not if Hunter was going to be hot on their tails.

They were the second group to tee off, based on the few divots in the tee box.

"Ladies first," Percy offered, making room for Cadence.

"I believe you'll need this." Matt slipped Harry the Husky off her driver and handed it to Cadence. "I did some research."

She wondered if Matt had googled "How to be a caddy." The thought helped her shake off some nerves.

"Thanks." Cadence wiggled her left hand into her white leather glove. She bent down and punctured her tee into the ground, placing her ball on top. In the background, Matt whispered something that made Percy chuckle. Cadence tuned it out, noting the minimal wind as she lined up her shot to avoid the bunker in the middle of the course. Settling into her stance, she tightened her grip, swung back, and let it rip.

"Whoa," Matt said in the most Keanu way, watching the ball's trajectory. The ball landed in the rough on the edge of the green.

Cadence griped as she stepped out of the tee box for Percy. "I should have come earlier to practice my chip shot." She noted Percy's good form as he reached back and followed through with a nice swing. His ball surpassed hers and bounced right on the green.

"This is going to be a good match," Percy said, making it obvious that he was not referring to the game. Cadence suspected Percy would try to get a decision from her today after his associate Ms. Huang refused to call her back after answering salary questions and clarifying the fine print over email.

"Great shot," Cadence offered, returning the focus back to golf. Everybody had a different agenda and she was caught in the middle of it. There were eighteen holes of ground to cover, so she had set the pace. She kept quiet as they drove to the green, letting Matt rebuild his rapport with Percy. Cadence managed to chip her ball out to make par while Percy scored a birdie.

Matt waited for Cadence to return her putter before throwing the bag over his shoulder. "Glad you changed your mind about letting him win," he whispered.

Cadence schooled her face, hiding her irritation. That wasn't her plan at all, but as luck would have it, she found herself trailing behind Percy hole after hole. It was a result of rushing through her shots, but she needed them to move through the course without running into Hunter. She was relieved when she finally caught a break at hole 7, when Percy's ball got stuck in a bunker after Cadence shot back-to-back eagles. Along the way, she overheard Matt and Percy discuss iStan's expansion plans. Percy was much more loose-lipped in this relaxed environment. A few times, she heard Matt mention her name, referring to the market report that she wasn't able to present when they met at the convention center.

Matt and Percy were deep in conversation by hole 8. Hunter was nowhere to be found, so Cadence allowed herself a little more time. She crouched down, using her putter as leverage to examine the long putt she had to make to take the lead.

"So focused," Percy commented behind her.

"That's how she is on every project," Matt replied. "It's why she's so good at what she does."

Cadence felt the small flutter in her stomach. Not that she cared much for flattery, but it was big of Matt to say this, since it sounded like he was vouching for her to her potential employer.

"It's funny, because when I spoke to Hunter earlier, he mentioned the 'excellent research team' he'd bring to L.A. I noticed he didn't mention you. I wondered what that could have meant," Percy said. "Perhaps he knew you'd be going elsewhere?"

"Um." Cadence pushed herself up to face Percy, but she looked back down at the green when she found expectant gazes from two men awaiting different answers. "I doubt that. Hunter and I don't work together very much." Planting her feet, she lined up her shot, giving the ball a firm tap. Cadence leaned back as the ball curved and clenched her fist when it dropped into the hole.

"It means he's not smart if he didn't think to include the best person on the research team," Matt said in heightened tone that he usually reserved for pitches. Cadence glanced over her shoulder. She had to see Matt's face to see his intentions because his statement felt bigger than his everyday praise. When their eyes met, Matt's lips pulled into a hint of a smile, an unspoken mutual understanding. This game was no longer solely for Matt's gain. Matt was showing up for her.

"Fore!"

Cadence instinctively ducked as a ball bounced three feet away from her.

"Sorry, Cadence," Hunter shouted as he jogged up, his group nowhere in sight. He lowered his bag and readjusted his cap, briefly exposing his sandy brown hair.

"We were just talking about you," Percy said. "All good things."

"Oh, I bet," Hunter said, shooting Matt a suspicious glare before he plastered on a fake smile for Percy. "Do you mind if I join you guys? The group I'm in are a bunch of duffers. Their best player is at a plus fifteen."

If his group was that slow, Hunter must have ditched them early to catch up to Cadence and Matt.

"There's not enough room on the cart," Matt said.

"I don't mind walking. It's a nice day out." Hunter tapped his ball in. "What do you say, Percy?"

Cadence wasn't sure if it was Hunter's persistence or the fact that he put Percy on the spot, but Percy obliged.

"Let's walk, then," Percy said, waving a signal to Ian, who

quickly loaded Percy's clubs. "Ian can follow behind us with the cart."

Hunter quickly swooped in and walked off with Percy, leaving Matt and Cadence scrambling.

"That asshole," Matt grumbled as he lifted Cadence's bag onto the cargo bench.

"Were you able to make headway with Percy? It sounded promising, from the bits and pieces I overheard."

"Yeah, but who knows what Hunter has up his sleeve?" Matt kept his voice low as they trailed behind Percy and Hunter. "Powerful friends with deep pockets?"

"It's not like that ever helped him close more deals than you," Cadence mused. "The only way he could make himself look better than you is . . ."

Cadence picked up the pace to a light jog to stay within earshot of Percy and Hunter. If her hunch was right, then she had gone about it the wrong way. Instead of avoiding Hunter, she should have kept him under close surveillance.

"What's wrong?" Matt whispered, catching up behind her.

"The only way he could make himself look better than you is to make you look worse."

"W hat's your deal, man?" Matt asked Hunter after he teed off. Cadence was trying to monopolize Percy's attention, asking him about his favorite golf courses. "We both know that my numbers are better than yours and none of my clients are my mom's or dad's friends, so whatever you're doing, it's not going to work."

Hunter chortled. "You're full of shit, Matt. You really think you had a shot? This job was always going to be mine. You're making things more difficult than they need to be."

"For once, it wouldn't hurt you to work for something," Matt retorted.

Hunter let out a deep belly laugh to cover up Matt's sharp tone, which made Cadence and Percy turn their heads. "Fuck off," Hunter said under his breath. *Clink.* "Nice shot, Percy!" Hunter turned his attention back to Matt. "If you can't close this deal, then maybe you're not as good as you think you are."

"Everything good over here?" Percy said, pulling his glove off, finger by finger.

"Just a little friendly competition. Right, Matt?" Hunter said, slapping Matt's back as if they were bros. Matt wanted to wipe Hunter's shit-eating grin off his fake-tanned face. Whatever orange tanning lotion Hunter had slapped on, he had forgotten to work it into his face. His pale skin peeked through his wrinkles whenever he laughed. It reminded Matt of those dried, forgotten baby carrots that he'd find in the back of his fridge.

Hunter blew out a low whistle. "Look at that," he said, jutting his chin at Cadence, who adjusted her stance, feet shoulder width apart, for a few practice swings. "Don't tell me you never tapped that."

"Shut the fuck up, Hunter." Matt didn't care if it was unprofessional or against clubhouse rules. Hunter had crossed the line. This wasn't some boys' club, and Cadence wasn't there for Hunter's entertainment.

"*Ooh*, you did, didn't you? And here I thought your type was more fun and enthusiastic, like Ashley. I ran into her at the mixer last week before you arrived and we had a nice chat about her life after Prism. I didn't know you had a thing for interns."

Damn it. Ashley was the mistake that kept on giving. Matt quickly glanced at Cadence. If she overheard their conversation, she wasn't letting on. Not wanting to take his chances, Matt stepped close to Hunter and lowered his voice. "If you have a problem with me, then take it up with me. There's no need to make it personal."

Hunter produced a haughty laugh. "You made it personal when you snuck down here to steal my job from under me."

"What the fuck are you talking about?"

"Don't play dumb, Matt. It would have been more believable if you'd said that you came down here with Cadence to fuck around.

But no. You pretended to come here to salvage this deal, but then you asked Kevin to work on some listing that turned out to be some teardown motel in the middle of nowhere. And here's what I don't get. You told Kevin you weren't going to take the listing, but when I called the owner, he said he promised the listing to you since you convinced the owner of the house next door to sell too."

"What?!" Cadence shouted as she swung, interrupting her momentum. Both men turned in time to see her ball plop into the water. "What is he talking about?"

Matt had no idea, but he had to think fast. "He's making shit up."

"Call Jack," Hunter goaded. "He'll tell you. Said the neighbor decided this morning."

Matt slipped out his phone from his pocket, thinking to himself how Kevin was going on his shit list, and his face fell when he saw several missed calls from Jack Shen.

"Gentlemen." Percy stood between Hunter and Matt. "Maybe you should take this off course. Cadence and I will finish the round."

"Percy, I'm sorry, but can I take a rain check?" During the fray, Cadence listened to her voice mail. Her frantic dialing confirmed that everything Hunter said was true.

"Cadence, let me explain."

Cadence ignored Matt, speaking Chinese into her phone at a fast clip.

"I can take her place," Hunter said, picking up his bag.

"You know what? I changed my mind." Percy signaled his assistant Ian to load his clubs onto the golf cart. "I'll finish the course on my own. I'd like to rest before I meet with other brokers. Matt, my office will be in touch with you."

Matt dragged his hand down his face as his shot for a promotion drove down the fairway.

"Looks like my job here is done." Hunter left one last departing jab. "No cell phones on the course!"

Matt clenched his fist, ready to punch Hunter's ugly-ass face, but from the corner of his eye, he saw Cadence shut off her phone and storm off toward the water to retrieve her ball.

"Cadence, slow down." Matt chased after her.

"How long have you known?"

"Since last Wednesday, after I met with Jack."

Cadence stopped and swung around, wielding her putter at him, forcing him to back away. "Why didn't you tell me? When did you speak to my dad?"

"Let's talk about this at home."

"Home? I might not have a home anymore, thanks to you!" Cadence spotted her ball at the edge of the water and took a reckless swing, missing it entirely, and slammed her putter into a rock. Cadence cried out in pain, reaching for her lower back. "Fuck!"

"Cadence! Are you okay?"

"I'm fine!" she insisted as she tested a few steps away from him. "I can walk it ou—ow!" Cadence gripped her knees as she folded in half.

"Let me help you." Alarmed, Matt looked around and waved down a nearby golf cart. "Please. I'll explain on the way back." Cadence agreed. She didn't really have much of a choice in the matter. The golf cart belonged to a Rolling Vista staff member, who was kind enough to call the valet to have Matt's car brought around while he drove them up through the side road that led to the front entrance.

When they reached his car, Matt first lowered her seat so that she could lie down before helping her up. The vulnerable position didn't stop her from letting her feelings be known, and she did not mince words.

"When were you going to tell me? When my childhood home gets demolished to make way for what? Another stand-alone plaza for some car insurance agency and knife-cut noodle shop? Displacing my family for that?"

"They're not being displaced," Matt said her as he drove back to their hotel. This was not how this conversation was supposed to go. He could hardly summon the will to defend himself when Cadence was lying in pain. "Your dad has been approached about selling the house for the last four years."

"Four years?" she repeated. "You mean when my mom died? He was clearly not in the state of mind to make a huge decision. One he should have informed me of, so I didn't have to find out after . . ." Cadence slammed her arm on the center console. "No wonder my room was packed up!"

"I'm not disagreeing with you," Matt said calmly. "If your dad didn't want to sell, then it was a nonissue. But the opportunity was on the table. I thought it could help everyone."

"How? Since when did you become an expert on my family?" *This week?* "Don't you dare answer that," she snapped, as if she read his mind. "You had no right to meddle," she said, suddenly choking back tears.

Matt reached for her hand, but she swatted it away, grimacing from overexerting herself. "I know I should have told you earlier, but you had so much on your mind this week with your mom and work. I didn't want you to worry if it was over nothing. I turned down the listing. When I spoke with your dad, he didn't seem interested, so I didn't tell you. I'm sorry. I really am, but I had no idea you would be so upset. Whenever it comes up, you make it very clear that you don't want to live there."

Matt knew before Cadence brought her seat upright that it was the wrong thing to say.

"I *don't* want to live there," she said, her voice wavering, "but, Matt. It's my childhood home. I don't have to live there for it to mean something to me."

When they returned to the hotel, Cadence didn't take off her shoes or complain about her clothes upon entering the suite. She ambled to her room like a zombie without saying a word.

Matt drove down to the nearest pharmacy and picked up a slew of pain medication—pills, ointment, Salonpas patches—not knowing what Cadence preferred. She accepted them all when he returned but stayed in her room. While he waited out the silent treatment, Matt followed up on his missed calls and emails. Sadie emailed for updates, but he had nothing. Matt requested another meeting with Percy before he left town, but to no avail. There was no way he would call Jack back. Accepting the listing would make matters worse.

Hours later, Cadence emerged from her room, smelling like menthol and wearing a new outfit, but not her home clothes. She had on her jeans, a plain T-shirt, and a red cardigan, the same one she'd had on at the airport. Puffy-eyed, she went to the bathroom to splash her face.

"What are you doing?" Matt asked from the hallway after she held up her hand, making it clear that she didn't want him to enter.

"I'm leaving," she replied, void of emotion, as she dabbed her face with a towel.

"You need to rest."

"I'm fine," she sniffled, filling up her quart-size plastic bag with her tiny moisturizers and cleansers. When she was done, she walked past him without meeting his eyes and packed the toiletries into her overstuffed duffel bag. She stood at her room's doorway for one final sweep.

"Cadence." Matt picked up her duffel for her so she wouldn't strain her back. "Let's talk."

She stood as tall as she could. Her voice was as cool as steel. "There's nothing I want to say."

"So you're just going to leave? What about us?"

"What about us?" Cadence repeated, incredulous. She blew out a shaky breath. "It was fun while it lasted, but this is not going to work. So let's not drag this out."

"Cadence. Please stay. I can explain—"

"What's there to explain? You told me that Best Eastern didn't work out, but you turned around and secretly spoke with my father because it would help *you*, not me."

Matt closed his eyes and tried to stay calm. "Do you really think I would do that?"

Cadence crossed her arms and bit on her quavering lip. Matt thought she might have lost some conviction, but then she said, "I don't care if you felt like you did the right thing. You crossed a line."

"I'm sorry. I really am, but you have to cut me some slack here. I'm not a mind reader." Case in point, Cadence's face was made of stone. "What was your plan? Run and hide like you always do?"

His barbed words were meant to stoke Cadence's competitive nature, a challenge for her to stay, but it backfired. Her face paled while her lips pressed into a tight line. Cadence tugged on the duffel bag's strap, but Matt refused to hand it over.

"Fine. Keep it." She walked around him, carefully slung her purse over her shoulder, and grabbed her carry-on. "I can travel light. I'm used to it."

"Cadence. Where are you going?" Matt was ready to follow her downstairs until she bore into him with her somber eyes, keeping him in the entryway.

"That house was the last place I saw my mother. I can't even . . ." Her voice trailed off while she held back a sob. Matt instinctively reached for her, hoping he could provide her comfort like he had this past week, but Cadence wedged her carry-on between them.

"Cadence," Matt begged. "You know I would never hurt you. I love you."

Matt winced, knowing that it sounded like a last-ditch effort to convince her to stay, but he meant it. Cadence didn't need to say it back, but Matt needed her to know what she was walking away from. That to him, it was more than fun and games.

Cadence shook her expressionless face. "I need to go home."

Cadence left and Matt had no idea which home she was referring to.

CHAPTER 29

CADENCE

C adence sank into the cushy tufted leather couch in the hotel lobby while her phone rang. Maddie picked up on the third ring.

"I'm sorry," Maddie said, acknowledging the loud banging noise and what sounded like a toy playing nursery rhymes on repeat, "James is destroying his room and my sanity. What's up? Wasn't today the big day? How did everything go?"

"Awful." The noise in the background subsided, so Maddie must have stepped away for a second. Not wanting to keep Maddie from James too long, Cadence quickly summed up the last twelve hours. "I hurt my back and Matt left early to take care of me, so the deal is still in limbo. On top of that, my dad's selling the house and Matt knew! He knew about it and he didn't tell me."

"Oh, you didn't know?"

"What?" Did the Salonpas patch seep into her brain and ruin her memory? "Don't tell me you knew too."

"My mom told me a few minutes ago. Your dad told my mom. You know news travels fast around here. Where are you?"

"I'm still at the hotel. I couldn't find a flight to SF." Not a cheap one at least. "How am I supposed to walk into the office on Monday morning? Everyone at work is going to think Matt and I were plotting something or sleeping together this whole time."

"Technically, that last part is true."

Cadence rubbed her forehead as she thought about her options. Everything in her life was in shambles. "Can I crash with you for the weekend while I clear my head?"

"You know you're always welcome here, but I don't think you wanna be around this," Maddie said when the banging noise returned. "Who cares what people think? The rumors never stopped you from getting work done before. You know the truth. On Monday morning, you will put on your best power suit and walk in there with your head held high."

"It's going to be hard to do while Matt is sitting next to me the whole time." Cadence was hurt. To think, she even offered to help Matt with the Best Eastern listing when he went around her and asked Kevin—Kevin of all people!—to look into the property for him.

"What does your gut say?"

The irony. Cadence spent most of her professional life using hard facts to help others make decisions. Here she was, getting advised to go with her gut. How did the gut get the final say on tough calls? She placed her hand on her solar plexus. In this case, Cadence's gut aligned with her brain. "I can't stop thinking about the house."

"Then maybe you should start there," Maddie said. James wailed in the background after what sounded like a bunch of plastic toys tumbled to a crash.

Cadence sighed after they exchanged goodbyes. She opened up her texts to tell Tristan she was on her way there. After she sent it, a new message appeared.

MATT: Sadie asked for an update. Don't worry about it. I'm
     going to tell her that I didn't close the deal.
MATT: I'm sorry.

Cadence couldn't account for the swirl of feelings that rose after reading Matt's messages. She was upset at him over the house, but she couldn't help feeling like she had let him down. They came to L.A. with a mission and they failed. It didn't sit well with her, so before she left for home, she had to take care of one last thing.

THE WAITER SEATED Cadence at a small private table and asked for her drink order. She was tempted to order a glass of wine to ease her nerves, but she thought better of it. She needed to keep a clear mind. She buttoned her cardigan with her shaky fingers, hoping it would make her a little more presentable since she was noticeably underdressed. The Beverly Hills clientele at the restaurant within Percy's hotel weren't in tuxedos or ball gowns. Quite the opposite. The patrons around her also wore jeans and casual attire, but still somehow managed to look more luxe.

Cadence paused her people watching and stood when Percy arrived. She reached across the table to shake his hand. "Thank you for meeting me on short notice. I hope I didn't interrupt your plans."

"Not at all. It may surprise you, but I have to eat dinner too." Percy perused the menu. The waiter returned and took their orders. "Are you in a hurry?" Percy asked in reaction to Cadence's salad order.

"I'm not too hungry." That was a lie. Cadence hadn't eaten since breakfast, but her stomach was twisted in knots.

"How is your back feeling?" he asked, as if he remembered his manners. "I saw the staff help you off the course."

"Better. Thanks." Cadence hoped that the smell from her Salonpas patch was not perceptible from across the table.

"Good." Percy buttered a dinner roll now that formalities were out of the way. "You asked to meet me, so tell me why we're here. Do you have questions, or should I ask for a bottle of champagne to congratulate you?"

"Right." Cadence released the napkin she was wringing under the table. "I do have a question. What are your thoughts on keeping Sansome for your headquarters?"

Frowning, Percy replied, "Don't tell me you're going to waste your time talking about that."

"I am. Thank you for the offer, but respectfully, I must decline. Some urgent family issues have come up and it's not the right time for me to start a new job." As much as the job appealed to her, she couldn't bring herself to accept when her priorities shifted.

"We can postpone your start date if that helps," Percy suggested.

"Thank you, but no."

Their food arrived, providing Cadence small relief from Percy's scowl. After the waiters left, Percy laid his napkin on his lap. "If I knew you were going to turn the job down, I wouldn't have invited you to dinner." He stabbed his piece of salmon to break off a bite. "I wouldn't have been offended if you declined via email."

"I wanted to tell you in person that I sincerely considered the position and I wanted to explain why you should close the deal with Matt."

Percy let out an incredulous *huh*. "Why should I listen after you admitted to a bait and switch?"

"Because I'm giving you some free advice."

"I'm paying for your dinner, so it's not free," he retorted, tearing a piece of bread. "It's just inexpensive advice."

"I can order more food, commensurate to my expertise," Cadence wryly suggested.

That earned Cadence another *huh* from Percy. He took a few more bites before he rolled his wrist, fork in hand, signaling her to continue.

"Please go on. I want to get what I paid for."

CADENCE LEFT THE restaurant with a little bit less weight on her shoulders, knowing that she gave it her best shot. During her ride home, she checked her email and found her inbox full of messages from Bill.

From: Bill Waterson
Subject: Q2 SF Rental Forecast Due

From: Bill Waterson
Subject: East Bay Trends Report

From: Bill Waterson
Subject: South Bay Retail Market Report

Cadence began to see red as she scrolled. The list went on and on, more than Sadie let on when she mentioned having projects waiting for her. Bill was power tripping. Handling a few projects was nothing new, but to have so many assigned to her within the last day seemed retaliatory. Rather than play his game, Cadence decided to cut her losses.

To: BWaterson@prismrealty.com
From: CLim@prismrealty.com
CC: SChan@prismrealty.com
Date: January 20, 2022 7:38 P.M.
Subject: Resignation Letter

To Mr. Waterson,

I'm writing to inform you that I will be resigning from my current position. While this letter serves as my two weeks' notice, I will not be returning to the office and will be taking my postponed vacation. The few personal belongings that remain in my desk can be mailed to my current address.

Thank you,
Cadence Lim

There was a burst of anxiety as she clicked send. Her therapist would have strongly advised her not to make such a rash decision, but once she pushed that email out of her hands, the immediate sense of relief knocked the wind out of her. So far her gut was doing an excellent job.

After an expensive and long ride home, Cadence lumbered toward the front house, dragging her carry-on behind her. Despite the dark winter night, the front house was visible, illuminated by the refracted light from the motel. The screen door creaked open before she made it to the porch.

"You look tired," Dad said. Cadence flinched, unprepared for his critical greeting. "You lost your match today, didn't you?"

In more ways than one. The day had beaten her up and left her bruised. Perhaps it showed, because by the time she reached the porch, Dad stood at the center of the doorway, not letting her brush past him.

"You should go to bed," he said out of concern, not the command she expected. "Tristan is shooting a wedding tonight, so we'll discuss things tomorrow."

Cadence nodded as she walked into the house and toward her bedroom. As she put down her things, her phone rang. Of all people, the last person she expected to hear from was Sadie.

Cadence answered with trepidation. "Hi, Sadie."

"Cadence. You must know why I'm calling. I received your resignation letter and I wanted to check in."

"Everything's fine—"

"People don't resign when things are fine. Did something happen or did you find a new job?"

Cadence didn't want to explain anything to Sadie, but she had to say something to keep her from pressing further. "I have some important family business that I'll need time to handle."

"Is there anything I could offer you to convince you to stay? A promotion? A bump in your salary?"

Oh. It was an odd feeling, being in the position to name her demands. It was nice, but it was all a little too late. "No, but thank you. I do appreciate the offer."

Sadie sniffed, seemingly understanding that Cadence's answer was firm. "I have to say, the CEO in me is sad to see you leave. I had a hunch when you came on board that you would quickly outgrow this job. So, what's next for you?"

"To be determined," Cadence replied.

"I see. Well, I will have Josie call you at the end of your two weeks to schedule an exit interview. If you change your mind or if you ever need a recommendation for your next job, you know how to reach me. One more thing before you go. Percy scheduled a call with me on Monday. Do you know anything about that?"

"No," Cadence lied. Nobody could keep secrets at the office and she didn't want to cause any more speculation. "I had to leave early from the golf tournament today."

When the call ended, Cadence threw her phone on her twin-size bed. She was effectively unemployed, and after ten years away, she was finally back home.

CADENCE WOKE UP the next morning to the sounds of clamoring pots and pans. She carefully got up and padded into the kitchen to see Tristan yawning while he made breakfast. Cadence took a seat at the table and studied him, trying to put herself in his shoes.

Dad shuffled into the kitchen with his house slippers and took the seat beside her. "You feeling better?" Before she could answer, Dad said, "Tristan. Bring two cups of hot water."

Tristan did as he was told and a steaming mug appeared.

"Thanks," Cadence said as she stared at it, waiting for it to cool.

"Leave that," Dad instructed Tristan, who had returned to his simmering pots. "There's something I want to say." Tristan joined the table with a mug of his own. "Listen, I know I surprised both of you when I decided to sell the house. I gave it a lot of thought and I don't want it to be a burden to either of you."

"It's not a burden," Cadence said.

"I'm not going to have you help me pay for a house that you don't even live in. You've done it long enough."

"But what if I did live here? I quit my job."

Dad's eyes were about to pop out of his head. "Why?"

"It wasn't a good job anyway and I need a break. I was hoping to stay here for a while. Can I . . . until it sells?" Cadence wasn't ready to go back to San Francisco and deal with moving out of her apartment, but her ulterior motive was to see if she could possibly live with Dad again. A trial run before she could commit to it and revolve her other decisions around it. "I can help out while I'm here."

"You don't need to ask if you can stay here," Dad replied. "The door is always open for you. And you," he said to Tristan. "I know about the baby."

Tristan recoiled slightly, even though Dad had said it in an even tone. "Are you mad?"

It was a fair question, considering Dad's old-school mentality that first came marriage, then a house, then kids. Now he was sitting before his two kids, one unemployed and the other having a child out of wedlock. They were far below the standards Dad set for them.

"Yes, I'm mad." Dad huffed. "I had to find out I was going to be a grandfather from Mr. Lee. I would have preferred to hear it from you." Dad exhaled after he sipped his water. "If we're all going to live together under the same roof, we have to tell each other these things. There's a lot to sort. Packing the house. Looking for a new place. We have to work together, okay?"

It was the most kumbaya speech she had ever heard from Dad. It was enough for her to hope for more.

"Okay," she said.

Tristan's eyes darted to Cadence. "You're really staying?"

"Yeah. For now."

CHAPTER 30

MATT

Matt laid low until his flight back to San Francisco on Saturday. Before everything crashed and burned, Cadence made him clear his weekend schedule to celebrate his anticipated promotion. Now he didn't have Cadence or a reason to celebrate. Matt had yet to receive a call or email from Percy. When Matt last checked with Josie, Sadie hadn't heard from Percy, either. With each passing hour, Matt knew his chances for the promotion were diminishing.

Back in his apartment, Matt rolled in his luggage and the duffel bag Cadence left behind. He considered dropping off her stuff, but she hadn't contacted him since she left. He texted her once, asking if she got home safely. No reply. Cadence was always clear about her boundaries, so he wanted to show her that he could still respect her space, even though he wanted to bombard her with texts. He could wait until he saw her at the office.

Holding the largest IOU coffee he could buy, Matt waited outside their building on Monday morning. Colleagues greeted him as they walked into the building. Nothing seemed out of the ordinary until Frank stopped to ask Matt how the meeting with Percy went. Everybody in the office must know if Frank knew about it. Matt kept an eye over Frank's shoulder as he answered, hoping that he didn't miss Cadence. Instead, he caught a glimpse of Hunter's smug face before he entered the building.

Matt waited as long as he could, but when the coffee became cold, he knew it was time to go in. Before he reached his desk, Josie accosted him.

"Sadie would like to see you," she said, personally escorting him down the hall.

"Hello to you too. What's going on?"

Josie refused to answer. Someone got out of the wrong side of the bed this morning.

Before Josie could knock, the door to Sadie's office opened. Bill huffed past Matt, while the rest of the senior management filed out, offering curt, foreboding greetings. Matt flapped his open jacket, airing out his nerves.

"Good luck," Josie said, leaving him alone to face his fate.

"Matt." Sadie gestured to the open seat in front of her desk. "We need to talk." She moved a stack of files aside and laid her crossed arms down on her desk. Matt gulped and took a seat as if he was in the principal's office. Twisting her jade stud earring, Sadie said with her ominous voice, "I spoke with Percy a few minutes ago." Matt kept his head down and spun the cardboard sleeve around the coffee cup. He was blanking out on excuses for his failure.

"Congratulations on getting iStan back."

Matt's eyes flew up. "What? Are you for real right now?" Sadie replied with an arched eyebrow. Why did he say that? Matt cleared

CIRCLING BACK TO YOU   293

his throat and proceeded with more proper decorum. "What did Percy say?"

"That his lawyer will be in touch with you soon to wrap up Sansome, so long as you give him the first month's rent free as an act of good faith for all the delays he'll anticipate with the construction." Matt couldn't believe this guy. Percy was trying to squeeze every last dollar out of this deal. He was ready to concede because this haggling needed to be over. Sadie lowered her voice, even though no one else was around. "Percy also mentioned that he did not find Hunter's comments about Cadence to be professional. Do you know anything about that?"

Matt nearly crushed Cadence's cup of coffee. "I probably shouldn't repeat them without Human Resources present."

Sadie seemed to understand the gravity of the situation. "Please document the incident so we have it on record. I will see to it that it gets taken care of." Matt thought she would explain, but she didn't. Instead she extended her hand for a handshake. Matt offered his hand, unsure what he was about to agree to.

"With that said, thank you for your hard work, *Director*."

Blood rushed in his body, mixing a heady cocktail of serotonin and adrenaline. The years of cold calls, late nights, drawn-out negotiations—all of it led him here. He was so pumped, he couldn't wait to tell his family the good news. The group chat was about to get lit.

"I'm happy for you, Matt. You have your work cut out for you. Josie will invite you to the next senior management meeting and you need to coordinate with HR to staff the L.A. office in time for the April launch."

"I want to hire Cadence," he blurted. When Percy mentioned Hunter bringing a team to L.A., Matt wondered why he never thought of that. As the director, he could hire anyone. The one person he had to have was Cadence.

Sadie's eyebrow reached higher this time. "I'm sorry. I don't understand."

What was there to understand?

"I want to hire Cadence," Matt repeated. He didn't know how else to say it. Was he supposed to say *please*? Did directors have to say please?

Sadie blinked. "You haven't thought this through, Matt. One, I don't think Cadence would want to work *for* you. Second, you can't steal my employee away from me. I'm still your boss."

Matt sank into his seat. He *was* supposed to say *please*.

"Although I suppose it's not considered poaching if they're gone."

Matt's ears perked up. "What do you mean, gone?"

"You really are the worst work husband, you know that?" Sadie sighed. "She didn't tell you that she resigned?"

Matt jumped out of his seat. "Resigned?! When?"

Sadie lowered a single pointed finger and directed Matt to sit back down. "I shouldn't have told you that now that it's a personnel issue. But whatever is going on between you two, please sort it out on your own time." She flipped open a manila folder, effectively dismissing him. "Congratulations again. See Josie on your way out."

Matt stormed out into the hallway and stopped at Josie's desk. If anyone knew what was going on, it was her. "Josie. Where's Cadence?"

Josie continued to type without looking up. "I am not to speak on personnel matters, nor am I obligated to answer you. As far as I'm concerned, directors are middle managers, and I am still higher than you on the org chart. You do *not* get to take that tone with me, *sir*."

Matt rolled his neck as he tried to collect himself. He was 0 for 3 with women this morning. Time to try a different strategy. He took a seat at the edge of her desk. "Hey," he said with a crooked smile and a honeyed tone. "I'm sorry. Did you have a nice weekend?"

Josie withdrew a sharp letter opener from her drawer and pointed it at his chin. "Get off my desk and stop that shit. It's not going to work on me."

"Aw, come on," Matt said as he stood up. "I thought we were friends."

"Whatever. You broke my ship," she said bitterly.

"What do you mean? Are we playing Battleship right now?"

"No, dummy." She gave him an exasperated look like she was trying to explain something to a kid. "A ship! I was hoping to see you and Cadence get together. Now I'll never have that chance."

"What do you mean? When is she coming into the office?"

"She's not. She took the next two weeks off and then she's going to Irish-exit out of this joint like it's a boring party."

Matt couldn't tell if he was breathing anymore. He had to call Cadence. Matt patted his pockets in search of his phone, which began to ping in quick succession.

"That's me," Josie explained. "I'm adding you to all the management meetings this week and with HR. This is only until you get set up in L.A. Then you're on your own until you get your own assistant. Got it?"

"You can't tell me anything else about Cadence?" Matt asked again.

"You better hurry." Josie swiveled her chair to pick up her office phone. "Your meeting with HR starts in ten minutes."

Matt took long strides down the hallway and through the open floor. Already, colleagues offered their congratulations, which he acknowledged with a nod and a short thanks. He didn't have time to engage with it. He had to make a small detour on the way to HR.

Matt stood on Cadence's side of their cubicle and placed the coffee cup on her desk. It was just as she left it, except for her weary plant, which slouched in its lopsided vase. There was her stapler labeled with her name, a sample bottle of moisturizer, and a wire mesh cup of her cheap pens that nobody stole. Next to her hand sanitizer, there was her box of ugly paper clips that she'd use whenever she returned documents to Kevin. If she had been here, Matt would certainly receive one. He deserved the whole box.

There was nothing of significance on her desk. No pictures. No favorite mug. Not even a nameplate. Matt picked up the keyboard. He flipped it upside down, and took out his frustration, shaking the hell out of it. Not a single crumb fell out. She left nothing behind. It was like she'd never been there.

CHAPTER 31

CADENCE

Two weeks had passed since Cadence moved back home. She thought moving back would be like riding a bicycle. She hadn't expected there to be a learning curve. She'd lived with Dad and Tristan before, but *before* was the operative word. Before, Cadence didn't know Dad had routine doctor appointments to attend every month. Before, she didn't know how many hours Tristan must have used up over the years to take care of Dad's affairs such as his Social Security and postponing his jury duty. Before, she didn't know Dad would swindle her into buying fast food, which she later found out was contraband in their house. So much for telling each other things.

On Friday morning, after breakfast, Cadence chauffeured Dad to run some errands. They first set off for the Chinese herbal store. Red Lunar New Year decorations were plastered in every aisle weeks ahead of the holiday, while a jaunty erhu tune projected from above. Dad waited at the counter for his supplements while Cadence browsed the clear plastic bins of preserved dried plums and beef jerky.

"Are you Mr. Lim's daughter?"

A group of aunties that Cadence vaguely remembered meeting once at her dad's shop surrounded her. They were grandmas now, though they tried to hide it with their stark bottle-black hair.

"Yes. Hello." Cadence laughed nervously as she searched for an escape route, but the aunties had her cornered.

"Wah," Tall Auntie marveled aloud, clasping her hands behind her back. "I almost didn't recognize you. Are you visiting for New Year's? I remember your mom saying you were living in New York. Or was it Seattle?"

"No, it was San Francisco," the middle auntie interjected, the angle of her tattooed eyebrow harsher than her tone.

"Yes, San Francisco," the third auntie said, clutching her potent bag of dried shiitake mushrooms against her quilted jacket. Cadence felt like an interloper, since they were really having this conversation amongst themselves. "Good thing you're back in warmer weather."

"You know what they say. 'The coldest winter I ever spent was a summer in San Francisco,'" Cadence said. The ladies laughed it off. They probably didn't know she was quoting Mark Twain.

Cadence was about to excuse herself when the third auntie said, "Your dad told us when we visited your house for your mom's death anniversary."

"Oh?" These were the ladies Dad invited? Cadence wondered how they knew her mom. If they were close. "I'm sorry I didn't get to see you then."

"It's okay," Middle Auntie said. "We know how important it is to work." She gave Cadence's wrist a quick squeeze and repeated it, making her way up to her elbow, as if to check her muscle mass. Cadence never understood elders who felt comfortable invading her personal space like that, but Middle Auntie didn't mean any harm by it. "You're a lot like her."

"I am?" Cadence supposed she resembled her mom, especially as she'd gotten older, though that wasn't the common response she received in the past.

"When we used to work at the factory, your mom used to say the funniest things. Kept us laughing while we sewed." Tall Auntie smiled as if she remembered something Mom might have said. "We're sad she's gone."

Cadence swallowed. "Me too."

"It's good that you're here for your dad," Middle Auntie said. "It was very hard on him."

Cadence turned to check on Dad. He was busy chatting it up with the herbalist. The image was similar to the way Dad had received guests at the funeral. At the time, it upset Cadence that he wasn't outwardly heartbroken like she was. It was hard to know how he was feeling when he was masking his grief by falling on what he did best. But wasn't that what she'd done by going back to work?

"We'll let you go. We have so much shopping to do," Tall Auntie said. "If you don't have any plans, you can come to our house for New Year's."

"Thanks," Cadence said, though she wasn't sure if she'd take her up on the invitation. Dad showed up after the aunties left with his bag of herbs. "How come you didn't come say hi?"

"Ah." Dad frowned as he shook his head. "I always see them. Why are you standing here? New Year's candy is over there." He pointed at the huge display with dried fruit trays and red lucky candy that always got stuck in Cadence's teeth.

"Maybe later," she said. "Is there anything else you need?"

Dad looked at her funny. She thought he was suspicious of her warm tone, but then he said, "We have all of this at home." He pointed at the boxes of red envelopes and firecracker decorations. "Unless you want some extra good luck? You seem to have run out these days."

Cadence rolled in her lips. What do you know? She didn't feel sad anymore.

"When we get home, can you fix my phone?" Dad shoved his phone in her face. "Why are there so many little pictures at the top? They bother me."

Cadence closed her eyes and counted to ten. Explaining (and re-explaining) technology in Hakka was not a competency she acquired yet. She swiped all his notifications away and moved on, wondering if she could convince him to go back to a flip phone. "All done. Let's go."

FATHERHOOD WAS DOING a number on Tristan because later that afternoon he pulled into the driveway in a white minivan. Cadence went out the back door to check out his new ride, surprised that it still had factory rims. After parking in front of the garage, Tristan stepped out to lift up the garage door and shuffle boxes around.

"Making room for the car?" Cadence asked, scoping out the minivan's interior. Tristan was going to learn the hard way that beige was a stain magnet.

"No." Tristan rummaged through a box, grumbling that he should have labeled them. "I'm looking for those thick red sticks of incense. The extra-tall ones."

ольории

"The ones for weddings?" Cadence opened a box to aid in the search. "Are you trying to tell me something?"

"I asked Linda to marry me and she said yes," Tristan said unceremoniously. "We're going to get married at the courthouse in a few weeks, but Linda still wants to do a tea ceremony with our parents beforehand."

"I'm happy for you guys." Cadence gave him a congratulatory pat on the back. "Tea ceremony would be a smart move. I think Dad would like that. Does he know?"

"Yeah. He should. I texted him before I drove home."

"You texted?" Cadence wanted to slap some sense into her brother, but her arm froze when he reached for the box on the edge of the second shelf. "Don't open that. It's from Mom's funeral."

"Oh." His arms fell and dangled by his sides. "I forgot. Thanks."

"Is it weird that we kept things from her funeral?" Cadence murmured, unsure how Tristan would react. After the funeral, Cadence flew back to San Francisco and tried to bury her feelings. She assumed Tristan did the same, since he hadn't brought up Mom's passing except to invite Cadence to Mom's death anniversary.

"It didn't seem right to throw away the program. It had her picture on it," Tristan explained as he stared blankly at the wall of boxes.

Tears pricked Cadence's eyes. She hated that her grief could come without warning, that she would mourn her mother again and again. "Is this how it's supposed to be? That we're destined to miss her for the rest of our lives?" Tristan hung his head, not giving much away. Cadence continued, uncomfortable in their melancholy silence. "I wish I came home more."

To cope, Cadence had gone to therapy, read self-help books, and had long, rambling conversations with Maddie. Still, she found herself back in the spiral of regret. She wished that it didn't take her mom's death to realize the missed opportunities.

"But you wouldn't have. If she was still alive, you would have done the same thing you've always done."

Tristan's accusation stung. Cadence crossed her arms, steeling herself. "Of course I would have."

"If things were the same, we all would have done what we've always done," he elaborated, lifting his head as he inhaled deeply, looking anywhere and everywhere except at Cadence. "Mom would have kept going to work, ignoring her symptoms. We would have all gone about our day—Dad and me. Nobody knew that there was anything wrong, so how could it have turned out differently?" Tristan said it like he was saying it to himself as much as he was saying it to her. "I miss her too. I'd rather miss her than forget her. It means she's never really gone."

"That's a nice way to look at it." Cadence blinked away her damp eyes, surprisingly soothed by Tristan's admission.

"Dad said it to me a month after the funeral. It's funny. I used to hear Dad talk to strangers and thought it was bullshit, but who knew it helped?" Cadence's skeptical eyebrows crinkled. "I know it doesn't sound like much, but sometimes, hearing the right words at the right moment . . ." Tristan's mouth pressed into a slight frown, the equivalent of a facial shrug. *You had to be there,* she interpreted. If she had been around, maybe the right words would have presented themselves earlier. Cadence wanted to hear more, but Tristan closed the topic, crouching down to open another box.

"Found them," he said, lifting a red box with a clear plastic window, revealing two red celebratory sticks of incense, a gold dragon wrapped around one and a phoenix circling around the other.

"I'm sure she would have been happy to see you marrying Linda. She used to tell me how much she wished you two would hurry up. She would have spoiled your kid with candy," Cadence said. "It would have driven Linda crazy."

Tristan nodded with a rueful smile, handing the box of incense to Cadence while he returned the boxes back to the shelf. A long creak alerted Tristan and Cadence's attention to the front house.

"Of course, Tristan told me about proposing days ago," Dad lied into his cell phone. The screen door casted an ominous shadow on Dad's figure. "I was napping when you called, so that's why I didn't know what you were saying at first. Yes, of course! We must have dinner sometime to discuss their engagement party."

"That's all you." Cadence shoved the incense back into Tristan's hands. "Good luck."

Tristan didn't seem to hear her. "Engagement party? Why do I need an engagement party? Isn't a wedding enough?"

Hadn't he lived with Dad long enough to know that Dad would want every opportunity to show off in public? Tristan was going to need backup. "Come on. Let's go talk to Dad before you end up with five hundred people on the guest list."

Tristan and Cadence jogged across the courtyard and through the back door of the front house and into the kitchen.

"Finally," Dad said as he ended his call. "What did I say about telling me things?"

Tristan pointed at Dad's phone. "I texted you."

Dad sighed his discontent. "When do you want to have the ceremony? We should consult the calendar for a good date."

"No," Tristan said. "We're not doing that. Linda wants a simple court wedding."

"Wh—What is that nonsense?" Dad gestured at Cadence to talk some sense into Tristan, but it wasn't her wedding.

"Let them do what they want." Cadence shooed Tristan out before he unwittingly agreed to host a huge wedding.

"Humph." Dad pulled down the tear-away calendar and checked the Chinese zodiac information as he flipped through dates one by one. "You kids don't know how to have a party," he mumbled to himself. "How about one month from now?"

"If they want your advice on dates, they will ask." Cadence started preparation for an early dinner, mincing garlic and rinsing choy sum. Dad stationed himself at the counter to supervise.

"Don't put too much oil or salt."

"*I know.*" Cadence rolled her eyes while her back was turned toward him and heated up the wok.

"You need to watch your tone. I'm just reminding you."

Cadence tossed in the garlic and vegetables to a sizzle. "I don't need reminding."

Dad grumbled. "You're so hardheaded. Always want to do things your way."

"Mom used to say the same about you." Cadence plated the choy sum after a quick stir-fry and warmed up leftovers from the night before. "So if anything, I learned it from you."

"She did say that, didn't she?" Dad paused. "I should have been better. I have many regrets, but I regret not listening to your mom." Cadence hoped Dad would specify what exactly he would have done differently. There were many arguments about finances, but also about Tristan's and Cadence's choices. Dad, however, went in an unexpected direction. "But there's something I want you to understand."

Cadence wasn't sure if she needed to hear Dad's defense, especially when Mom wasn't here to share her side of things.

"We did fight a lot, but what you might not know was that your mom and I discussed things in private. Sometimes we came to an understanding. Sometimes we agreed to disagree. But every time, she would say, 'You're lucky that I won't divorce you, because who else will want you?'"

"That's harsh." Cadence wasn't sure what she was supposed to take away from that.

"But it was also true, and maybe I took that for granted. I should have sold the store earlier. It was failing longer than I wanted to admit. It was a gift that she still saw something good in me, even when we didn't see eye to eye." Dad rapped his fingers on the counter and glanced out the window toward the main house.

There was a solemn pause that allowed Cadence to let his words sink in. At first she thought this was as close as Dad would get to offering an apology. Then she wondered if this was Dad's way of extending an olive branch. It was possible that she was reading too much into it, since he didn't explicitly request another chance, but it didn't matter. She wanted to hope that it wasn't too late for them to repair their relationship.

Dad helped her set the table while she placed the dishes in the center. She was about to sit and eat when her phone buzzed in her pocket. It was a text from Josie.

JOSIE: Can you confirm your mailing address for your last paycheck?

"Tell your brother to come eat and put away your phone."

"Tristan, come eat!" Cadence shouted as she typed, much to Dad's chagrin. She entered Dad's address and hit send.

JOSIE: Thanks.

JOSIE: If I knew you were down there, I would have sent Matt
with the few personal belongings on your desk.

Oh?

CADENCE: He's down here?

JOSIE: Yeah, at the new office.

"Who are you texting? Matt?" Dad asked as he scooped a bowl of rice for himself.

"No, it's work. They're sending my check here."

"Mmm." Dad tapped his chopsticks on the table to align them. "You know what your Matt said when he asked me about selling the house?"

Cadence liked how Dad referred to Matt as her Matt, even though she wasn't sure if that was accurate anymore. She wasn't very nice to him when they last spoke. "What did he say?"

"He said that it could be a new beginning for all of us. I liked the sound of that."

"Me too." It was simple but effective, and Matt said it apparently at the right time.

Cadence's phone suddenly exploded with texts. That could mean only one thing. Matt's ears must have been burning. As she read each of his messages, she had to admit that he had good timing.

When Tristan approached the table, Cadence offered him her seat.

"Where are you going?" Dad asked as Cadence grabbed Dad's car keys.

"I'll be back!" she replied as she slipped on her shoes and exited through the back door. She didn't want to admit to Dad that she had been hardheaded. That she hoped that someone still saw the potential in her.

"A nak ko," Mom said, placing her palm on Matt's forehead. "Are you feeling sick?"

"Just tired," Matt replied, blinking his stinging, red eyes.

Once his promotion became official, he had been working nonstop for the past two weeks. There were deals in the Bay Area that he had to close out as soon as possible and prospective candidates to interview in L.A. It would have been convenient to interview over Zoom, but real estate was all about connections and he thought it would be better to get to know his candidates in person. So he flew down late Wednesday evening and crashed at his parents' house in Glendale.

Mom set down a plate of sinangag with tocino and a fried egg. Garlic rice wasn't the ideal choice for breakfast, since he'd be conducting interviews all day, but he wasn't about to pass up a plate of comfort food. Matt dug in with his fork and spoon.

"Can you leave the gate unlocked? I'll be coming home late," Matt said in between bites.

"Is this what it'll be like when you move down here? Leaving early in the morning and working until the middle of the night?"

"For now, while I'm transitioning out of my old office."

Mom closed her eyes as she sighed one of those long, hopeless sighs. "How is this different from being in San Francisco? I'm never going to see you."

Matt grimaced after sipping his coffee. What was this? Instant coffee? "I have to leave early to beat rush hour." He couldn't wait to find his own apartment so he wouldn't have to slog through traffic each morning. Could an assistant do that for him? He'd check with HR.

Mom tsked at him. "Is this why Cadence dumped you?"

Matt choked on his drink. "Hey!" He turned to the side and coughed. Blah! It didn't taste great going down and it didn't taste great coming back up (and down again). "Who told you that?"

"Lola did."

How did Lola know already?

"Cadence didn't dump me," he said bitterly, pushing rice onto his spoon with his fork. "She found another job."

"Doing what?"

"I don't know." Matt waited for Cadence to text him, but she never did. Then work consumed his life to the point that he didn't have a chance to text her until late at night. He didn't think a "You up?" text at midnight was the right way to break the ice.

"Then you were dumped," Dad chimed in as he helped himself to breakfast. "You should have waited until I got some help on my swing before you got dumped."

"Thanks for the advice," Matt deadpanned as his dad left to eat by himself in the den. Why did everyone think that *he* screwed it up? It was true, but it wasn't nice to assume.

"It's too bad. I really liked her," Mom said wistfully.

"You met her once."

"But I could tell there was a spark. That was enough for me."

Matt wished it was enough for Cadence. "It's complicated."

"When is it not complicated? You think when you find someone and get married, you live happily ever after? Look at your father and me. I supported his career, raising you and Celine on my own at home. When he had the chance to transfer, I had to convince him it was time to move. Do you remember how much we argued during that time?" It was such a distant memory, Matt hardly remembered that. "And he did it for me. I missed my family too much. And then when you and Celine moved out for college, it was like I had to learn what it was like to live with him again." She leaned in close and whispered, "And now that we're retired, he's home all the time and he drives me crazy."

"Mom."

"My point is, no matter who you end up with, both of you will have your own needs and they're not always going to be compatible. You will grow and change in ways that will sometimes pull you apart, but you have to work at keeping it together. Sometimes that work is done together and sometimes that work is done alone. Like your dad golfing. I tell him to go golf and leave me alone."

Mom made good points, but he could have done without the disapproving looks. Matt finished his breakfast and put his plate in the sink before giving his mom a kiss on the cheek. "Bye. I'll be home later."

The new office was completely done, save for a few final touches. Gone were the paint cans and plastic tarps. Everything was unwrapped, plugged in, and set for business. Now all he needed were employees. Three days after the job posting went live, Matt received hundreds of applications for the administrative and broker job openings in the office. But first he desperately needed an assistant to help him stay organized while he split his time between San Francisco and L.A.

As his day went on, he thought more about what his mom said. He waited all this time for Cadence to contact him, assuming she'd call when she was ready. But life was bound to throw shit their way. As long as both of them were willing to problem-solve together, then there was no such thing as good timing. Besides, waiting was overrated.

In between reading applications, he sent her two weeks' worth of texts.

MATT: Hi.

MATT: I'm in L.A. Did Josie tell you? I got the promotion.

MATT: Why did you quit? I need you.

MATT: Not for work, but I need you period. Who else is going to tell me when I'm being annoying?

MATT: Let's do it. Long distance.

MATT: PRO: You'd get to see this again.

He attached an old shirtless selfie from last summer. He wasn't above selling himself with his body. It worked last time, so why reinvent the wheel?

MATT: CON: I'd still miss you, but not as bad as I do right now.

MATT: I can fly up to SF and spend the weekends with you.

MATT: Your face soap is really good btw. My pores are so clean!

MATT: Are you there?

MATT: Where have you been?

MATT: I'm sorry I didn't tell you that I talked to your dad

MATT: fwiw I didn't take the Best Eastern listing

By the time his sushi dinner had been delivered, Cadence still hadn't responded to any of his messages. Matt paced around his office as doubt about this plan creeped in. He was about to shoot one last text to apologize when three dots appeared.

She was typing something back!

Matt pushed his takeout box away and placed his phone on his desk. If he stared at it any harder, his eyes would pop out.

CADENCE: Sending a bunch of texts is annoying.

Matt didn't know whether to laugh or cry.

MATT: Can I call you?

His phone rang right away. Matt quickly inserted his earbuds and picked up.

"Hi." The sound of her soft breath nearly toppled him over. God, he missed her voice.

"How are you?" he asked. "I'm sorry." It couldn't hurt to say it again.

"I'm sorry too." There was a hint of a smile in her voice. "I should have responded earlier. I've been busy, trying to settle in."

"Oh." Matt leaned back into his chair. He tried to ask Percy about Cadence once, but Percy dismissed the question, muttering,

"The balls on that woman." Cadence would have appreciated the sentiment if it weren't anatomically incorrect. "I'm in L.A. right now, but I'll be back in town on Sunday." Hell, he'd change his flight and fly up right now if she'd say the word.

"Um . . ." The phone went silent, long enough for Matt to check if his earbuds were working. "I've been staying with my dad."

"You what?" Matt shot straight up from his seat. He pulled his jacket off the back of his chair and tapped the front of his pant pockets to check his keys. Where was his phone? He flipped over stacks of résumés and job applications. He'd just had it! Matt checked underneath his takeout box. Where was his goddamn phone?!

Oh. He was holding it.

"Stay where you are. I'm going to be there in one hour." He checked the time on his phone, the one in his hand. Traffic was going to be hell. "Two hours tops."

"Wait. Don't do that. I—"

"No, Cadence. I can't wait anymore. This is the longest I've gone without talking to you and I hate it. Josie hates it too. She says I'm not as interesting when you're not around. What the hell is that supposed to mean? Whatever. Let's do long distance. We can FaceTime and I'll fly up on the weekends. I'd rather see you sometimes than not at all."

Matt could imagine Cadence's poker face. His heart couldn't take her nonresponse. He literally laid it all out for her.

"Are you done yet?"

Was she . . . laughing at him?

"What more do you want, woman?" Why was he smiling when she was driving him crazy?

"Do you negotiate all your deals this way? Opening with your best and final?"

Oh, now she had jokes.

"I'm telling you that I'm in it to win it. So what's it gonna be, Lim?"

"Before you started running your mouth, I was trying to tell you . . . to open the door."

"Don't play with me." Matt ran out of his corner office and down the hall. Natural light from the setting sun filtered into the office. When he rounded the corner, the motion-sensing lights flickered on section by section until he reached the main floor, announcing his presence. Cadence stood on the other side of the glass door, holding up her phone against her slightly flushed face.

With his hands in his pockets, Matt stood at the end of the center aisle that divided the rows of cubicles. "How did you know that I was here?"

"Josie texted me about my last paycheck and she told me." Matt heard Cadence's voice twice, once through the phone and on the other side of the door. It made him feel off-kilter, or it could have been that she was finally here. She came to see him.

"That's not fair. She wouldn't tell me where you were."

Cadence shrugged. "Girl code," she surmised. "What's with that look? Come open the door."

Matt released his bottom lip from his teeth and sauntered down the main floor. His eyes scanned down from her bare face to her Chucks, searching for a body that was surely somewhere underneath her oversize T-shirt and thankfully tight jeans. "I haven't seen you in two weeks and you come and meet me in your home clothes, Lim?"

She sandwiched her phone between her shoulder and her ear while she pulled her shirt away from her body, examining it. "I left all my nice clothes in my duffel bag. You should know that since you found my cleanser."

"I'm not complaining." The power of this woman. She was essentially wearing a potato sack and she still made him weak-kneed over a flash of exposed midriff. "What brings you all the way over to the Westside?"

"Some things are better discussed in person." Cadence's eyes stayed on his as he stood in front of her. "Aren't you going to unlock the door?"

"Not until I get an answer."

"There's a small problem with your plan."

"Which is?"

"I turned down the iStan job and I'm staying with my dad until the house sells." Her eyes filled with mirth as he struggled to unlock the door with shaky hands. "I won't be here the entire time. I have to take care of things in SF. Move out of my apartment—"

Cadence dropped her phone when Matt hooked his arm around her waist to bring her inside. He pushed her back against the door with a kiss, charged with the relief of being reunited. Like all great pairings—peanut butter and jelly, hoisin sauce and sriracha—they were great individually, but enhanced by each other's presence.

Cadence palmed his shoulders, her elbows wedged between them before he got ahead of himself. "I'm still going to be busy. I'm trying to make things work with my family first. So I want to do things differently. Slower this time, until we figure out what's best for both of us."

"Okay," he said, catching her hands as he took a small step

back. That sounded fine by him. "I can do dates and discounted touristy things."

"Oh, now you're speaking my language." She grinned, holding his hands tighter. "What are your plans for tonight?"

"Reading job applications. Wanna help me?"

"Tempting," she said, pretending to consider it, "but I don't work for free."

"I ordered sushi."

The lure of free food was too strong for Cadence, though she made it clear that she would read zero job applications. Instead, she sat at his desk, gobbling up the salmon nigiri while they traded updates of the last two weeks.

"HR required Hunter to attend sensitivity training, but then he resigned after HR received more complaints." Unfortunately, Hunter's behavior with Cadence wasn't an isolated event. Matt grabbed the last California roll before Cadence cleared the plate. When it came to food, Cadence seemed to think it was a free-for-all. Matt might have to order a pizza. He was still hungry. *Medium?* Cadence picked at the last grain of rice that was stuck to the to-go container. *Better make it a large.*

"They should have fired his ass when they had the chance." Cadence rattled the cup of ice after sipping the last of his green tea. She leaned back in his leather chair, drifting slowly into a turn. "At least I won't have to see him again."

"You're really going to quit?"

"I have my exit interview on Monday."

It was really happening. Matt had been in denial about it, but there was a finality in her response. "It's the end of an era. I'm going to miss seeing you in the office."

"We can see each other outside of work, you know."

"It won't be the same. Did Sadie tell you that I tried to hire you and then she handed my ass back to me?"

Cadence swiveled back toward Matt, appalled. "I can't work for you. We're dating, and besides, do you know how many times you'd write me up for insubordination?"

"What are you talking about? We get along well. *Very* well." Matt would be more than happy to remind her if needed.

"Yes, I know," she replied, not picking up on Matt's invitation. "But I didn't report to you, and analysts work for the entire company. Not just you."

Matt loved having Cadence back, but sometimes she was a dream killer with her facts and technicalities. "Picture it. The memo would go out and the subject would read: Matt and Cadence—Cadence and Matt," Matt corrected after he got side-eyed, "helm the new Prism L.A. office, taking Southern California by storm."

Cadence rolled her eyes. "You know it would probably have a boring subject like, 'Introducing the Prism L.A. Team,' maybe with an exclamation point." She leaned back in his chair once again, eyes closed, and laid her hands one over the other, on top of her stomach. Matt assumed that was the end of their conversation, but then she said, "Tell me more."

"More what?"

"Give me the whole spiel. I want to hear about this imaginary life you cooked up for me here. Come on, it'll be fun. For me, at least."

"Like a pitch deck?"

"The works."

Cadence's definition of fun was different from Matt's, but he was game. He took out a legal pad and a pen. But his best ideas took a little time and—

"Pizza. For that, we'll need pizza."

CADENCE AND MATT'S L.A. TAKEOVER

1. Cadence's New Job: Director of Analytics aka Data Guru aka ~~Moneyball~~ (this is not the same thing)
2. Free lunch provided (by Matt)
3. Cadence will have her own office. Noise startles the formulas
4. Don't want to commute home? Stay at Matt's conveniently located future apartment
5. Long walks on the beach with Matt
6. Cheap dates with Matt
7. Back rubs (and everywhere else rubs) with Matt
8. Be with Matt, please

CHAPTER 33

CADENCE

To: SChan@prismrealty.com
From: CLim@prismrealty.com
CC: JHill@prismrealty.com
Date: February 7, 2022 8:02 a.m.
Subject: Re: Exit Interview

Hi Sadie,

Could we schedule some time to meet privately before we meet with HR? I'd like to propose a different option for us to move forward. A new opportunity, if you will.

Cadence

To: CLim@prismrealty.com
From: SChan@prismrealty.com
CC: JHill@prismrealty.com

Date: February 7, 2022 8:08 a.m.
Subject: Re: Re: Exit Interview

I have time in 30 minutes. I'll call you.

SC

AFTER HIS PROPERTY had been on the market a few weeks, Jack Shen called Dad to let him know that there was a developer interested in Best Eastern. They were still early in their talks, but it seemed promising. It was only then that Dad allowed her to clean out the garage, but he wasn't giving up his things without a fight.

Dad gripped his box of brand-new red envelopes like they were full of money. "This is still very useful." He pointed his chin at the box at Cadence's feet. "And that box. We'll need that for Tristan and Linda's tea ceremony."

"There aren't enough holidays to use all of this stuff," Cadence argued as she sorted through Dad's inventory. "If you don't want to throw it away, then give it to someone. You can't possibly want all this at your potential new home."

That was the other thing they were still fighting about. He refused to look for another house, avoiding the subject whenever Cadence brought it up. While they had discussed their inevitable move, Tristan, Cadence, and Dad couldn't come to an agreement. With an offer on their house coming, they had to make some decisions, and fast.

"Call one of your many friends, Dad. I bet they would be happy to pick up some free stuff."

Dad grunted as he dropped the box and stormed back into the front house.

After she separated out the items she wanted to keep for herself, Cadence entered the front house through the back door. Dad sat at the head of the dining table, flipping through the weathered, dog-eared pages of his thirty-year-old address book. He didn't know it yet, but entering all of his contacts into his cell phone was Cadence's next project.

"I'm not moving outside of San Gabriel," Dad said when Tristan showed up. "All of my friends are here."

"Here we go again," Cadence muttered under her breath. It was like he transformed into a teenager. "You don't have to base your decisions around your friends."

"It's also close to all the shops I go to."

"There are stores in other neighborhoods, Dad," she countered. "If you wanted to stay here so much, why did you agree to put the house up for sale?"

"How did your mother put up with your big mouth?" he scolded. Cadence had more to say with her big mouth, but she held back to keep the peace. "This property is too big for me to take care of without your mom."

"What about me?" Tristan asked.

"It was never your job to take care of this house. Both of you are grown now. You should be able to live on your own," he said to Tristan. "You have your own family to take care of now. When we sell the house, you'll be able to put in an offer on any house you'd like. And you." Dad turned to Cadence. "I'll pay back the money you sent so you can save up for your own place."

"You don't have to do that," Cadence said. "That was yours to keep. You'll need it to get a three-bedroom house around here."

"Who needs three bedrooms?" Dad asked.

The three of them kept looking at one another, utterly confused. Once in a while, unspoken rules had to be said out loud as a reminder that they were on the same page.

"I thought I would live with you for a while," Cadence said.

Dad's jaw dropped in abject horror. "For how long?"

"For as long as you need me?" Cadence almost vomited as she said it, but she chose to step in for Tristan, so she'd see it through the way that he had.

"No," Dad said firmly. "I don't want you to live with me. You're so bossy and you scare away my friends. It was easier to make you look good when you weren't always at home, looking jobless."

Was he implying that *she* cramped *his* style?

"I wouldn't have been able to help you if I still had a job." Cadence pinched the bridge of her nose. Living at home hadn't been all sunshine and rainbows, but she never once anticipated her dad kicking her out. "If I don't live with you, then who's going to take care of you?"

"For what? I know how to feed myself and take my medicine."

"But we separate it for you," Tristan pointed out. "And what if something happens, like you falling again?"

"I'm fine. My legs work great now." Dad slapped his thigh as if it demonstrated its sturdiness. "If you're so concerned, you can install a camera in my house like a baby monitor. A baba monitor," he added in English, punctuating his sentence with a "ha!" He laughed at his own dad joke.

"And what about your errands?" Cadence asked.

"I have friends who can drive me. I could take the bus. For more important things, like doctor appointments, one of you can take me." To Cadence, he said, "You already pay for my bills online and check my email. I don't even know what my passwords are anymore because you don't like writing things down on paper. Call me if there's something important."

"Are you sure, Dad?" Cadence asked. "I thought you'd want me here."

Dad let out an exasperated sigh. "I wanted you to come home more, not live with me again."

"I can do that," she said. Truth be told, it was for the best. She nodded at Tristan. "How do you feel about all of this?"

Tristan shrugged. "Works for me. Linda doesn't want to move too far from her parents because they're helping us with the baby, so I'll still be close by if something urgent comes up."

"I can help out," Cadence offered. "Maybe we can set up a shared calendar, so we can split up his appointments and errands."

"If you want." One of Tristan's shoulders shrugged, as if it was too much work to shrug both of them. "If you'll be around."

"Yeah." Cadence exhaled. This she could promise. "I'll be around."

THE FOLLOWING FRIDAY, Tristan and Linda married before a judge, him in the only suit he'd ever owned and her glowing in a white maxi dress that had a high-low hem, courtesy of her baby bump. Cadence and her dad, along with Linda's parents, were their witnesses. With the Prism L.A. office launch approaching, Matt couldn't get out of work. He sent the bride and groom his best wishes. Tristan fidgeted in his suit, unaccustomed to formal wear. Luckily for him, the judge fed him all the words he needed to recite. He was on his own for *I do*, but he got those right.

The ceremony was short, and to appease Dad, Tristan and Linda held a reception of sorts for the six of them in a private room at Dad's favorite banquet-style seafood restaurant. Above the dark wood wainscoting, the room was plain white, whereas the main dining room had chandeliers and red panels worthy of grand celebrations. Dad must have called in a favor with the restaurant owner because on the wall behind the happy couple hung a red panel with a golden phoenix on the left, a floating dragon on the right, and a round plaque in the center for 囍, double happiness. Tristan and Linda sat together, with their parents on either side of them, and Cadence sat next to her father.

"I can toss it to you, if you'd like," Linda joked when she caught Cadence admiring the massive bouquet of fluffy pink peonies.

"No thanks," Cadence replied. "They're beautiful, though."

"Tristan called up a florist that he met through a client. I'll save her contact info for your future wedding."

"Ha-ha." Cadence laughed nervously before flicking her hand across her neck to nix the wedding talk. She didn't want Dad to get any ideas. A waiter arrived with a tureen of crab soup and ladled it into the adjacent bowls. "How are you feeling?"

Linda leaned back into her seat to stretch her legs underneath the table. "Except for my swollen feet, I feel good." The elders each picked up their own bowl of soup from the lazy Susan, followed by Tristan, who placed a bowl in front of Linda before getting his own. "Today I got married. I have a baby and soon a house on the way. Life is good."

Linda smiled as she rubbed her belly before her parents whispered something to her in Mandarin. She then translated the message into Tristan's ear. Dad minded his own business, spooning red vinegar into his soup. It was the mark for new beginnings for everyone. There were newlyweds, new in-laws, soon-to-be parents, soon-to-be grandparents. New homes over the horizon. It was beautiful, seeing everyone content.

"My mom would have liked it," Cadence relayed to Matt over the phone. "She preferred smaller gatherings. It seemed that way when we had guests over at the house versus the times she accompanied my dad to big community functions."

"I'm sorry that I couldn't come," Matt said. "I promise I won't miss any more events after I move down. My cousins already committed me to that big night market by your house. Jason's playing a set there on Saturday night."

"Can I come?" Cadence's self-invitation came out rather timid. It would be the first time she'd seen Matt's family since the birthday party, but the night market was a big event. It was all over social media and billboards around town. There would be food stalls with a wide range of pan-Asian dishes and pop-up shops selling stuff she probably didn't need but that was too cute to resist.

"If you come, all eyes will be on us," Matt warned.

It was cute how Matt worried over this, but the more Cadence thought about it, it was perfect. The more the merrier.

There were way too many people waiting in line for an eight-dollar spiral-cut potato on a stick. Was it sprinkled with gold flakes or something?

"This potato better be worth it," Matt complained as the teenager behind him stepped on the back of his white sneakers. Matt had been working tirelessly to get the Prism L.A. office ready. Sadie was scheduled to be there on opening day to welcome the team, so everything had to be perfect. The last place he wanted to be was at the insanely popular night market.

"Why are you so salty? If I can stand here with a sweaty baby strapped to me, you can stand there by your skinny-ass self." AJ cradled baby Sofia, who slept peacefully against his chest. Two weeks ago, AJ and George received the placement call and instantly became parents. At four months old, Sofia had already managed to wrap AJ and George around her tiny little finger. While there was some concern about the possible future involvement of Sofia's birth parents, AJ and George dove in with full hearts, and they couldn't be happier or more tired.

"Sorry. I'm nervous about the launch on Monday," Matt said as he inched closer to the vendor stall.

"You'll be fine. You got this." The sun was mellowing against the cotton candy sky, but AJ still secured a tiny bucket hat that protected Sofia's innocent face. If anything, AJ should be concerned with the sound. How could the baby sleep with Jason bumping his mix of throwback hits?

"I know. I just want everything to be perfect." During his whirlwind summer, commuting back and forth between San Francisco and L.A., he had hired twelve brokers and ten administrative staff members to support marketing, research, and office operations. By April, he was going to have a full house to kick off this brandnew chapter in his career.

"Are you settled into your apartment yet?"

"The movers brought everything, but I haven't unpacked yet." Matt found a nice two-bedroom apartment a few miles away from the office that currently had no decent place to sit. He'd much rather be there with Cadence. Speaking of Cadence, she was late. Matt peered across the open dance floor to Jason, who shook his head. He hadn't seen Cadence, either.

Matt was about to order his potato when his phone rang. "Order one for me," he said to AJ when he saw the caller ID. "I'll pay you back." Matt left the line and covered his ear as he picked up the call.

"Percy, how can I help you?"

Ever since Percy closed the deal with Matt, he called Matt enough times to rival Lola. Unlike Lola, however, Matt put up with Percy's calls with the hope and promise of a commission worthy of all the headaches Percy inflicted on him. None of the properties he'd shown Percy for iStan's future L.A. base met his particular set of standards.

"Am I interrupting something? Are you at a party?"

"Something like that," Matt said, searching for a quiet place. "I'm free to talk."

"It's okay. I'll send you an email. I talked to Cadence and I want to revisit the building you showed me in Venice. If we can get a better deal, I think we should go for it. I'm going to be traveling for the next couple of weeks, but let me know if the deal goes through."

"When did you talk to Cadence?"

"This morning. She didn't tell you?"

Since when did Cadence and Percy become so cozy? "Tell me what?"

"That woman." Percy chuckled. "She has a lot—"

"Of balls, I know," Matt interjected. Speaking of the devil, Cadence was calling him.

"She has a lot to tell you," Percy clarified. "We'll talk soon."

Matt switched the calls and weaved through the crowds to make his way back to AJ. "Where are you?"

AJ was standing where Matt left him, holding his now-cold Torpedo Potato. Instead of gold flakes, it was rolled in furikake.

"I'm starving," Cadence said. "Can I take a bite out of your potato?"

"I hope that means what I think it means." Matt made a 180-degree turn as he searched the crowds for her. She must be close. "Where are you?"

"You don't see me? I'm the one wearing red."

"You and a bunch of others in this place."

Cadence laughed. "I'm at the noodle stand at the side gate."

"I'll be right there."

AJ tapped Matt's shoulder and told him that he had to meet George at the dumpling booth. Matt nodded and split off toward Cadence. On his way there, Matt texted Jason, "She's here." Jason immediately replied with a thumbs-up.

Cadence was waiting away from the crowd, who was watching a chef pull long noodles by hand. She was wearing her red cardigan over what looked like a new dress. Her smile grew with each step. If her twinkling eyes were any indication, she was seventy-five percent happy to see Matt. The remaining twenty-five percent was for the spud in his hand.

"Hi," she said, greeting him with a chaste kiss that managed to steal his heart and his skewered potato at the same time. "Not bad," she said through her stuffed mouth.

"I have to watch out when I'm around you," he started to say. Over her shoulder, on the main stage, Jason flashed two fingers at him. Matt had a few minutes to spare before he needed to get Cadence to the dance floor. "I got off the phone with Percy and he told me about the interesting conversation the two of you had."

Cadence stopped eating and handed back the half-eaten skewer. "Are you upset?"

"Oh, I'm so pissed." He had no idea what he could possibly be mad about, but he was going to let her tell him. "How could you do that to me?" He was surprised that he managed to keep a straight face as he said that.

"When I had dinner with Percy, I told him—"

"You had dinner with him?" he squeaked, forgetting for a second that he was supposed to be upset. "When?"

"After the golf tournament . . ." She tilted her head, giving him a wary look. "Is that not what we're talking about?"

Matt took a bite of his potato, which was not eight dollars good. "What kinds of things are you hiding from me?"

"Let's find something else to eat," she suggested, trying to change the subject. "I think I see ramen burgers."

"Spill it, Lim."

"Fine," she relented. The jig was up. On the stage, Jason started to cue in the next song. "After the tournament, I had dinner with Percy. He thought I was there to accept the job offer, but I went to advocate for you, since you had to leave early. I don't think I said anything you wouldn't have said about yourself."

"Is that all?" he said, taking her by the wrist after he tossed his skewer in the trash. They had to hurry before the next song played.

"You don't think I overstepped?"

Matt didn't quite look at it that way. Perhaps it was a bit unorthodox, but so was their symbiotic work relationship. She knew him better than anyone else at the office, so if he had to choose a proxy, she would be it.

"Why are you looking at me like that?" she asked while Matt dragged her into the crowd in front of the main stage. He held his finger against his lips and then tapped his ear.

"How's everyone doing tonight? We have a special request from Cadence," Jason announced as an intro looped in the background.

"*From* Cadence?" she shouted over the scattered *whoo*s that likely came from all his cousins and their families. "Did he mean *for* Cadence?"

Matt shook his head and started swaying side to side while the intro to "My Boo" by Ghost Town DJs swelled. He tried to keep his grin in check as her face grew annoyed at the opening lines of the song.

"Admit it! You love this!" he cackled, dancing as he sang along. His falsetto was so off pitch, it cracked her hardened face.

"You're the worst," she said, trying to stifle her smile. He held her hands, dancing for the both of them as she stood there, thoroughly displeased. Thankfully, she started moving her feet on her own, albeit reluctantly, before people thought he was a puppeteer and she was a marionette. "You better get this out of your system before we open the new office."

Matt stopped dancing. "What did you say?"

Cadence proceeded to dance on her own with a mischievous smile. "I spoke to Sadie and we worked out an agreement. I thought about asking for my old job back and working remotely, but you made a compelling case. So I told Sadie that I wanted to handle larger transactions, that I had experience interfacing with brokers and clients. On top of that, Percy personally vouched for my contributions toward the iStan deal. He said if I wasn't going to work for his company, then I should at least work for him during this next phase of iStan's expansion. So, long story short, you're looking at the new director of research for the Pacific Southwest Region."

"Wait. Who do you report to?"

"Technically, it would have been Bill, but Sadie arranged it so that I would report to her."

Matt nearly tackled her in his bear hug. "How could you keep this a secret from me!?" He couldn't stop shouting. He didn't give a fuck that people were staring at him, swinging Cadence around.

Cadence wriggled herself free from his arms. "I was waiting until I could ask you . . ." She got down on her knee, eliciting some gasps from people passing by.

"Cadence," he whispered, "there are children around."

That earned him a stinging slap to his leg. He knew he shouldn't have worn shorts.

"Don't ruin the moment!" she hissed. Cadence presented her phone with a document displayed on the screen. The print was too small for Matt to read.

"Matt," she said, looking up with those gleaming doe eyes, "would you do me the honor of completing this affidavit for HR, declaring our relationship, to officially become my work husband?"

Cadence used to tell him that he never knew when to shut up, but he was genuinely speechless. He covered his mouth with both hands and nodded.

"Yes!" He picked Cadence up and spun her around. "I said yes!" he shouted over the applause, letting the crowd cheer and snap pictures at their misleading scene. Lowering her, Matt pressed a firm kiss on her lips.

"You love me." Matt brushed her hair away from her face, feeling the warmth on her cheeks. "Tell me you do, because I love you."

There, standing in the middle of the dance floor, with the aroma of deep-fried foods wafting in the air, surrounded by cousins who appeared out of nowhere, blowing up the group chat with photos, Cadence said, "I do."

EPILOGUE

After an anxiety-ridden night, Matt arrived at the office building an hour early. He was at his desk, answering emails, when Cadence called. She'd left her dad's house early, expecting there to be traffic, but she would be arriving shortly. He tried to convince her to stay over at his apartment so that she wouldn't have to commute at all for the launch, but it was a hard sell when most of his things were still in boxes and his mattress was lying on the floor.

While he waited, Matt opted to bring an old tradition into their new office and left for the coffee shop around the corner. When he walked back up to the office, the door was unlocked. He heard the click of heels down the hallway, followed by the recognizable thud of Cadence's heavy purse being set on her desk.

Matt made his way toward her office, which was on the corner opposite his. From the doorway, he saw her place a picture frame and a fresh new plant on her desk.

"Good morning," he said, setting the coffee on her desk. He leaned down for a kiss that landed on her cheek after she turned away.

"Not at work," Cadence reminded him. Last night, she texted all the rules. No kissing at work. No hand-holding. No flirting. No anything. Work Cadence was no fun.

"Come on. I signed the affidavit and sent it to HR. Everybody knows already," he said, going in for another kiss. He nabbed the corner of her lips before she pushed him away.

"Everyone in San Francisco knows," she stated, unbuttoning her blazer before she sat down, revealing the white silk blouse under her sleek gray suit. "The staff here haven't seen us together yet. We need to set a good example, and we—meaning you—need to be on our best behavior. I know we're going to be transparent about it, but I don't want to advertise it."

"What about this?" Matt flipped the picture frame around, assuming it was a picture of them. Instead, it was the grayscale picture of a generic white couple that came with the frame. There was still a sticker on the bottom corner with the price. "What is the point of this frame if there's nothing in here?"

She snickered. "I'm waiting for a picture of my future niece."

Matt returned the frame to her desk. "I'll let you settle in, then, *Director.*"

He went back to his desk across the hall. A few minutes later, with discreet glances over his computer screen, he watched Cadence take a tiny sip of her coffee while she sat at her desk. He wondered if she missed the message he had left for her when an interoffice chat popped up on his screen.

CADENCE: Stop looking at me, creeper.

His eyes darted up and were met with hers, which were unobscured since her computer was positioned on the corner of her L-shaped desk.

MATT: You stop looking at me. I'm trying to work.

CADENCE: I'm going to buy blinds.

MATT: Noo!

MATT: Check your coffee.

He watched her twist her coffee cup until her eyes landed on the small *IOU* that he had written along the bottom edge.

CADENCE: You don't owe me anything.

MATT: Look closer.

MATT: Do you need to get your eyes checked? I can lend you my reading glasses.

She squinted at her cup, blushing when she saw the heart that replaced the *O* in the center.

CADENCE: I love you too. Now get back to work.

ACKNOWLEDGMENTS

In 2019, I conceptualized this book, wanting to write a workplace rom-com. In 2020, I started this book over in the midst of the pandemic as the world paused and work culture underwent a dramatic transformation. Like many people, I reflected on my priorities and what brought me joy. I loved writing this book, but it was difficult to do so during uncertain times. This book would not have been possible without the following people.

Thank you my editor, May Chen, for helping me find clarity in my chaotic draft. You gave me constructive feedback in a way that made me laugh and allowed things in my brain to click into place. It is always a pleasure to collaborate with you. Thank you to Alivia Lopez, Diahann Sturge, Jessica Rozler, and everyone at Avon/William Morrow/HarperCollins for your talents in getting this book in tip-top shape.

Thank you to my agent, Laura Bradford, for your patience and sound advice. I'm grateful to have you in my corner.

Thank you to the Sloth and Steady Writers group: Linh Pham, Daphne Dador, Evalyn Broderick, C.H. Barron, and Cecile Ferro. I don't write kidlit or sci-fi and yet, you welcomed me with open arms. You've all been an amazing source of support during my debut year and helped me brainstorm as I wrote this book. Linh and Daphne, thank you for beta reading and providing invaluable feedback.

Thank you Joanne Machin for providing notes on my early chapters. Always love our chats!

Thank you to Joyce and Laura for reading my horrible first draft and cheering me on until I finished. I don't know where I'd be without either of you and your fast reading skills.

Thank you Brianne and Komal for introducing me to your commercial real estate professional spouses. Max and Ankush, thank you for simplifying the complexities of your jobs and for being so professional as I asked the most inane questions. I took some creative liberties and any errors are mine.

Thank you Tracy for helping me with the Tagalog in this book. I take full responsibility for any mistakes. Save me a plate (or two) at the next big party!

Thank you to all the comforting kdramas, Mike Schur shows (*The Office, Parks and Recreation, The Good Place*), and Doritos that kept me company in 2020.

To my Superfriends, I love you for life. Shout-out to your "cool dad" husbands and their very, very cool Supreme stickers.

To my family, I wouldn't be anywhere without your support. Thanks, Ma, for feeding me whenever I wrote at the house. Thanks, Ba, for waiting until after a writing session to pitch your story ideas. Phuong and Sue, I always appreciate your advice. Jared, Mitch, Lauren, Roman, Emily and Logan, thanks for keeping the kids busy.

To David, thank you for loving me as is and for taking care of the house and kids so I could write. To Alice and Sophie, thank you for not touching Mommy's computer.

Thank you to the librarians, bloggers, and bookstagrammers who supported *The Donut Trap* and continue to shout about my writing. I am so appreciative of your time and energy.

And last but not least, thank you, readers. I know there are many books available, and I am grateful that you chose to spend time reading mine.

ABOUT THE AUTHOR

JULIE TIEU is a Chinese American writer, born and raised in Southern California. When she is not writing or working as a college counselor, she is reading, on the hunt for delicious eats, or dreaming about her next travel adventure. She lives in the Los Angeles area with her high school crush husband and two energetic daughters.